RELIC

Book 3 of the Mars Fr...

Get the prequel to the Mars Frontier series FOR FREE

Sign up for the no-spam newsletter and get exclusive content, all for free.

Details can be found at the end of RELIC.

COPYRIGHT

First published by P&J Books 2020

Copyright © 2020 Paul Rix

All rights reserved. No part of this publication may be reproduced stored or transmitted in any form or by any means, electronic, mechanical, photocopying, recording, scanning, or otherwise, without written permission from the publisher. It is illegal to copy this book, post it to a website, or distribute it by any other means without permission.

This novel is entirely a work of fiction. The names, characters and incidents portrayed in it are the work of the author's imagination. Any resemblance to actual persons, living or dead, events or localities is entirely coincidental.

Paul Rix asserts the moral right to be identified as the author of this work.

First edition

Am I dead? Grant wondered. *If this is heaven, why am I strapped to a bed in the dark?* He didn't feel dead. But there was something different about him he could not define. And, if he wasn't dead, how had he survived the fall? There were too many questions and no obvious way to get answers.

"Megan!" he called out. "Georgia? Is anyone there? I'm awake. Can someone please turn the lights on?" There was no reply. The ominous and oppressive silence closed in on him, making him feel anxious. *None of this makes sense!*

Grant lay there for a long time, trying to piece together the different elements of the puzzle. It frustrated him to have absolutely no information to help him, only his memories. And they only created more questions for him. Without knowing it, he eventually drifted into a light sleep.

***

A sudden burst of light disturbed Grant's sleep as a door silently opened. He squinted as his eyes became accustomed to the light, but he could not see who, if anyone, had walked in. "About bloody time," he called out. "Can you release me from these straps and explain why I've been tied up and left in the dark?"

If Grant expected an immediate response, he was disappointed. The room remained deadly quiet. *Perhaps the fall has damaged my hearing.* He waited for someone to move into his limited field of vision. All he could see was the ceiling and some strange equipment he didn't recognize hanging from it. He was getting a terrible feeling about his situation and was close to panicking.

"Okay, the joke's over. It's not funny anymore. Can you please get over her and release me!" He tried to sound assured but was dismayed to hear the slight tremor in his voice let him down.

He heard a faint sound that he thought was an intake of breath. And then, from somewhere to his left and out of sight, someone spoke. "I am sorry for the restraints, but they have been necessary for your own safety." Grant didn't recognize the voice, but it had a melodic quality that quelled most of the anxiety he was feeling. But he was unable to tell if the speaker was male or female.

"Who are you? And, where am I? I know for a fact this isn't Alpha Base."

"I understand you have many questions. I promise I will answer them in good time. My name is Falmas. I have brought you to a safe place where your injuries have been tended. Your body is still rejuvenating, which is why you find yourself in your current position."

The name sounded familiar, but Grant couldn't remember where he'd heard it before. It wasn't one of his Expedition Two crew mates. "Where is Doctor Betts? Why isn't she taking care of me?"

"There is no need to worry, Jim Grant. You are receiving the most advanced surgical treatment known to us. The repairs to your body will be complete within the next day and then I will answer all of your questions. May I get you any refreshment?"

The relaxing sound of Falmas' voice was easing some concerns Grant had. But the refusal to answer his questions was disturbing. He realized, however, that he was suddenly very thirsty. "Thank you, Falmas. I could do with a drink. And can I see your face? I'd like to know who I'm talking to."

Falmas replied, "I shall see that you receive a drink immediately. As I said, we shall talk properly tomorrow and I will answer all of your questions. It is pleasing to see you awake."

Grant heard some footsteps before the door closed, and the room returned to complete darkness. He lay there, helpless and annoyed. The brief conversation had only raised more questions in his head. What was the reason for the secrecy? Where were the rest of the crew? If his injuries were almost healed, how long had he been there?

The almost imperceptible hum of a tiny motor interrupted his thoughts. He felt the soft tap of a tube against his lips and instinctively took a sip. The cold liquid tasted like water but had a bittersweet aftertaste. As his thirst was eased, he wondered if he should have taken a drink. There could be any number of drugs in it. That was his last thought as the anaesthetic took hold and he fell into another deep sleep.

***

This time when Grant awoke, a soft light illuminated the room, allowing him to see the surrounding space. Once again, it took him several moments to remember where he was. This time, however, he was able to turn his head as someone had removed the restraint. He tested his arms and legs and noticed that they were still tied down tightly. Cautiously, he turned his head slowly to the left, hoping that Falmas had returned. There was no sign of either Falmas or the door, just a blank wall. The view to his right was exactly the same. With some effort, Grant raised his head and saw that they had covered him in a glossy metallic fabric that clung closely to the outline of his body. Beyond the end of his bed, the wall was also bare. He couldn't see any corners so wasn't sure if the room was square or round. *This is one of the strangest medical rooms I've been in,* he thought. *Where is all the medical equipment?*

He lay his head back down and closed his eyes to concentrate on the facts he knew. His surroundings suggested it was almost certain he was no longer in Alpha Base. His doctor's name was Falmas, and he had suffered severe injuries. The only logical conclusion was he'd been in a coma and transferred back to Earth for surgery and other medical treatment. But that would have involved waiting two years for the next suitable transfer orbit from Mars to Earth. Surely there was no way he'd been unconscious for that long.

The name 'Falmas' continued to resonate in his mind. *It must be one of the doctors at Houston*, he thought. There had been plenty of fresh-faced doctors at the space center during training, all far too eager to carry out physical and psychological experiments on the trainee astronauts. He couldn't be expected to remember all of their names. So why did he think he'd heard that name more recently?

And then, with a recurring flood of panic, he recalled Georgia telling him that one of the aliens she had encountered was called Falmas. Suddenly, several more pieces of the puzzle fell into place. He was on the Sentinels' ship. They must have saved him, as they had done with Georgia. They had applied their advanced medical knowledge to save him. So, he was still on Mars after all and, in all likelihood, the Sentinels presence meant that Georgia had succeeded against Redmayne.

The secrecy made perfect sense now. Georgia had said that the Sentinels weren't supposed to intervene in human progress. He was being kept like this so he didn't have access to any of their technology. That was fair enough. He would have liked to experience the technical advances possessed by alien civilizations, but at the moment he was happy to have had his health restored.

Satisfied that he'd been able to work out the mystery, he relaxed with a smug smile and waited for Falmas to return.

The faint hiss of a door sliding open interrupted Grant's thoughts. He opened his eyes and turned his head in time to see a tall humanoid being walk into the room. Grant tried to suppress any feelings of fear as he stared into the large eyes and blue face, rationalizing that the Sentinels had proved to be a peaceful race. So far. They'd not harmed Georgia.

Again, the soft, tuneful voice rang out as Falmas spoke. "Hello again, Jim Grant. As promised, I am ready to answer some of your questions." Falmas' facial expression contorted into what Grant assumed was a smile as he moved closer to the bed. "You are not surprised by my appearance. I therefore assume more of your memory has returned during your time of contemplation."

"Hello Falmas," replied Grant, not knowing if it was morning or afternoon. "Yes, your name finally registered with me a few moments ago. You saved Georgia Pyke's life several days ago. My last memories are of crashing to the ground, and I guess you have performed similar procedures to heal my broken limbs and other injuries. For that I thank you. I cannot express how grateful I am for your saving my life and Georgia's. Can you tell me she is okay?"

Falmas paused for a moment. "I can confirm that Georgia Pyke is safe and well. When I left her, she was about to return to your base. That is the good news. The injuries you suffered were far more serious and extensive than the ones she experienced. Not only had you fallen from a great height, falling machinery from an explosion in your vessel had also crushed your body. When your doctor could not save you, I offered to assist and evaluated your condition. We immediately determined that my ship did not have the medical facility to save you."

"And yet I'm here and alive," said Grant, not sure where the conversation was heading but needing to say something.

Falmas nodded. "Indeed, you are. And it is most gratifying that you have recovered. I gave Georgia and your doctor a choice. You would die where you were, or I could return you to my planet where we have more extensive medical facilities. Georgia chose the latter so you would survive. It was the only way to save your life."

The revelation stunned Grant. "So, you're telling me I'm no longer on Mars! In that case, where in hell am I?"

"You are on Nikari. It is my home planet, located seventy-eight light years from Earth."

"Seventy-eight light years! How long did that take?" Grant couldn't believe it.

"Not as long as you think. Eleven of your Earth days. We placed you in a stasis chamber for the journey so that you did not die from your wounds."

Grant was shocked by the numbers. All those years studying relativistic physics had been a complete waste of time. Einstein had a lot to answer for. "How many days have I been in this room?"

"We arrived thirty days ago. You are currently in one of the recovery rooms in the Science Ministry located in our capital city, Prema." Falmas pressed a button, causing the wall to the right of Grant to dissolve and transform into a panoramic window overlooking a city.

There was too much information for Grant to take in as he took his first look at an alien world. His senses were still reeling from the knowledge that he was so far away from home. The whole experience felt like a dream. The vista outside the window was unlike anything he could have imagined. The sky was a clear deep blue with high altitude clouds but that was as far as the similarity to Earth went. Although he couldn't see the sun, it cast long harsh shadows. His room must have only been several floors up because he could see the ground less than fifty feet below him. Metallic vehicles of different shapes and sizes buzzed through the air and along transit ways. There was no obvious sign of life that he could see. He counted five tall majestic buildings in the distance, but the closer buildings were no taller than twenty stories. Science fiction movies had gotten alien worlds totally wrong!

"Did anyone else travel with me?" he finally asked.

"No, that was not possible. I am in enough trouble returning here with you. But at least I could use medical research as an excuse. It would not have been workable to have a healthy human returned. I assure you that Georgia gave a lot of thought to her decision and she knew you would be here alone."

"Okay, I understand. Falmas, I am grateful for everything that you have done for me, especially if it has caused you any trouble. Now that I am healed, can you tell me when you'll be taking me back to Mars? You must understand that I'm eager to be reunited with my friends. I'm sure they're worried about me."

"I am sorry, Jim Grant. This trip was one way only. Again, Georgia was aware of this. It is not possible for you to return to your friends. In time I hope you understand."

Falmas' words left Grant dumbfounded as their meaning sank in. "So I'm trapped here, alone? Maybe you should have left me to die!"

Chapter 2

Falmas stood and walked to the window, allowing Grant a few moments to gather his thoughts.

"I appreciate this is too much news for you to process fully. You have been through a most traumatic time and your recovery has taken longer than we expected. After all, you are the first human to experience the procedures we had to undertake. That is part of the reason we have waited until now to explain your situation."

"I'm sorry," said Grant. "I don't mean to sound ungrateful. I wasn't prepared for any of what you just told me. And I naturally assumed I'd be allowed to return home. I cannot even comprehend how far seventy-eight light years is or in which direction my home is. It's too much to absorb in one go. But if you brought me here why can't I go back? What future do I have on your planet? Am I simply going to be an interesting specimen for your scientists to experiment on?"

"Nothing like that, I promise. There are ongoing discussions among our senior ministers. We do not yet have a consensus over what to do with you. That is my fault for being too compassionate toward your species. I didn't consider the consequences of my actions. My motives were purely to save your life and to help Georgia after she prevented my ship from being taken. Even though I have no regrets for what I did, I expect I'll be reprimanded for my actions."

"Where does that leave me? Why can't I return? Can't you carry out a mind wipe like you did with Georgia?"

Falmas returned to his seat next to the bed. "I'm not sure you're ready for the explanation. You've already learned so much today. It may be better that we wait until tomorrow."

"That's not good enough!" Grant almost shouted. "You have brought here me without my permission and you're telling me I can't return home. I deserve to know the truth now. It can't be any worse than being trapped here, never being able to see my friends or loved ones again."

Falmas shrugged. "You're right. I cannot imagine the distress you are going through at the moment. I am not sure there is a good way to explain, but I will try." Falmas paused and looked directly at Grant, a look of sorrow on his face. "When we returned to Nikari, it took ten days for our scientists to confirm what treatments they could apply to your frail and broken body. The bones in your legs, hips and hands were badly crushed. Despite the stasis field, infection had set in during the flight from Mars. It was the first time they had worked on one of your species and several of them expressed concerns you could not be saved. They were fearful that your anatomy wouldn't be able to deal with the required adaptations."

"What do you mean by adaptations?" said Grant slowly. It wasn't the term he expected to hear when it came to medical procedures.

"It's probably easier if I show you." Falmas stood and gently pulled back the fabric that had been covering Grant's body to reveal the procedures that had been performed.

As Grant looked down the length of his body, he noticed a myriad of fine scars along his chest and over his heart. He gasped in horror as he looked to his right and saw that the whole of his arm had been replaced by a metallic mechanical arm, seamlessly joined to his shoulder. He could see where the metal blended into his skin. He looked across at his left arm to see that the Sentinels had also replaced it with an artificial arm..

"So, you've kept me tied down to ensure I wouldn't discover the truth," he said through gritted teeth. "You've turned me into a monster!"

"Not at all. The restraints were necessary to allow the bonding process to complete. Not just with your skin but also to your internal nerve endings. Nano-tech is currently connecting all of your nerves so that your brain can operate your hands and fingers. You'll be able to feel, and touch as you did before. In time, your dexterity will return. Think of it as an enhancement. You'll be stronger and we can always replace the parts should they wear out or malfunction. These adaptations are natural for our people and have sustained us for thousands of years."

Grant was only partially aware of what Falmas was saying. He was trying to see his legs but couldn't raise his head high enough to see over his chest. "What about below my waist? You said my legs were crushed. Have you replaced those as well?"

Falmas nodded. "Again, there was no alternative. Your legs had to be amputated to counter the infection that was threatening to spread through your body. In any event, we wouldn't have been able to repair the bones. At the same time, your hips were also removed. Every bone below your vertebrae had to be replaced. You will be able to walk and run, and much faster than you ever could. The advanced alloys used to construct your arms and legs are virtually indestructible."

"No doubt you think I should be pleased that you saved my life and give me enhanced limbs. But what is left of me? You've turned me into a cyborg! My legs and arms may have a lifetime guarantee of one thousand years but the rest of me doesn't. So, I don't see any advantages at the moment. In fact, you've taken away most of who I was. What am I left with?"

Falmas looked at Grant quizzically. "You're left with your core. Your brain and mind are still yours. You are the same person on the inside with the same knowledge, preferences and dislikes. They are the important parts. Your physical body was merely a weak and badly designed container. You will soon forget that we have replaced your limbs."

"Is there anything else I need to know? Any more enhancements your scientists decided to add as a joke? Should I change my name to Inspector Gadget?" Grant couldn't hide the bitterness in his voice, although Falmas didn't seem to notice.

"I do not know who that person is. We have had to make alterations to some of your internal organs. We have installed a micro generator to power all of your systems, an interface directly to your brain to download data from our neuro-net, and we have upgraded your lungs because of the lower oxygen content in our atmosphere. Other than that, we have kept as much of your original body as we could."

"Good God man, I think that's more than enough. I hope your scientists are satisfied with their handy work. They made damned sure that I can never return to my own kind. In fact, am I still human?"

"That depends on how you define what a human is. I understand that many humans have prosthetic limbs, mechanical hearts, and organ transplants. Does that make them less human in your eyes?"

Grant was quiet and looked out of the window as he contemplated Falmas' words. They hit close to home. Back on Earth, he'd been inspired by stories of courage and valor from soldiers who'd created new lives after life-changing injuries. They hadn't given up when faced with devastating losses. "I don't know," he said quietly. "Perhaps I over reacted. You can't really blame me. I've just discovered I'm half machine. I am still alive, which is the important thing. I guess I need to reset my expectations. When will you be freeing me from this bed?"

"Later today," Falmas replied cheerfully. "Initial tests show that the nano-tech is adapting to your alien body. I must warn you that it can take some time for you to learn how to control your new enhancements. Coordination is a difficult skill to master after such extensive work. Even with minor enhancements, it has taken me several hours of training to be able to utilize the new components effectively."

"I love your positive attitude Falmas. I can tell that you're a can-do type of guy," said Grant, before hastily adding, "I assume you're a guy, anyway."

"Sentinels are an androgynous species. There are no males or females and procreation is somewhat... complicated. I will share the details with you one day, if you would like."

Grant shook his head. "No, I think you've shared more than enough with me for the time being. What I really want is to be out of this bed and to start exploring your wonderful planet. For now, though, I think I need some time alone to absorb what you've told me. Can you leave the window open this time though? I want to look at your world."

"Yes, I understand," said Falmas, as he stood to leave. "I will return later to begin your rehabilitation."

***

Grant managed to control his emotions for several minutes after Falmas left. But then the tears began, and he sobbed uncontrollably. Eventually, he wore himself out and his body subsided. He turned his head to stare, unseeing, out of the window, feeling his tears as they made tiny streams over his nose and across his cheeks before ending their journey dripping onto his bed.

He couldn't recall the last time he had cried like that. But then, he had never been so full of absolute despair. He couldn't decide which was worse; his new body parts, the loneliness or being so far from Earth or never being able to return to see his friends and family. The situation was hopeless. His destiny was to die on an alien planet where the locals would keep him alive by swapping out worn out components. He recalled Georgia saying that Sentinels could live for thousands of years. He didn't think he could face that future. It would be torture.

Despair slowly turned to anger. He needed someone to blame for where he was. After all, he'd never had a say in the matter. Why had Georgia allowed this to happen? What was she thinking when she had made her decision to send him in exile to this planet? Had her emotions overruled her head? He was sure she wouldn't have wanted him to die. But would she have wanted to see him like this either? *Georgia, you really need to think about the consequences of your actions. What you want is not always for the best!*

He was now faced with an uncertain future with no one to speak to. Life couldn't get any worse and he wasn't sure if he was strong enough to move on. Or even if he wanted to.

Chapter 3

Three floors above Grant's room, Falmas reluctantly walked toward Director Mortak's office, guessing the reason for his urgent summons was unlikely to be positive. Mortak had spent his entire life on Nikari, choosing a career as an eminent historical scientist. He'd become famed for researching information received from hundreds of star systems and had developed a reputation for holding very prescriptive and traditional values. This had made him popular among many in the Nikari Council Chamber and there had recently been discussion that he would be seeking political office in the near future. It was therefore a bad time for Falmas to have breached several core principles imposed by the Confederacy. Mortak would have to demonstrate strong leadership to correct the transgression.

The aperture to Director Mortak's office was open, allowing Falmas to walk straight in. "Good day Director Mortak. I understand you would like an update on our guest from Earth."

The director was standing by the window, preparing a speech he was to make later that evening. He was fifteen inches shorter than Falmas, having chosen not to be fitted with the extended limbs favored by the field researchers such as Falmas. He looked irritated. But that was his natural expression. "Ah, Falmas. Thank you for coming to me so promptly."

Falmas nodded to acknowledge Mortak's appreciation, although in reality he'd had no choice but to treat the director's request as a priority command.

"I've been advised that the human has recovered consciousness. That is good progress indeed. Have you been able to converse with him?"

"Yes, Director. I spent some time with him earlier today. He is quite lucid and seems to have recovered full memories of his time prior to being brought to Nikari. I explained why he is here and the procedures we undertook to save his life."

Mortak squinted at Falmas. "How did he take the news? I'm sure it must have been a huge shock for him."

"He took the news better than I or the psychological team anticipated. We have taken our time to determine the appropriate moment to share his situation. Clearly, he was shocked by his new reality. But that's to be expected. He seemed most agitated by the news he is unable to return to his home planet. We have him under constant observation to observe his reaction over a period of time. The intent is to remove the restraints and allow him to become accustomed to his enhancements."

"Good work so far. As I've previously advised, proceed with caution. There is no baseline to determine success and failure. We have no idea if his less advanced intellect will enable him to use the enhancements or what the long-term effects of his time here will have."

"He did ask if we had any plans for him. I advised we were still discussing options."

"That's not entirely true, is it? I'm still waiting for you to present me with suggestions for how we handle the human. You brought him here against protocol and without permission. It has created many questions for me to address and a problem for this facility. You still have an opportunity to make it right but, so far, I've seen nothing. Do you not cherish your career?"

"As you know, Director, I have spent most of my life off-world observing other species and cultures. I want to continue carrying out those duties. I get a lot of pleasure from watching species develop and bloom. I get less satisfaction from observing similar cultures self-destruct and implode while I passively stand by. But I have an exemplary record and continue to provide excellent research material for your academics. So yes, I cherish my career and want it to continue."

Director Mortak wasn't impressed. "I do question your judgment, Falmas. You've shown recent signs of weakness. I've been shown the reports of your encounters with other humans. You've put your research mission at risk. And I fail to understand why."

"With respect, Director Mortak, you've never carried out field work or had the opportunity to observe alien species at first hand. It can be difficult on occasion not to feel compassion for individuals or cultures where you see great potential being wasted or destroyed. The humans may be considered brutal savages as a race, but their individuality and spirit are characteristics we have not in any other systems. I accept that I may have become too involved in my research and that I have shown compassion in circumstances where I should have stayed more remote. But in this particular case, I think the positives more than outweigh the negatives. We can learn so much more from interacting with humans than we ever could by hiding in the shadows."

"So you think you know better than the law makers who established the protocols thousands of years ago? That those protocols don't apply to you?" snapped Mortak. "You're attempting to undermine fundamental principles that were established to protect all parties. You have no idea what damage you may have caused. And you have the temerity to stand in front of me and tell me your actions were justified. You bring disrespect on yourself and this facility."

"That was never my intent. You should come and speak to the human. Maybe you should take time to talk to him and experience his feelings. Then you may understand how different and amazing humans are."

Mortak looked repulsed by the suggestion. "I think it better if I remain unbiased and maintain a healthy distance from your subject. I will let you continue your curiosity with him, but I still have to make a final decision on his future. And yours. You must appreciate that I am under a lot of pressure to deal with you harshly. There have been calls for me to set an example to others who may be developing similar weaknesses for their own subjects."

Falmas knew there was some resentment from the older Sentinels. He could guess which ones were whispering in the director's ear with their grievances and suggestions for retribution. His crew mate, Falment, has already been reassigned to a remote outpost. Yet, he had to hold firm to his own values. "I don't feel that I need to be punished for my actions. I had hoped you would see that I've created a unique research opportunity. I'm not looking for praise or recognition, but I am disappointed if you believe my actions merit a punishment of some kind."

"You cannot expect to do what you've done and not receive some form of rebuke. There would be anarchy. The trouble is that you're too impulsive. So, let me assure, I will insist that action is taken against you. I have arranged for a disciplinary session to take place shortly. You'll have full capacity to explain your actions to a wider audience before I decide on what to do with you. Perhaps the experience will deter any subsequent lapses in your reasoning process. And allow me to trust you again. I'll let you know my final decision in the next few days. Now, get out of my office."

Falmas didn't need any more prompting and knew there was no point attempting to defend himself any further. He turned on his heals and left the director to his own dark thoughts.

Chapter 4

Despite his situation, Grant was fascinated by the alien world outside his window, although it still seemed too fantastic to be true. The analytical part of his mind had switched on, enabling him to suppress the flood of emotions that had threatened to overwhelm him. He knew that the color of the sky must mean there was water vapor in the atmosphere, but the deeper shade of blue indicated there were also other chemicals present. He could only hope that none of those chemicals were toxic. As he watched the clouds glide leisurely across the sky, he reasoned that there must be weather patterns. Perhaps Nikari was more Earth-like than he had first appreciated. He wondered if this type of planet was a prerequisite for intelligent life across the galaxy.

The harsh sunlight also signaled the planet orbited a different type of star to the Sun. He'd noticed the shadows of buildings shorten as the sun reached its zenith. It would soon come into view and he'd be able to see his first alien sun at first hand. He was intrigued to see its size and color.

He couldn't help but compare everything to Earth. That was his baseline after all. Earth was all he'd ever known. Although he'd visited the Moon and Mars, they were just lifeless rocks. But the comparisons made him increasingly realize that he was no longer on Earth and, if what Falmas had said was true, unlikely to ever see it again.

"What are your first impressions of Prema?" asked Falmas, surprising Grant as he entered the room.

"From what I can see from this window it looks very peaceful. I expected it to be buzzing with activity. The architecture is fascinating though. I cannot begin to imagine the materials you have at your command to be able to build many of the complex buildings. They look impossible and would not be possible on Earth."

"It may not be a modern city compared to other planets in the Confederacy, but I think it has a certain style and sophistication," replied Falmas. "I was raised less than two hours from this location. My twenty years of orientation and training was spent in this city, so I know it very well. I will gladly give you a tour when you are allowed to leave this facility."

"I would welcome that, Falmas. And I hope that day is soon. Have you returned to remove my restraints?"

Falmas shook his head. "That is not my responsibility. Norgal, the engineer who designed your enhancements, will be here in a few moments to carry out a system check and perform any final calibration of your new limbs. Norgal took great pride in being nominated to perform the procedures on you and it will go well for his career if you survive."

"Well, that's reassuring to know that my engineer has some motivation to succeed," said Grant, raising his eyebrows. "Although I am more used to having doctors deal with my ailments. Talk of an engineer makes me sound more like a machine. You may not be aware, but I am the chief engineer for the Expedition Two mission. Or, at least I was before I ended up here! I'm not sure what I am anymore."

"We will find a use for you, Grant. I have no doubt of that. I think there is a saying you have. 'You need to learn to walk before you can run'. I think that it a most appropriate way to consider your situation."

Grant laughed unexpectedly at Falmas' correct use of the idiom. "I've never heard it used more literally. I need to learn the basics all over again. How long do you think it will take to get me walking again?"

Before Falmas could answer, another alien entered the room and walked over to Grant's bed. Although still humanoid, this alien was about five feet tall and stockier than Falmas. His skin was pale yellow and, unlike the hairless Sentinel in the room, this new arrival had fine gray hair on the top of his head. His all-in-one dark blue suit looked like a uniform with what looked like insignia across his chest. The new alien was staring intently at a device in his hand and, so far, had failed to acknowledge either Falmas or Grant.

"Is this Norgal?" Grant asked Falmas as the alien began to check the restraints on his legs.

"Yes," replied Falmas. "You are his first experience of a human. I'm not sure he knows what to say."

Grant couldn't see what Norgal was doing, but he suddenly felt a strange tingling sensation in his left ankle. "Falmas, I don't mean to be rude but I'm guessing that Norgal isn't a Sentinel."

"You are correct, human," interrupted Norgal, in a slow deep voice. "I am an Elassian from the Belachis system. My people have far superior technological expertise than the inhabitants of Nikari and have been supporting their enhancement program for many thousands of years. You have no need to worry that we have provided the best possible replacement parts. While you have been a challenge, it has been refreshing to test my expertise on a totally new species."

Grant wasn't sure what to say. "I'm honored that you should view me as a test subject." He paused for a reaction, but his sarcasm seemed to be lost on Norgal. "What I would like to know is has your work been a success? Will I be able to walk again?"

Norgal glanced up from his device. "Of course you will be able to walk. I have yet to fail in establishing neural connections with any of my projects. It may take a while for your simple brain to work with the impulse generators in your new limbs, but it should soon become second nature to you."

"When can I try? Can you remove the restraints now?"

"You can try as soon as you like. The restraints were taken away a few moments ago, and I have disconnected all external sources required to complete connections to your nervous systems. Try lifting your right arm."

Grant closed his eyes and concentrated on his right arm. He could feel it rising several inches above the bed. However, when he opened his eyes, his arm was still laid where it had been since he's woken up. "It's not working," he said, with some concern in his voice. "It feels like my arm is moving but nothing is happening. What's gone wrong?"

"Relax," said Falmas. "You need to learn the correct commands. It requires patience and concentration."

Norgal looked unimpressed. "Falmas is correct. I can see that your brain is transmitting signals, but the neural inducers don't understand what they mean yet. This is all part of the process. I have installed signal translators into your neural pathways. But, because we have no experience of human physiology, the translators have to learn what your brain signals mean. Stay centered and focus on one command at a time. In fact, let's start with something simple. Move your finger."

Grant took several deep breaths and tried to relax. His only thought was to bend his index finger. He couldn't tell if it was working but his brain was registering some movement. He could see Falmas and Norgal looking at his hand, waiting for any sign. "Is anything happening?" he asked.

Falmas looked concerned. "Norgal, can you detect any activity in the hand?"

"I am registering electrical stimuli. That is a very good sign that the subject's nervous system is functioning. You must remember that he is a new species. It may take longer for the translators to fully calibrate human brain activity. I am, however, confident it will be only a matter of time. All systems appear to be ready to function."

"Jim Grant, there is no cause for alarm," said Falmas, calmly. "You simply need to practice the movements until your brain has synchronized with the nano-tech."

"I don't understand," replied Grant. "I've been able to feel the resistance from the restraints. I've been pulling against them to release myself. Why can't I move now?"

"You didn't feel anything," said Norgal. "It's been your mind playing tricks on you, probably as a result of the nerve fusion activity taking place inside of your body. They were phantom signals, based on your brain's established understanding of your body."

"The sensation was real. I could feel myself moving," said Grant, feeling dejected. "And you tell me it's my imagination playing tricks. How will I be able to tell if I am actually moving any of my enhancements?"

"You will know, with practice," replied Norgal. "From the initial data, I see no reason why you won't have full mobility in time. I will return to check on your progress later. I do have other subjects to monitor." And with that, Norgal left the room.

"He doesn't exactly have a great bedside manner," Grant said to Falmas.

"Elassians aren't known for their pleasantries. But they have been excellent cohorts for our enhancement program. There are countless modifications that are available thanks to their ingenuity and reliability. If Norgal says your enhancements will work, then you should believe what he says. I don't recall that he has ever been wrong. I suggest you heed his advice and continue to practice."

"It sounds as if you're leaving me as well," said Grant.

"I have a disciplinary session to go to. It concerns my actions in returning with you to Nikari. I expect there will be a censure of some kind. Several ministers, including Director Mortak, have already shown their displeasure."

"I'm sorry to hear that. I trust that any punishments are not too severe and you are able to continue your visits."

"Thank you. I shall let you know."

Falmas walked from the room and the aperture returned to being a solid wall. With nothing else to occupy his time, Grant continued to concentrate on moving his artificial limbs. He was intent on mastering the movements and proving Norgal wrong. Nothing would make him more satisfied than showing the miserable Elassian what humans were capable of.

***

One hour later, and after much frustration, he was rewarded by seeing his right arm lift six inches off the bed for several seconds, before dropping back. Within another ten minutes he was able to keep the arm in the air and flex his fingers. Shortly after that, he was able to repeat the exercise with his left hand.

It felt very odd, yet satisfying, to see his metallic arms and hands respond to his mental commands. He knew it would take some time to become used to his new look and considered that it may not be so bad if he wore gloves and a long-sleeved shirt.

Once he'd mastered his arms and hands, he was ready to try his legs. The translation implants were very effective because he was able to bend his knees within a couple of minutes. But the effort of learning the movements had exhausted him and it was time to rest.

He lay for a few moments, content with the progress he'd made so far. *Perhaps I'm not going to be a cripple after all*, he thought. *I'm going to be a bionic man.* He smiled at the idea. It sounded better than being a cyborg. Maybe having enhanced limbs wouldn't be quite so bad after all. He'd be able to do more than he did before. If only he could play basketball again. All the NBA teams would want to sign him up.

When he felt suitably rested, Grant focused on using his arms to pull himself into a sitting position. He'd been lying flat for far too long and wanted a new perspective on his surroundings, as well as an opportunity to see what his new legs really looked like. So, with much effort and grunting he used his arms to lever himself upright so that he was leaning against the wall behind him.

Once he was comfortable, Grant attempted to pull the sheet away from the lower half of his body. Having tried several times to grip the material in his new hands he gave up in frustration, instead finding a way to sweep the material away with his arms. The cover dropped to the floor to reveal a pair of shiny black legs and chrome looking feet. Between his stomach and the top of his legs was a metallic gauze type material which hid where his new legs joined his torso, He imagined the join would be seamless as it was for his arms.

The initial impression of his legs was that they looked very sleek. His engineer's mind couldn't help but be impressed at the craftsmanship that had gone into designing and manufacturing his limbs. His knee and ankle joints had numerous servos which he guessed would give him flexibility and mobility. It was only when he saw his feet that he was shocked to find he had no toes. They had been replaced by two plates that hinged as his toes would have done. He wiggled the plates, but they'd never be as good as his old toes. He briefly wondered what the Sentinels had done with his body but soon decided it was probably best not to know.

***

Thirty minutes later, Grant was standing next to the window, taking a good look at the outside world. Slightly breathless, he had one hand resting against the wall to prevent himself from falling over. The whole sensation of walking on artificial limbs felt clumsy, like walking on stilts. However, he couldn't help but be encouraged by the first faltering steps he had made. It had been difficult, but he was sure his determination would see him through.

From his position, he was now able to see Nikari's sun. As he had correctly surmised, the sun shone much whiter than the Earth's sun, but appeared to be about fifty percent larger. He wondered how that would affect the outside temperature. Looking down, he found it strange that he could see no aliens moving around. So far, all he could see was the occasional vehicle. There had to be a reason for that. If Prema was the capital city, it should be heavily populated. It was a question he would have to ask Falmas.

Having recovered his breath, Grant began to walk slowly around the room, holding his arms out to balance as he carefully took each step. He noticed that he didn't have to concentrate quite as much on his arms as they seemed to move subconsciously into the correct position. The problem was coordinating his knees and ankles, bending them at the right time and placing one foot in front of the other. There wasn't any feeling in the sole of his feet which made it impossible to know when they were in contact with the floor. With some practice, however, he was able to find a rhythm that worked without fear that he may topple over.

Grant approached the point in the wall where Falmas entered and left. There was no obvious sign or switch on the blank wall. As he stepped to within two feet of the wall, however, the aperture appeared in front of him, revealing a featureless empty corridor beyond. Without pausing to think about his actions he stepped into the corridor and looked left and right for any signs of life or direction. The corridor was straight and was about fifty yards long in each direction without any obvious doors or signs. The walls were a plain pale iridescent blue. There were no lights, but the ceiling glowed a soft white light.

Grant decided to turn right, walking toward what appeared to be a dead end at the end of the corridor. He was conscious that his feet made a loud drumming sound each time he took a step, but that was the only noise. There didn't appear to be anyone else about to hear him.

As he reached the end of the corridor, another aperture opened in front of him onto what looked like an elevator. He stepped inside, hoping to find buttons that would take him to different floors. There was nothing other than blank walls. He stepped close to each wall but failed to find another way out. *Perhaps it's voice operated.* "Up," he said, but nothing happened. "Top floor," he tried. This time the aperture closed, and he felt himself ascending.

Five seconds later, the aperture reappeared in front of him. He stepped through into a large room that had continuous views across the city. He was alone but now much higher than he had been in his own room and he could see large parts of Prema that had not been previously visible. There were far more low buildings that stretched into the distance. And for the first time, he saw flying vehicles converging on a large tower that he guessed could be an airport or transit point.

Grant refocused on the contents of the room. It was similar in size to many conference rooms he'd been in at Houston and Florida. He remembered that Falmas had said the building was a research facility. Perhaps the Sentinels held lectures or meetings in the room. To his right was a long white bench, about waist height. It was empty except for a small pile of clothes that appeared to have been just dumped. And next to the bench was a tall steel cabinet with a mirrored finish.

Do I want to see what I look like? Grant was unsure if he was ready to see the dramatic changes that had been made to him. He didn't know if he'd ever be ready. Reluctantly he walked over to the cabinet, pausing for several moments to take some deep breaths before stepping in front of it to look at his reflection.

He gasped in disgust at what he saw. Norgal had turned him into a monster! With his long metallic arms and legs, and most of his abdomen covered in a gray gauze material, there wasn't much of his old self left. And now that he could finally see himself, he saw there were implants in the side of his neck, his head had been shaved and there was a metal plate across his forehead. "What have they done to me?" he cried out, reaching a hand up to touch his forehead, tapping the metal several times. He was filled with revulsion at the sound. He was now more Frankenstein's monster than bionic man. *Who have I been kidding to think that I'd be okay?*

Grant reeled in horror from his reflection. All he could see were the new artificial components. So much of him had been replaced. Although Falmas had explained what had been done and why, being confronted with the changes was far too much for him. He spun around, consumed by fear and loathing at what had been done to him, not knowing what to think other than he was a man now trapped inside a mechanical body. The one thing that was clear in his mind was that this no life for him. He saw a railed balcony on the far side of the window nearest to him and blindly charged toward it. The window became another aperture as he approached it and he found himself on a small balcony no more than eight feet wide. The air was freezing on his naked face, but the rest of his body felt nothing.

He grabbed the railing and screamed in anguish at his plight. He didn't deserve any of this. His life had been turned into a living nightmare. Looking down at the ground one hundred feet below, he knew what he had to do. Without another thought, he clambered over the railing and jumped.

Chapter 5

Grant opened his eyes to find himself back in his room and laying on his bed. *Did I just dream of jumping off this building?* He tried to move his hand to see if there really was a metal plate on his head but found that the restraints were back in place. Looking out of the window, he could see the sun beginning to set over the distant hills, causing the clouds to turn a deep shade of violet.

He sensed someone sit next to him and saw that it was Falmas. "What happened?" Grant asked. "What am I doing back here?"

"You were found on the grounds outside. It was lucky we found you when we did. Another ten minutes and we may not have been able to resuscitate you and repair your internal organs. I am sorry for the restraints, but we felt they were prudent until we discover the malfunction in your enhancements. Norgal is currently running through diagnostics data with his team to establish what caused you to fall from the balcony. We will sort discover the cause and make all the necessary corrections. I hope this setback has not changed your mind about the adaptation. I promise that this type of reaction is extremely rare."

Grant sighed. "I can save you all the trouble. There isn't anything technically wrong with any of the adaptations. I didn't fall from the balcony. I jumped on purpose."

"I don't understand," replied Falmas. "We were taken by surprise when we found that you weren't in your room. Norgal did not expect you to adjust to the implants so quickly. We thought it would take your mind many weeks to master the complex controls. Then, when we found you had fallen, we believed that you had not learned sufficient control and subsequently lost your balance. I blame myself for not being here to watch your progress."

"It wasn't your fault, Falmas. The fall was no accident. I saw a reflection of myself and was appalled at what you have done to me. The enhancements are far more extensive and brutal than you explained. I know that the procedures you carried out on me are entirely normal for your own people and that they saved my life. That doesn't prevent me from hating and being disgusted by what you have turned me into. I'm no longer human. I deliberately jumped from this building because I wanted to kill myself. I don't want to go on living like this."

Falmas looked puzzled. "That is a most strange reaction. I will need to advise Norgal that his design is overwhelming your sensibilities. Georgia Pyke told me that humans have a strong sense of survival. It seems as if our work has somehow overwritten your core values."

"It's nothing like that. I didn't like what I saw. I was horrified to see that there is so little of me left. I don't think you understand how much this matters to me. I've found myself on an alien world, with no friends and discover my body has been replaced by machine components. I look like a freak."

"You should have spoken to me. Occasionally, some Sentinels are dissatisfied with their enhancements. But the joy of having artificial parts is that they can be designed to suit the taste of the host. If you tell me which aspects you would like to alter, then we can see what further modifications may be possible."

"You still don't understand. I hate the whole concept of enhancements. I'm now more machine than human. I realized that was something I didn't want and, in a moment of weakness, decided I wanted to end my life. Jumping from the top floor of this building was the most instant way of achieving that wish."

"So, you're telling me you intentionally tried to end your life? I am not aware of that concept. It runs contrary to what Georgia told me."

"It's not so unusual," said Grant, quietly. "On Earth, if someone is terminally ill, desperate or has emotional issues it is not uncommon for those people to take their own lives. I don't know how you've not picked up on it during your observations of humanity."

"An oversight on our part. I will enter a record in our archives to conduct more research on this phenomenon. Does this feeling continue or is it transitory?"

"It depends on the source of the problem and the support that other people provide. In my case, it's likely to be permanent. I didn't want to be saved," said Grant, bitterly. " I have no place here on Nikari and I don't want to live with all of these mechanical parts attached to my body. You never told me about the implants and metal plate in my head. What are they for?"

"Norgal installed some neural enhancers into your frontal cortex and brain stem. They helped to speed up your recovery process but also act as inhibitors should your body's immune system react against our nano-tech. I agree that the aesthetic appeal of the plate on your forehead is less than appealing, but it is only a temporary measure. If you are displeased with the look of your enhanced limbs, we can coat them in synthetic skin. Norgal's team will be able to match your skin tone to give your limbs a more natural look. In time you'll forget that you have any enhanced body parts."

"Maybe externally I'll appear normal. But I can't forget what I've become or where I am. How are you going to resolve those aspects?"

"There are ways, but I fear you may find them distasteful. We have had the occasional case of a Sentinel having non-physical issues. In such circumstances, they are re-programed. There is a ninety-eight percent chance of success in those situations. Re-programing may not work for you, but we could eradicate parts of your memory so that you don't remember those aspects that upset you."

Grant shook his head vigorously. "You've already taken away most of me as it is. You're not taking anything else. And I saw with Georgia how successful your mind-wiping processes are."

"What would you have us do?"

"Release me from these restraints for a start."

"From what you've just told me, I don't think that would be a good idea!"

"In that case, give me something constructive to live for. Anything to take my mind away from the dark places that may drive me to suicide again."

Falmas' lips curled into a knowing smile. "At my disciplinary session earlier, I was indeed punished for my insubordination. There was unanimous agreement among the ministers that I should be taught a lesson and set an example for all other Sentinels that none of them are above the Confederacy's principles. I have been instructed to devote all my efforts into researching you at first hand. Once Norgal had evaluated your enhancements, you will be placed into my care."

"As your prisoner?"

"As my project. You will be free to go wherever you wish, on Nikari. But I shall be with you so that I can observe and better understand complex humans through your behavior."

"That sounds as if I am being punished," replied Grant, less than enthused by the prospect of spending the rest of his life with Falmas. Although the Sentinel seemed friendly enough, Grant doubted that the two of them had anything in common.

"You are being honored. No other species representative has had a dedicated Sentinel. As far as I am concerned, though, my career is forfeit. I will not be heading off-world any time soon. Not until you die at least."

"In that case, I suggest you leave me next time you see my crumpled body at the bottom of a long drop! That way, we both get what we want."

Falmas had no idea that Grant was being serious and ignored the comment. "Let me show you around Prema when you have had more time to recover your strength. You will learn to love it like so many others do."

"If it's that great a city, why do I feel you'd rather be anywhere other than here?"

"Because I'd rather be out exploring the galaxy. There's nothing left to discover on Nikari. I yearn the excitement of research. Director Mortak knows my feelings which is why he imposed the harshest punishment he could on me." Falmas looked dejected as the prospect of his own future hit him.

"We're going to make a great couple!" noted Grant. When Falmas didn't respond, he added, "I'm going to have to teach you about sarcasm."

Chapter 6

One month later, and Grant's concerns about his future were coming true. It had been two weeks since he'd been discharged from the research facility. Two long weeks that he had spent, living in the same underground, yet spacious, dormitory as Falmas being continually monitored every day and regularly questioned about all decisions he made. And if living with Falmas wasn't bad enough, Grant had to return to see Norgal every three days to have his implants tested.

Grant quietly admitted to himself that the enhancements looked far better now that they were coated in an artificial coating that mimicked the look and touch of real skin. The coating contained millions of micro-sensors that fed constant data to Grant's microprocessors, which in turn filtered out the majority of information so that his brain was not overwhelmed. The ghastly metal plate had been removed from his forehead and replaced with more synthetic skin. His hair was also starting to grow back so, from a distance, he was looking like his old self.

After many hours of practice, his dexterity had improved so much that he was now able to pick up delicate objects. Walking and running had also become easy, and he had long forgotten any fear of falling over. If it wasn't for the regular testing, he could almost forget that his limbs were artificial.

Nutrition remained an issue. Sentinels were vegan and their food was unpalatable, consisting largely of purple vegetation and soft fruit with an overpowering odor that made Grant feel nauseous. He was living mainly on a concoction of vitamins and minerals, washed down with water. He could give anything for a strong black coffee and a pepperoni pizza.

As promised, Falmas had given Grant a tour of the city, most of which was underground due to the effects of the Nikari sun's rays and the long winters where temperatures failed to rise above freezing for up to two hundred days at a time. Below the surface were a labyrinth of tunnels, walkways and transit systems. This was where the millions of inhabitants existed, going above ground to work in self-contained buildings.

Grant had lost count of the different number of species that lived in the city. Falmas had explained that there were many off-worlders who either had made their home in Prema or traveled from planet to planet seeking seasonal work or offering their particular talents. The strength of the Confederacy lay in its diversity. Species were free to travel wherever they desired. There had been no conflicts for more than eight thousand Earth years and that had been only a minor disagreement between neighboring worlds that resolved itself within a week.

Falmas was a very patient and knowledgeable teacher. He had answered all of Grant's questions about the history of the Sentinels and the Confederacy. Grant was finding that each answer only created more questions. Although he'd never been concerned on learning about diverse human cultures, he had surprised himself at how fascinating it was to delve into the details behind rituals, religions and habits of alien civilizations. And he knew he was only scratching the surface of the Sentinel's knowledge. Perhaps it was due to the enthusiasm with which Falmas explained the subjects, bringing otherwise dull stories to life.

While Grant found it incredibly interesting to learn about the multiple alien species, he couldn't help but feel he himself was nothing more than a long term experiment. The tedious testing, taking of specimens and the constant surveillance were intrusive and wearing him down. He had nothing constructive with which to fill his days and Falmas was always vague whenever Grant suggested that he should be trained up to do something useful.

During the long thirteen hour nights, he would often lay awake, staring at the ceiling thinking of his friends and family back on Earth and Mars. He knew it was unhelpful to have such thoughts, but he felt so isolated and out of place on Nikari. Although he'd not had many close friends at home, he missed the companionship of another person. Someone to go for a beer or watch a ball game with. Everything he had ever taken for granted was now gone from his life. Even the simplest of pleasures.

The Sentinels had no obvious entertainment or hobbies and instead were devoted to researching other cultures. They had a thirst for knowledge that took priority over every other pursuit. Grant had not seen any artwork and was unaware of any music or literature. Creativity seemed to be totally lacking from their society. As a consequence, everything was bland.

Even though he should be excited about being on an alien world, he had quickly found it be underwhelming for most of the time. Falmas' teachings had convinced him he must be on one of the least exciting planets in the Confederacy. He wished that he could speak with Georgia to let her know that advanced civilizations were not all they were cracked up to be. Maybe the information would cool her obsession for humans to more actively search out alien life.

As he followed Falmas onto the Prema underground transit system that would take then both to the research facility Grant was feeling particularly despondent. The prospect of another round of needless checks with Norgal was almost more than he could bear. He'd been unable to sleep for three days despite feeling weary and lethargic. He'd also lost his appetite and guessed that these were all signs of a deepening and lingering depression. Falmas had commented that Grant had been less responsive in recent days and although he took notes of Grant's explanations, it was for research rather than as an aid to address Grant's emotional state.

He stood, staring into space, as the four-person transit vehicle made its familiar way to the research facility. Once they reached their destination, Grant jumped from the stationary vehicle and walked in time with Falmas' steps toward the elevator.

"How many more times do we need to do this?" he asked. "The implants are working perfectly and Norgal has not found any issues in the last six visits. The routine is becomingly increasingly monotonous and unnecessary. It's a waste of my time and yours."

Falmas sighed. "We have this conversation every time we visit the facility. Norgal will decide when he no longer needs to see you. I believe there will be many more visits to come. Norgal is part way through writing a thesis on how he treated your injuries and adapted the implants to suit your physiology. He will want to ensure your body does not reject the enhancements before he publishes his work. There is no denying that he is very proud of his work. Your case will be famous and studied for a long time to come."

"So, these regular check-ups are for Norgal's benefit rather than mine."

"I hadn't thought of it that way. But yes, you are correct. However, you should be reassured that Norgal is doing his best to ensure you have no issues. You are receiving the best aftercare available."

If Grant was supposed to feel honored by the attention he was receiving, he wasn't feeling it. If anything, Falmas had confirmed the checks were a complete waste of time. He was tempted to turn around, but he had nowhere else to go.

When they stepped out of the elevator, Grant immediately noticed they were not on the usual floor. The shade of the walls was a subtly different shade to that on Norgal's floor. "Where are you taking me?" asked Grant, suspiciously. It was unlike Falmas to spring any surprises.

Falmas' skin darkened, an indication Grant had picked up as a sign of embarrassment. "Grant, it has been decided that, due to your erratic behavior, a thorough medical examination needs to take place. We want to determine what is wrong with you and then find a cure, if there is one."

Grant stopped walking and re-entered the elevator. "I don't need a medical to tell me what's wrong. I'm lonely and depressed. I'm a trained engineer. I need something constructive to occupy my mind. You may think I'm inferior to you, I need a purpose and I need a future I can look forward to. Are you able to help with any of those?"

Falmas turned and looked back at Grant. "I'm sorry, I don't have the authority to address any of those issues. But you really should come with me now for your examination."

"No, Falmas. I've tried it your way for long enough. It's as if you refuse to acknowledge my self-diagnosis."

Grant stepped back from the aperture and directed the elevator to go up, leaving Falmas in the corridor. Grant leaned against the wall and closed his eyes, trying to compose himself. He had no idea where he was going to go or what he was going to do. His anger had been a simple reaction to Falmas lack of consideration and respect. The secrecy around today's tests was the final straw.

The elevator stopped at the top floor from where Grant had previously jumped. He stepped out to find that this time the room was filled with about one hundred individuals who were in the middle of a meeting of some kind. He recognized only a few of the species and it seemed as if they were being lectured by a Sentinel who was standing alone at the front of the room. Grant's sudden appearance was an immediate distraction for most of them as they turned their heads to stare quizzically in his direction.

He sensed Falmas' presence behind him. "Come on Grant, we can sort this out. We don't need to do the checks today."

Grant moved away from the elevator into the room, brushing past an Elassian who gave him a dark look. "I'm okay, Falmas. Just leave me alone."

The Sentinel who was standing at the front of the room was irritated by the interruption. "Excuse me, but I'm teaching a class here. Please take your debate somewhere else. Falmas, you need to keep your friend under control. I'm disappointed in you but I'd heard your standards have slipped."

Falmas ignored the Sentinel and moved slowly toward Grant who continued to retreat through the room until he was close to the windows. "That's far enough Grant. There's no need to cause a scene here. Let's go and watch the transports arrive. I know that's something you enjoy."

"That's the only thing I enjoy," replied Grant as he took one more step backward, opening an aperture in the window. "Doesn't anyone here know how to have any fun. You're not taking me for any more tests. I'm done here." He took two more steps until he was standing outside on the balcony.

"Don't do anything stupid," called Falmas, finally aware of Grant's intentions.

Grant gave him a cold stare. "Don't revive me this time. I want to die."

Falmas ran forward, but he was too far away from preventing Grant leaping over the handrail and falling one hundred feet to the ground below. As he fell, Grant was filled with a sense of relief that his nightmare was conclusively over.

Chapter 7

Grant opened his eyes to find himself back in the familiar surroundings of his room at the research facility. *They just won't let me die!* The thought rang bitterly in his mind. It felt like he was being subjected to a bizarre regime of torture, seeing how far he could be pushed before he broke, only for him to be resurrected. Whilst it proved the durability of Norgal's craftsmanship, the experience was less than beneficial for Grant's mental wellbeing. The fact that he was still alive confirmed that he faced many years on this planet, playing a macabre game of finding an effective method of suicide that was permanent.

He sat up, surprised that there were no restraints this time. His chest ached but otherwise there were no other physical signs that he'd attempted to take his own life.

Falmas entered the room, a grave expression on his face. "How many times do you intend trying to destroy all the hard work our teams have performed to give you a more efficient body? It is proving very tiresome and shows a lack of gratitude on your part."

"How many times are you going to repair me when you know full well that I'd be happier if you didn't rebuild me? I have no life. Can't you see how desperate I am to end this existence. What you're doing to me is cruel. Humans need a purpose in life in order to sustain them. That is missing from my life. You're not allowing me a reason to live."

"We thought survival was a purpose for humans."

"Survival is an instinct. Purpose is what gets us up in the morning. I'm an engineer. My purpose on Earth was to design and build bigger and better rocketry. I was able to apply my mind to solve problems or establish different manufacturing practices. It was something I was very good at and I enjoyed myself. Here on Nikari, what do I have to occupy my days or wake up for?"

Falmas looked confused. "What more could you possibly want? You have our research, regular sessions with Norgal and unlimited access to my time. You are helping us to build a better understanding of humans."

"But you're not building a better understanding. You're seeing how I engage with you in your surroundings. You can research how I adapt to my new life but I'm not acting normally, as I would on Earth. There are no social interactions with friends and family. I'm not able to demonstrate my technical abilities. Instead, I'm coasting from one day to the next. You're only researching an artificial representation of a human. A very depressed human who doesn't want to play anymore."

Falmas shook his head. "What would you suggest that we change so that you behave in a more natural manner? Other than return you to Earth."

Grant didn't hesitate in responding. "Give me something meaningful to do. I know you think humans are a lesser species, but we are intelligent. Find me something where I can use my skills, even if it means sitting me alongside your children. You can then test how intelligent I really am and if I am able to learn. And monitor me in a less obtrusive way. I don't enjoy having physical examinations every few days. Treat me more like an equal and less like a high school project."

"You ask a lot. It is not within my authority to be able to accede to your requests, but I will raise them with my superiors."

"You do that, Falmas. I'm even prepared to trial it for thirty days. That should be enough time to prove to both of us if I'm right or not."

"Will you stop harming yourself? We do not wish you to self-terminate."

Grant nodded. "If you give me the freedom I'm asking for, and something to stimulate my mind, then there will be no reason for me to consider any further suicide attempts."

***

Two days later, Grant was unwinding alone at his favorite location in Prema, the domestic transit station, watching various transports arrive and depart from different cities on Nikari. He had spent many hours here over recent days and was fascinated by the different types of vessels, which all appeared to be unique and designed for specific purposes. They ranged from small pods capable of transporting two individuals, up to enormous liners that could probably carry several thousand in comfort. How each of the vessels was powered was still another mystery as Grant had spotted at least seventeen different types of propulsion systems, none of which he understood.

There were numerous different alien species swarming around and through the station in a steady and organised stream. They seemed to come in all shapes, sizes and colors with the only common element being that nearly all of them were bipeds. When he was here with Falmas, he would ask lots of questions, seeking as much information as he could about each new species that he spotted. And, with the help of his neural implants, he had found that he was able to process and remember for more than he ever used to do.

He had spotted one transport arrive with a group of four-legged creatures dressed in furry jackets and metallic helmets on their large oval heads. He recognized them as Haj'lons, a species largely devoted to agriculture who had learned to farm on a wide range of planets. He hadn't spoken to any Haj'lons so far but was intrigued to discover how they could be so adaptive.

The most surprising thing for Grant was that very few aliens had paid him any attention. They all seemed to take his presence for granted. He wasn't sure whether they had been warned about him or if they were used to new species turning up on their planet. He assumed it was the latter. But all the species appeared to co-operate with one another as they made their way to their destinations. He certainly felt the transit station was peaceful and harmonious.

The building reminded him of any large American airport he'd ever been to. All individuals were walking with intent and the whole process was organized to ensure thousands of individuals got to their destination. The only thing missing was the sight of anyone tearfully saying their goodbyes or greetings to loved ones. Family units and emotion was another area of life here that he would need to understand better.

Out of the corner of his eye he noticed Falmas coming up to him. From the speed of his walk, Grant guessed that Falmas was eager to share some news. He was right. "I have just left a meeting with Director Mortak. He has reviewed all the research activity we have conducted on you and is aware of yourself harm. With some reluctance, he is permitting you to take part in an aptitude test to determine the possibility of placing you on an education course."

Grant couldn't resist a huge smile. "That's fantastic news. Thank you so much, Falmas."

Falmas raised his hand in caution. "This is only a test, and it's not going to be easy. You're not guaranteed to pass and, even if somehow you do, there will still be further decisions to make as to what you are taught."

"I understand. It's a start though, that's the main thing. When am I supposed to take the test?"

"In one hour."

Grant was taken aback but knew it would be unwise to request a delay. "There's no time like the present," he said as he followed Falmas toward the research facility. For the first time since he'd arrived on Nikari he had a spring in his step.

Chapter 8

Ten days later, Grant found himself connected to the engineering education computer via the interface in the back of his neck that fed information directly into his neural cortex. He was excited yet wary at receiving his first tutorial in this way, with information being directly downloaded into his own memory. Falmas had attempted to explain the process, which sounded harmless enough, but the Sentinels were unable to describe how the receipt of large packets of data would feel.

Grant was sitting in a darkened room with only Falmas and Norgal present. "Remember what I've told you," said Norgal, who sounded anxious. "I have prepared a simple tutorial to prepare you. Are you ready?"

Grant gave a thumbs up before realizing after several moments of silence that neither alien understood the gesture. "Yes," he said. "Switch me on."

For a few moments he felt nothing. He was beginning to wonder if the connection was working correctly when he felt a strange tingling sensation start at the base of his neck before quickly spreading to the top of his head. It wasn't painful and was as if someone was tickling the inside of his skulls with a feather. All of a sudden, his vision was replaced with thousands of images, numbers and symbols, flashing by in fractions of seconds.

"There's too much information," he called out. "Can you slow it down?"

"No," replied an irritated Norgal. "I've already turned the machine down to only five percent. My youngest child could use the computer on at least sixty percent. Relax and focus on the information being received. It's down to you to process the information into an order that you can comprehend and access."

"You can do this, Grant," added Falmas in a more reassuring tone.

He took another deep breath and tried to sort the myriad of information that was continuing to flow through the interface. Gradually, he was able to discern distinct shapes and colors before, finally, he pulled together a data file on star maps. Once the information was sorted, he filed it away in the memory storage and re-focused his efforts on finding the next piece of information.

After an hour he stopped for a break. "My brain hurts!" he exclaimed as he sat up. "But I'm getting the hang of it. I can't begin to tell you how happy I am to get this chance. This is such an effective education tool."

The excitement he was feeling was immediately quashed by the sour look on Norgal's face. " Wouldn't call it a resounding success," the Elassian said. "You're still only receiving data at eleven percent capacity. Do you know how much information you have left to process? I'm going to die of old age before you're complete."

"But you've seen I'm a fast learner. By this time tomorrow I'll be much better."

"We'll see," replied Norgal. "I can't recall having anyone this slow before. Unless they had learning difficulties."

"Give him a chance," said Falmas', encouragingly. "There may be an issue with the interface. This is the first time a human has used this device. Maybe you've made a mistake when making the modifications."

"That's not very likely," Norgal sneered. "But I will take a look at the feedback loops." He disappeared down the corridor, returning five minutes later with the same irritated expression on his face. "Okay, human. Let's try this one more time."

Grant lay back down and re-established the connection. He immediately felt a massive improvement in his ability to sort the data that was being relayed into his brain. He noticed he was able to perform the process much quicker and with far more information. It wasn't long before he'd downloaded the complete schematic for a transit vehicle. He now understood how the vehicles were propelled at high speeds.

"Thanks, Norgal. Whatever changes you made are working. How much faster am I processing date now?"

"It required only a minor adjustment," said Norgal who was not going to admit his original modifications were flawed after all. "You're up to eighty percent already. Far more like it."

Falmas was more enthusiastic. "Well done, Grant. We'll soon have you flying interstellar craft."

***

"I hear the training is going well. The human has potential after all."

Falmas was in Director Mortak's office.

"Yes, Jim Grant has shown a surprising aptitude. He is processing and storing information at a remarkable rate. And I have observed a change in his character since his education began."

Mortak looked concerned. "How so? Is the computer damaging him in any way?"

Falmas shook his head. "The opposite. He's finding the whole experience very positive. He's more talkative and is eager to learn more every day. I am disappointed in myself for not suggesting this sooner."

"Is the human ready to pick up additional responsibility? I have plans for both of you. But only when the time is right."

This time, it was Falmas' turn to be concerned. "I don't know what those plans are, Director Mortak. But I have found Grant to be very resilient and determined when he puts his mind to a task. I'm confident he'll be able to perform admirably."

"That's reassuring to hear, Falmas. I need to give you some news about one of your other transgressions. Norgal has reported to me that, as a result of testing the human, he has discovered with some disturbing findings that you will certainly be interested to know. It appears that using nano-tech on humans has an unexpected side-effect. There is something unusual about human DNA that means it fuses with Sentinel DNA used to effect a speedy recovery. It's a property we have not observed in any other medical trials."

"That is indeed interesting. But what is the impact of the fused DNA strands? And how does this discovery affect anything else I've done?"

Mortak walked back to his desk and sat on his contoured chair, pausing for effect. "Norgal doesn't know for sure. The new hybrid DNA strands lay dormant, possibly for months or even years, until they're activated. Computer modeling indicates the subject may gain abilities we've witnessed in other species."

"So, you'll want me to continue my observations in order to spot any of those changes. I have no issue with that."

"The human is only part of my plan. In your last report from Mars you detailed how you had almost killed a female human until you had the compunction to restore hr health. I believe it likely that she now also is carrying hybrid DNA in her genes. Obviously, if that is the case, then I want someone close by who can observe and take action if necessary."

"Georgia Pyke? You think I've altered her DNA?"

"We can't be sure but it's highly likely that your ineptitude has resulted in changes within her. We need to discover what damage you've done."

Falmas ignored the contempt in Director Mortak's voice. He was more surprised at the implied message. "It sounds as if you want me to be the one to make that discovery?"

"You wouldn't me my first choice. My fellow ministers, however, feel it appropriate that you be the one and, if necessary, right the wrong that you created. And they want you to take the human with you. They believe he can offer valuable insights that may help you determine if she has changed. He knew her fairly well, apparently.

Note, however, that you are strictly forbidden from making contact with Georgia Pyke. Confederacy protocols still apply."

"You trust Grant? How can we be sure he'll be ready for the mission?"

"I trust the human less than I trust you, Falmas. You have one hundred and fifty days to have him ready for your first trail mission. Only after that will I evaluate his readiness to accompany you to Earth and Mars to recommence your research."

Falmas couldn't believe that his punishment may be coming to an end. He was being allowed to head back into space. It still meant dealing with Grant's company, but that was a small price to pay in exchange for getting off planet again.

"Thank you, director. I won't let you down." He excitedly returned to the research facility to inform Grant of his news.

Chapter 9

PRESENT DAY

The pale Sun was still low in the sky as Georgia Pyke looked down across the vast Hellas Planitia from her vantage point atop the escarpment five miles above Alpha Base. Below, the crater floor was multiple shades of dull orange and brown, as rocks and dust co-existed as they had done for an eternity. The towering spaceships from Expeditions Two and Three cast long shadows across the ground. All except *Yorktown*, which was laid on its side like a lonely beached whale; a reminder of how close the base had come to being wiped out.

This was only the second time she'd used the Jetcopter in two years. The flight up the side of the cliff had brought back painful memories of the first time she had been forced up to this location. She quickly pushed the memories aside; she couldn't change the past, but the past had certainly changed her.

"I told you it would be an amazing view from her," she said turning to her brother, Jackson. She could see through the faceplate in his helmet that he was staring in wonderment.

"I cannot believe that all of this was created by a meteor impact," he replied. "Can you imagine the size of the rock and the devastating effect it must have had on impact? I've seen the satellite imagery but seeing the impact crater for myself gives a whole new perspective. No wonder the base seems so insignificant at the foot of this cliff face."

Georgia nodded, wishing she had made more time to visit this location. "It may be insignificant at the moment, but I'm hopeful that you'll find the minerals that will suck in the huge amounts of investment necessary to grow our colony. I'm sure you're probably already seeing details that I've not picked up on."

"You're right, sis. I'm studying the walls and they're truly inspiring. There are no sedimentary layers as you find on Earth. I'm more interested in the gullies and ravines that have been created over millions of years. There are signs of rock falls but there's also clear evidence of liquid erosion, probably as the result of ice and water as it's slowly made its way down to the floor of the crater. I can only imagine that there once used to be glaciers that carved into and broke up the rocks. Mars is going to give me one amazing field trip."

"You know that you have all the resources available to you in order to carry out your survey work. If there's anything you need, then you only have to ask."

"Thanks sis. The drones should be returning from their initial reconnaissance in the next few days. The data they provide will allow me to narrow down the search parameters further. All of my equipment has been unloaded by Joe and Vicki, so I don't envisage any delays in starting the prospecting part of my mission."

Georgia looked back out over Hellas plain, trying to find inspiration for what she had to say next. "Jackson, I know I can always rely on you to give me an honest opinion, whether I like it or not. I need to ask you a question."

"Okay, shoot. I'll try to be as forthright as I can be. It sounds like a serious matter."

"Am I becoming too obsessed with my desire to re-connect with the aliens? Is my goal to turn Mars into a new home for mankind that transcends nationality and religion even achievable?"

Jackson took a deep breath. "Wow! Some serious questions. Before I answer, what do you think?"

Georgia didn't need to hesitate. "I'm certain that I'm doing the right thing. Not just for myself but for the future of Earth. Yet most of the time I'm worried that all I have is a personal crusade and I'm working in isolation. Perhaps my experience with the Sentinels has blinkered my rationality and I'm forcing mankind to change rather than let human development take its natural course."

"Revolution rather than evolution," said Jackson.

"Exactly. Except I never saw myself as a revolutionary. I've seen what happens to them throughout history; they end up with a target on their back and wind up dead long before they achieve the outcome they've strived for."

Jackson smiled. "In that case you become a martyr. And you somehow get a wider following and a footnote in history."

"Very funny," Georgia sneered. "I want to stay alive to see the future. I don't just want to be the catalyst for change. Am I strong enough to be a force for change? Some days I'm not sure. Only a handful of people know that we've made contact with aliens. It's not in the forefront of their minds that they have the opportunity to expand beyond the solar system. They're far too focused on their daily problems."

"Okay, this is what I think. You can't do this on your own, however pure and altruistic your motives may be. You need to change public opinion. As you've said, politicians won't instigate change because they're fearful of undermining the power they cling in to. That's why they've held back so much information that needs to be shared. But there are enough people who know the truth and eventually it will leak out. Until then, you have to remain patient. I'm sure you'll be a power for good when the time is right. And for what it's worth, I believe you'll achieve your goal. You're too determined not to succeed."

"Thanks, Jackson," replied Georgia. "I know I can be reckless and impatient at times. I'm finding it harder to work within the rules set by Ground Control."

"It's only natural that you've lost confidence in them. They lied to you about the particle beam technology. And now you're left with two scientists whose mission was to militarize Mars."

Georgia nodded. "I still don't know what to do with Molloy and Anna. They're like two lost sheep at the moment."

"Recruit them. They're highly intelligent people who have recently both lost close colleagues. They've had almost one month to consider what their research cost in the way of human lives. Perhaps they're ready to reform. If you're going to succeed in your quest, then you need everyone on Mars to be converts."

Georgia took a few moments to consider Jackson's words. He made sense. If she couldn't influence opinion on Earth, the least she could do was ensure the rest of the colony were bought in to her ideals. She was their commander, after all. And she would need to understand if there were any dissenters.

A message suddenly appeared on the heads up display in her helmet. It was from Mancuso, informing her that there was a newly arrived report from Earth requiring her urgent attention. So much for the sightseeing tour, but a few more minutes wouldn't hurt.

"Thanks for your confidence in me," she said to her brother. "And you're absolutely right that I need to be patient. I am seeking the biggest change in human history and can't expect overnight success." She smiled ruefully.

"To answer your initial question, I do think you're becoming obsessed with the Sentinels. There's so much that needs to be done at the base and to establish the colony. The crew are looking to you for leadership. My suggestion is to step back from any thoughts of alien contact for the next few months. Allow yourself to see the wood for the trees again after all the trauma you've experienced."

Georgia was slightly surprised by Jackson's answer. She'd convinced herself she was acting rationally and had expected Jackson to confirm it. Maybe she had been avoiding certain issues at the base. "Maybe I should listen to you more often," she said. "Unfortunately, I need to cut this visit short as I'm need back at Alpha Base. But I can't tell you how much I've enjoyed this time out with you." She made her way back to the Jetcopter and climbed on to the platform.

"Likewise," Jackson smiled nervously back as he followed her. "We need to do this more often." He held on tightly to the bar in front of him as Georgia piloted the jetcopter over the rim of the crater and down the sheer drop back toward the base. As the jetcopter dropped at a dizzying speed close to the cliff face, he remained silent, aware that she was taking advantage of his fear of heights. He closed his eyes, hoping it would help, and made a mental note to exact his revenge. If only he knew what her weaknesses were.

***

Mancuso was waiting for Georgia in the Control Room. "I was watching as you landed the jetcopter. That must be some ride from the crater rim."

Georgia nodded as she sat in her command chair in front of the main display screen. "There's no denying that it's a long way down. It scared the shit out of Jackson, even though he'd never admit it. His silence spoke volumes."

Mancuso laughed out loud. "I'm sure you didn't enjoy that for one moment. Was he impressed with what he saw from up there? It must be an amazing view."

"He's the first trained geologist on Mars, looking out at a whole new world for him to explore. Of course he was impressed. I think he was more interested in rock formations and the limited effects of erosion than either you or I would be. Anyway, where's the message?"

Mancuso pressed a button in front of him causing the frozen image of a grizzled General Stockton to appear on the main screen. The general was in his best dress uniform and appeared to be alone in his office at Houston. Georgia could immediately tell from Stockton's expression that he was about to share some bad news. With a knot in her stomach, she asked Mancuso to hit the play button.

"Commander Pyke," General Stockton began. "Georgia. I've just finished a teleconference with President Wyndham, the secretary of state and the national security advisor where I tendered my resignation. The president reluctantly accepted it and I will be stepping down in two days' time. In the circumstances I felt I had no other option.

"Over the past four weeks, I have thought long and hard about my actions before and during the disastrous exercise with the particle beam device. I realize now that I should have kept you informed or our plans. Instead I've broken your trust and I don't think that situation can be repaired. For that, I take complete responsibility and offer my heartfelt apologies. Although it would not have prevented the Russian and Chinese devices from also arriving on Mars or prevented the death of Captain Bailey or Professor Duncan, I should have had more faith in you.

"I should also let you know that at midday today, the president will be speaking to the nation to advise them he is stepping down and Vice President Ramsay will be assuming his role. To be honest, he also has no choice. There has been public condemnation not only at the deaths of American astronauts at the hands of the Chinese but also the billions of dollars spent on a secret weapons program that no one believes is designed to protect Earth from asteroids. The whole exercise has been an unmitigated disaster.

"The Mars program is now at risk of being pulled. I've been fire fighting as much as I can to ensure funding is maintained for Expedition Four and beyond but it's tough. So, time for a fresh administration with new ideas and no baggage to step in and deal with this cluster-fuck.

"Georgia, I know we've had our differences, but I can truly say I've enjoyed working with you. You have continued to uphold the traditions and values of the Astronaut Corps." The general paused, visibly struggling to contain the emotions he must be feeling. Georgia knew that he was a proud man and had served in the military for over fifty years. This was a sad way for his career to end.

Stockton quickly recovered his composure. "I have done my absolute best to support you and your crew. I have nothing but respect for all the courageous astronauts currently on Mars and wish you well for the future. And there's no need to worry about me. I was close to retiring anyway and Mrs Stockton has been stockpiling brochures for cruise ships in the last two weeks. It's been a long time since we took a vacation together. If you ever return to Earth, make sure you come and find me. Stockton out."

Georgia glanced across at Mancuso. "I can't say I'm surprised by the news but it's sad to see the general leave. He's a good man and I doubt we'd be on Mars at all without his determination and willpower."

Mancuso nodded. "I only met him twice, but he was a force of nature. There aren't many like him anymore."

"I wonder who we'll end up with. There are a few obvious candidates at Houston, but they may be tarnished by the current scandal. The vice president may be forced to bring in an outsider." Georgia was concerned by the possibilities. If there were issues around the future of the program, then Stockton's replacement needed to be dynamic, powerful and most of all enthusiastic. What she needed for Alpha Base was some stability, no more accidents and for Jackson to have some quick wins with his geological surveys. If he could find rich mineral deposits, it would be easier to persuade the major corporations to extend their funding. It felt like her tenure on Mars was on a knife-edge and she wasn't ready to be ordered home.

Chapter 10

Deeper inside the pressurized lava tube that contained most of Alpha Base, Doctor Megan Betts was sitting at her workstation in the medical facility. She was aware she was frowning as she tried to make sense of the results from Georgia latest medical. Although she'd been closely monitoring all personnel, and Georgia in particular, the information in front of her was entirely different to anything she'd seen so far.

Because of Georgia's unique medical issues shortly after Expedition Two landed on Mars over two years earlier, Megan had observed several minor anomalies which had been resolved once Georgia was able to recall the medical procedures performed by the Sentinels. But what she was looking at now was beyond her comprehension.

Across the small room, Doctor Benjamin Coleman was quietly reading a medical report on his computer terminal. He'd been there when Megan had arrived almost two hours earlier. It was an easy decision to not share any pleasantries with him; he'd made it clear when they were first introduced that he didn't appreciate his concentration being interrupted. In the month since then, the atmosphere had remained frosty between the pair of them. He seemed unable, or unwilling, to let go of his resentment that she had chosen to remain on Mars. As far as Megan was concerned, any anger he felt was his problem to deal with, not hers.

With Georgia's information in front of her, Megan now faced a dilemma. Should she send it directly to Ground Control to get a second opinion from the doctors based there, or should she consult with Doctor Coleman first? Involving him was the proper thing to do, even he was acting like a complete asshat!

She took a deep breath and made her approach. "Excuse me Doctor Coleman," she said in the politest voice she could muster. "Would you mind taking a look at these results? I'm having trouble trying to make sense of them."

Doctor Coleman had an irritated expression as he removed his glasses and looked up from his computer. "Is it urgent, Doctor Betts? I'm halfway through a research paper on the long-term effects of exposure to gamma radiation on the nervous system."

Megan controlled her frustration as she replied, "I thought you might find this of interest. Not to worry if you're busy. I'll send the information to Houston. I'm sure they'll be only too happy to get to grips with these abnormalities."

"No, no. You don't want to do that," blustered Coleman, clearly fearful of how it would appear if he was left out of the loop. "I could probably do with a break from my reading. It's a very complex subject after all and the research was completed by the World's leading experts from Toronto and San Francisco."

Megan smiled to herself as he pushed his chair across the room and sat next to her. *Definitely an asshat.*

"What do you have for me?" he asked, peering at the information on Megan's screen.

"These are Commander Pyke's latest medical results. I've been monitoring her closely since the escape pod accident last month." She gave Doctor Coleman several moments to absorb the details.

"I don't see any particular issues other than an elevated white blood count and a large number of B cells. Both indicative of an active bone marrow that may require some further investigation. But other than that, these look like the records of a very fit person. I don't understand why you felt the need to share the results with me." The last sentence was said with a sneer and he looked eager to return to his workstation.

"Yes, you're absolutely right. All of the commander's wounds have healed. Now look at this other screen. It identifies her injuries when we picked her up at the crash site."

Coleman put his glasses back on so that he could read all the details. After several seconds, he began shaking his head at what he saw. "Remind me. When did the accident happen?"

"Twenty-nine days ago."

"So, she arrived with typical trauma injuries for an accident if this type. Severe contusions, mild concussion and a broken rib are standard, and I would expect a full recovery after four weeks. But then you mention she had two crushed vertebrae and her right knee suffered a grade three posterior cruciate ligament tear and a dislocated patella. Ouch! Those injuries normally take a minimum of three months to recover, with surgery and extensive physiotherapy. I'm not aware you performed any such treatments. I don't even recall seeing the commander wearing a back brace."

"She didn't wear a brace, and there's been no surgery. Her body has somehow healed itself in rapid time. And I do not know how."

"I understand now why you've come to me. I'm sure it wasn't easy for you to request my assistance. Of course, I'm more than happy to share my expertise. Can you send me the commander's medical records?"

That was enough for Megan, whose temper finally snapped. She stood up and glared down at him. "Let's get one thing straight, Coleman. I've included you as a courtesy only. I don't expect you'll be able to determine a prognosis. But the commander is my best friend and I want what's best for her. Stop being an asshole and get over yourself. Otherwise, I will be going straight to the Medical Board to lodge a formal complaint about your attitude. Is that clear?"

Doctor Coleman wasn't the type to be intimidated. "There's no need to react like that," he calmly replied. " You really do need to be less emotional, Doctor Betts. It would absolutely improve our working relationship if you were less confrontational."

"You have got to be joking!" Megan exclaimed. She realized she no longer wanted to be in the vicinity of her colleague and headed for the door. "Just take a look at Georgia's files on the medical system and let me know if you have any theories. I'm going for a coffee." She slammed the door behind her, regretting her decision to remain on Mars instead of returning home when she had the chance.

Chapter 11

Jackson was in his geochemical laboratory at the rear of Alpha Base, eagerly awaiting the return of two of his drones. Each drone was transporting four rock samples from their designated survey zones, collected from three inches below the Martian surface using a bespoke drill. The drones were also equipped with basic spectrometers, giving them the ability to perform rudimentary tests of the samples and identify which minerals were present.

The initial findings sent back by drone number three appeared to be the most promising, with high concentrations of magnesium and titanium detected. Drone one had so far drawn a blank, finding only carbonates and sulfides; Jackson had re-directed it to its second survey zone.

Drone two was also returning to Alpha Base with samples that looked as if they contained aluminium, although it was difficult for Jackson to interpret the information.

Lieutenant Charlie Molloy was with Jackson, helping to calibrate the delicate equipment that would be able to provide accurate confirmation of what substances were within each of the samples. "I can't do any more, Jackson," he said from underneath the control console next to the large Spectroradiometer. "There's no one else that can finely tune this instrument better than I have. It even exceeds the parameters stated in the instruction manual."

"Thanks. Charlie. I'm really grateful for all the help you've given me this week."

"I'm more than happy to assist," Molloy replied. "After all, it'll help to occupy my time here. Now that my weapons research has been canned, I have plenty of spare time. It looks as if I'm going to be assisting the chief engineer to repair the construction robots to allow the rest of the base to be built. Not exactly what I signed up for. However, I understand there's a need for all personnel to be flexible."

"Okay, Lieutenant Grumpy. I think you'll find that most of the residents are multi-skilled and willing to help each other. You can't carry on being inflexible."

Molloy, stood up, absently brushing away a thin layer of dust of dust from his trousers. *The dammed stuff gets everywhere.* "I have a meeting with your sister later today. I'm going to be presenting my ideas of how productivity can be improved, together with a list of projects I think I'm well suited for."

"Good for you, soldier. And do any of your plans include the very attractive Professor Kozlovsky? I've seen the pair of you getting closer over the past few weeks." Jackson smiled as he noticed Molloy's face redden.

"I've just been trying to make her feel welcome," stammered Molloy. "Anna's been through a very traumatic experience. Her base was destroyed, and all her colleagues killed. She knows no one here. We've connected because of our similar backgrounds in particle beam research. I've included her in some of my projects but that's through merit. She can be a very valuable member of Alpha Base for the remaining time she has here. It would be crazy not to make use of her skills."

"So why are you blushing?" laughed Jackson, making the most of Molloy's discomfort. "Your feelings for her go beyond sympathy for her situation, don't they?"

"Can we change the subject please? You're becoming tedious. Tell me how your work is going."

Jackson accepted that Molloy didn't want to discuss his personal life. "Progress is slower than my employers would like. They're not interested in the delays we suffered in being able to unpack the prospecting drones. The executive board want results as soon as possible and are reminding me on a daily basis."

"Do they expect you to perform miracles?" asked Molloy, shaking his head in surprise.

"You have to understand the large corporations have invested billions of dollars to support this program. That's an enormous risk they've taken in the expectation of big rewards." Jackson sat down and took a drink water. "While I don't need reminding of the urgency, the corporations and NASA will be planning the equipment, cargo and personnel for the next two Mars missions. They're reliant on what I discover. They also need me to confirm the existence of rich sources of minerals before they're willing to invest further funding."

"That's a lot of pressure on your shoulders. Is there anything your sister can do to assist you?"

"Not until the drones return later today. She did prioritize the unloading of the key instrumentation as well as making this space available for my work. But the real activity will take place when I'm able to confirm the contents of the return samples. That's when I'll need to make some field trips. There's nothing to beat empirical research."

"In that case, good luck Jackson. Let me know if I can help. But please stop mentioning Anna." Molloy smiled as he stood to leave.

"I can't promise that," laughed Jackson. "But thanks for the offer of help. I will take you up on it."

***

Guided by their autopilot systems, the two drones landed gently in front of Alpha Base just before sunset, allowing the samples to be carefully retrieved and taken to Jackson's lab. Each sample came sealed in a metallic container no larger than a beer can. From the outside, each one looked nondescript but Jackson knew how precious the contents were. They had the potential to change the very future of the fledgling Mars colony.

Jackson opened the lid of the first, pouring the rocky contents onto a metal plate. The sample resembled the orange rocks and dust that covered Hellas Planitia but he hoped that the delicate spectrography instruments would detect the key elements he was desperate to find. He had warned everyone not to raise their hopes too much on the first samples being a success, but he couldn't help but be optimistic.

"So, this is what's going to make this base rich," said Georgia as she entered the lab. She bent down next to Jackson to take a closer look at the pile of dust and rock. "It doesn't look very impressive," she said, disappointedly.

"That's because you don't know what you're looking for," replied Jackson. "If you take your time, you'll notice dark specks running through some of the smaller rocks. There's also one stone that has a smooth dark side with what appears to be a vein of a metallic ore. Of course, it may just be worthless iron oxide."

"Or it may be one of the minerals you're looking for," Georgia replied encouragingly.

He nodded. "Absolutely. But that doesn't mean that there's a sufficient concentration to start mining. I keep telling you, there are so many unknowns. If geology was easy, then I'd be out of a job."

"When do you think you'll know for sure?"

"I've seven other samples to test as well. I can conduct some simple checks to rule out any samples that don't look promising. For the more interesting specimens, I have a series of fourteen different experiments to examine the composition and ratios of metallic elements. By the morning I should have a clear idea if any of these canisters deserve the full treatment."

"And then what?"

"You are impatient!" Jackson teased. "If there is sufficient evidence to warrant it, I'll need to carry out more detailed site surveys. What that means is me taking one of your extravehicular vehicles and heading out on a field trip for maybe one week. I can get far better results if I'm in situ. I assume you'll make one MEV available as you know the importance of my work."

"You know you can have a MEV. Who will you be taking with you? You can't go on your own."

"To be honest, I haven't thought that far ahead. Maybe Charlie Molloy as he's offered to help. But I'll deal with it when I actually need to go. I've already reprogrammed the prospecting drones for their next mission, and they're primed to leave at first light. It could be weeks before we find a viable site."

Georgia shook her head. "I have more faith in you. You'll see."

"Let me do my work and you'll find out."

Georgia smiled. "I can take a hint. I'll be waiting to hear your good news in the morning."

Once Georgia had left, Jackson started his meticulous experiments knowing that he faced a long night. However, he couldn't help but feel a quiver of excitement at the prospect of success. He'd had the sensation on numerous field trips on Earth and he'd developed a reputation for sniffing out rich mineral deposits in remote locations. This was what he was sent to Mars for and he was going to prove to everyone that he was the right man for the job.

Chapter 12

Georgia woke at five the following morning and was instantly disappointed to have not received any messages from Jackson overnight. *No news is good news,* she tried convincing herself. *Perhaps he's being excessively thorough to confirm his results.* She knew that he wouldn't present anyone with positive results unless he was absolutely certain. There was too much at stake for him to make any embarrassing errors. She ignored the voice in her said that was asking how she'd react if the results were negative; it simply wasn't an option at that moment.

To take her mind off the subject, she went to the gym. As usual, it was empty at this time. Georgia knew that other members of the crew wouldn't show up until nearer six. She enjoyed having the time to herself before having to face the daily workload of being base commander. She plugged in her headphones and spent the next forty-five minutes on the treadmill, letting her mind drift as she listened to Billy Joel.

Feeling relaxed and ready to face the day ahead, Georgia was making her way from the showers to her quarters when she saw Megan walking toward her. "I don't often see you this early, Megan. Have you started house calls?"

Megan smiled nervously. "Good morning, Georgia. Yes, I was coming to see you, but I can promise I'm not going to make a habit of it. I was hoping to catch you in your quarters, but I can see you've been following my instructions to exercise regularly. Is it possible to have a word in private?"

"Of course, follow me. Is it anything to do with Doctor Coleman again?" asked Georgia as she continued along the corridor with Megan falling in step beside her.

"Not this time," she laughed. "But I'd still prefer if he wasn't here. I need to talk about your recovery and the results from your last medical."

They stepped into Georgia's quarters, with Megan closing the door behind her.

"Is everything okay?" asked Georgia. She'd heard the tone in Megan's voice before and it usually meant bad news.

"Yes. Don't worry. Your results couldn't be better. They show that all your injuries have completely healed since the crash. Just to be sure, did you notice any pains or swelling this morning when you were exercising?"

Georgia knew, despite Megan's relaxed tone, that there must be a good reason for the question. But she couldn't imagine what it could be. "There's no reaction at all," she said, shaking her head. "In fact, I could have run further if I'd had more time. I can't remember the last time I was this fit. Even though I started exercising again only four days ago."

"Don't you think that's strange. How much training do you normally require to achieve this level of fitness?"

Georgia gave it some thought. "Months at least. But that was on Earth. I assumed the reduced Martian gravity was aiding my recovery. Why do I feel you're about to tell me I've been mistaken?"

Megan sat down on the one chair in the room, studying Georgia as she sat on her bed. "The injuries you suffered in the crash were severe, but not life threatening. I know you think I'm a miracle worker, but I had nothing to do with how quickly your injuries healed. If we were on Earth, you'd still be sitting in a back brace and receiving light physiotherapy to strengthen your knee. To allow you to walk! I've never known anyone recover so quickly. And neither has Doctor Coleman."

"You actually spoke to him! Now I am beginning to worry."

"It's no laughing matter, Georgia. I required his second opinion to confirm I'd not missed anything or made a mistake in the initial assessment of your injuries. I think he was secretly happy that I asked him, but he'll never admit it."

"I hope this doesn't mean you want to run more tests on me. I have the base to complete and I don't have time to be treated as a test subject for one of your experiments. I feel great so why do you feel the need to discover why I've recovered so easily. Surely, it's related to being here on Mars. You should throw out your Earth-based medical assumptions. They're not relevant here."

"Don't you want to know what's happening to your body? I know I would. There has to be a reason for its amazing healing properties. We could make a discovery that will help others. Can you imagine that?"

"Don't try to blackmail me, Megan. There's too much going on right now. Establishing this base has to be my priority. I don't think you appreciate how precarious our position here is." Georgia immediately regretted snapping at her best friend.

But Megan wasn't easily intimidated. "And your welfare is my priority. I've patched you together more than enough times since we arrived on Mars. I understand that your role as base commander keeps you busy. Can't you delegate more? Joe Mancuso is more than capable of taking on more responsibility as your second in command. And Commander Dunn has leadership experience."

Georgia knew that her friend would not let the matter go easily. As one of the base's physicians, Megan had the ability to declare that any member of the crew, including the base commander, was medically unfit to carry on their duties. It was the ultimate threat and Georgia wasn't sure Megan would use it. "Look Megan, I do understand that my health is important," she said. "I will submit to your examination, but it needs to wait until the current situation at the base has stabilized. Four weeks maximum and I'll let you do whatever you need to. Is that okay?"

"No, but do I have a choice?"

Before Georgia could answer, there was a knock on the door. It opened to reveal Jackson looking tired and disheveled. He'd obviously been up all night and was fidgety from too much caffeine.

"Sorry sis, I thought you were alone," he said. He smiled warmly at Megan. "Good morning, doctor. I hope I'm not interrupting anything important."

Megan shook her head and replied. "Only your stubborn sister's health. Although it doesn't seem important to her."

"It never does. Georgia, I need you to come with me now. I have something I need to show you. I think you're going to be very happy."

Georgia beamed. She could see that Jackson was finding it almost impossible to contain his enthusiasm. He was like a child with a new toy. Which meant only one thing. He'd found the evidence for precious metals that they were all looking for.

***

"How sure can you be?" Georgia asked once they'd returned to Jackson's lab. She was doing her best to contain the exhilaration flowing through her. She wanted to see the facts for herself. Could she really be this lucky so soon?

Before Jackson could reply, Mancuso burst into the room followed closely by Megan and Dunn. Each of them had eager expressions on their faces, knowing that this could be a momentous moment for the future of Alpha Base as well as human colonization.

"I hope you don't mind the interruption," said Mancuso. "Megan told us that Jackson may have some exciting news for us."

"Relax," replied Georgia. "Jackson was about to provide me with the details."

Jackson took a deep breath and ran his fingers through his unkempt hair. He felt slightly daunted by the four pairs of eyes staring intently at him. The tension in the room was palpable as everyone waited to hear his news. "I've run all the tests that I can, some of them twice. I would appreciate if someone could verify my work as I've been up all night," he said. "However, my results show that two of the samples returned by one of my drones contain excessive concentrations of magnesium and titanium. The percentage content ratio of each of these minerals strongly indicates that there are large deposits present in that location."

"Sufficient for mining purposes?" asked Georgia.

Jackson shrugged. "There's no way to be absolutely sure from such small samples. We could simply have chanced upon a small deposit left by a meteor strike. It requires a more detailed survey of the area. I need to analyze drill samples at different depths to at least fifty feet. Remember, these samples are from only just below the surface. If I can get to the area, I'll need four or five days to carry out the necessary tests."

"So, it sounds as if it's too early to celebrate," Megan said with more than a hint of disappointment.

"I wouldn't crack open the champagne just yet, Megan. There are many reasons why the results have come back as they have. And, assuming I've not made any mistakes, there is much work ahead of me to be able to determine the potential quantities of these metals. However, I am cautiously optimistic from what I've seen so far."

Georgia felt deflated. She'd been sure that Jackson's initial enthusiasm was due to absolute proof. Now he was telling them all to rein in their excitement. It was an unexpected roller-coaster of emotions and she was currently lost for anything positive to say.

Fortunately, Joe Mancuso was harder to disappoint. "Which area are you talking about?" he asked. "Do I need to give you a ride in *Lexington*?"

Jackson pulled up a map of Hellas Planitia on his computer screen. "The survey area is roughly three hundred and eighty miles north of Alpha Base," he said pointing at the screen. "Still within the confines of the Hellas crater. That means I can drive an MEV there in less than two days. I would suggest that's more efficient, and safer, than using our main spaceship. I can load all the necessary supplies and equipment onto the MEV's trailer."

Georgia nodded in agreement. "Joe, I've already agreed that he can take an MEV, on the condition that he takes someone with him. Jackson, have you decided who you would like to accompany you?"

"Not yet. Who is going to want to spend a week with me looking at rocks?"

"That's why I think I should go with you," said Georgia.

There were surprised looks from everyone in the room, except from Jackson who simply smiled.

"Is that wise?" said Dunn. "I thought you were continuing to supervise completion of the base. I don't want to question your decisions, but I would have thought your place is here, as base commander."

Georgia smiled. "We've not worked together for very long, Dunn. So you may not be aware that I like to be closely involved in the action. You and Mancuso have been doing a fantastic job to coordinate all the activity around the base over the past few weeks. And, as my doctor has reminded me, I should be delegating more to the pair of you. I am confident that you can carry on without me for a week or so. And you have plenty of expertise to fall back on if necessary."

"Thank you for your faith in us," replied Dunn. "We'll do our best not to let you down."

Georgia cringed inwardly at Dunn's formality. She was still trying far too hard to impress everyone. "While I'm away, can you also try to relax? You're not stationed on a military base now. We're adventurers. Although we're faced with dangers every day, it doesn't mean we can't inject a little fun into our daily lives. I've never been one for deferring to rank. I know what everyone here is capable of and that really is all I need to know to let you get on with your job."

Georgia noticed that Mancuso and Megan struggled to keep straight faces, but Dunn looked embarrassed at having been called out. She didn't feel guilty about the outburst; the uptight commander had been getting on her nerves for several weeks.

"Jackson, I'll ask Professor Kozlovsky to review your analysis," she continued. "Anna may not have a geology background but she understands the principles associated with the correct analysis and research. I believe she wants something to do and this exercise should be ideal. She'll be able to verify that you've not made any obvious errors. In the meantime, get some rest because you look like shit. And you've got plenty of work ahead of you."

***

Before Georgia was able to settle down for the evening, she unexpectedly received a video message from Libby Selznick, the NASA Administrator. Looking at her wall clock, Georgia calculated it must be approaching nine P.M. in Houston. Intrigues by why Selznick was contacting her so late in the day, she opened the message.

Libby Selznick was sitting in her office looking immaculately dressed as she always did. Next to her was a military man that Georgia didn't recognize. "Good evening, Commander Pyke," began the administrator with a warm smile. "I wanted you to be the first to know that Colonel Eugene Byrne has been appointed as General Stockton's replacement, with immediate effect. The colonel comes with very impressive credentials and has been selected by the White House. He's not worked directly for NASA before but has been involved in some very significant government projects over the years. I'll let him explain more about himself."

Georgia was surprised by the haste with which General Stockton had been replaced. It seemed almost as if he was now an embarrassment to be swept under the carpet and forgotten about. She hoped that was not the case; he was a great man and had made a massive impact on the Mars program. This new colonel looked like a typical military man. Regulation hair, intense blue eyes that stared unblinking into the camera and an impeccable dress uniform. Even before he had spoken, she knew he would be difficult to work with.

"Hello, Commander Pyke. I understand that you had a very strong working relationship with General Stockton. That is until he chose to keep you out of the loop on the particle beam development. He may have had good reasons to do so and I intend to discover the reasons for his actions. I don't expect there will be any significant changes under my tenure although I will be introducing more rigorous controls and reporting structures to prevent what I perceive as relaxed processes that have gradually found their way into the program.

"As Administrator Selznick has said, the White House has brought me in to correct the wrongs that have plagued the program. My last ten years has involved working with the air force's hypersonic fighter project. I've more than proved my ability to bring failing projects back into line with the right people and strong chains of command. I trust that you will respect my decision and act upon my orders with unquestioning obedience."

Georgia could see that Libby Selznick appeared decidedly uncomfortable by the colonel's confident tirade. She knew it was highly unlikely that the administrator had had any say in his selection. And it was clear that the colonel intended taking no prisoners. Georgia wondered what the extent of his remit would be. It was likely to be extensive if he had White House support. It spelled bad news for her; she'd never been good at following orders.

She felt it only appropriate that she respond to the message. "Colonel Byrne. May I be one of the first to welcome you onto the program? You have some very large boots to fill. General Stockton has cast a large shadow across the project for many years and I'm sure you would agree it would not be the success it is if it wasn't for him. I'm happy to hear that don't intend to make any significant changes. I've always said, 'if it's not broke why fix it' and I'm confident you have enough experience to appreciate that's a good motto to follow. I'm sure we'll learn to work well together, and I am more than happy to share my plans with you so that we can pro-actively create a thriving and sustainable Mars colony."

She left it there, feeling she'd done enough to let the colonel know where she stood. She was mildly interested what his reaction would be, but her gut told her that Colonel Byrne was going to be a thorn in her side for the foreseeable future.

Chapter 13

The sun was rising slowly over the distant horizon as the MEV, containing Jackson and Georgia, pulled slowly away from Alpha Base early the following morning. Georgia, sitting in the passenger seat, leaned forward to look out of the side window and was able to see most of Alpha Base's crew standing by the large window in the control room, watching her departure. She knew that everyone realized the importance of the next few days; it hadn't escaped anyone's attention that there was a lot of pressure from Earth for the Martian base to prove its viability. Georgia was sure the pressure would only act as a catalyst to bring the crew closer together.

She turned to glance across at Jackson who was sitting in the driver's seat. The navigation computer was currently driving the MEV, leaving him as another passenger. He was staring out of his window at the distant supply ships that towered over the plain. "We have an audience," she said. "There's a lot of hope pinned to your broad shoulders, little brother."

Jackson, as ever, was laid back. "I've tried not to set expectations too high. You're the one that's made everyone excited. I really don't know what we'll find when we arrive at the site."

Georgia smiled. "I have a positive feeling about this. We're due some good luck and I'm sure this is it."

"I hope you're not disappointed. While your enthusiasm is encouraging, I'd rather reserve judgment for now. One of has to remain impartial."

Georgia kept any other thoughts she had to herself. She knew that Jackson had a point and there was little point debating what they might find in two days. Instead, she looked out of the front window at what lay ahead. Barren rock and sand as far as the eye could see. From satellite imagery, as well as from the vantage point at the top of the cliff, she knew that the landscape didn't change for the first two hundred miles. The relatively flat surface was covered with small rocks and boulders which would be quick and easy to traverse, allowing the MEV to maintain a steady thirty miles per hour. Then the terrain altered dramatically with the ground turning into a large series of regular undulations that looked like ripples. Imagery had revealed that these undulations were ten to twenty feet high and up to five hundred feet wide, but it had yet to be determined how solid the ground was. Ground Control had speculated that that the undulations were likely to have collected large deposits of dust and sand that could potentially bog down the MEV if it carried too much speed into a sand dune.

With not much to worry about for the next two days, Georgia say back in her chair and opened a romance novel to read on her small computer pad, letting Jackson monitor the data on the nav computer. She couldn't remember the last time she'd found time to read any fiction and was thankful that she finally would have some time to herself.

***

One hour after the MEV had departed Alpha Base, Mancuso received a priority video message from Ground Control. He raised an eyebrow as soon as he saw it was marked confidential and sent by the newly appointed head of the Mars Colonization Program, Colonel Byrne. Mancuso immediately called Commander Dunn to the control room to see what the colonel had to say.

The colonel was in General Stockton's former office, sitting next to a senior looking official who neither Mancuso nor Dunn recognized. While the colonel was in his army uniform, the stranger was sitting stiffly in a suit.

"Gentlemen," began Byrne, his steely blue eyes staring through the screen as if he could actually see Mancuso and Dunn. "The actions of General Zhang, one month ago caught us with our pant down. Some people had become complacent with the program, believing that each country would behave ethically and independently of one another. That naive and short-sighted type of behavior is something I will not tolerate under my tenure.

"During the past few days, I have engaged the services of Mr Kyle Buckley, sitting to my left, to review opportunities to extend our reach on Mars as well as better protect our interests there. Mr Buckley is the best strategic analyst I know, having worked with him on several projects before I joined NASA. He now works as an independent consultant and he formerly spent twenty-five years working for the FBI. Already, he's suggested a very interesting possibility that I want you to consider."

Buckley nervously cleared his throat and began. "The remit the colonel gave me was to review the assets currently on Mars, or in orbit around the planet, in order to improve the safety of you and your fellow astronauts, and to increase efficiency. I understand there is a strict window of opportunity to prove the reliability and viability of Alpha Base following a series of unfortunate incidents.

"The first question I had for the colonel was whether I was restricted to American assets only. He has allowed me to extend my research to the destroyed Russian base, Derzost, as well as their orbiting spaceship, *Moskva*. What I have to share with you next is highly confidential, for obvious reasons. The destruction of Derzost is likely to be a fatal blow to the Russians who do not have the resources to fund another mission in the near term. Definitely not in time to launch in two years. Although Derzost is of no use to us, there may be some equipment that could be re-purposed for our own good.

"My preliminary analysis has determined that there is a landing craft close to Derzost. Recent satellite imagery shows little if any damage to that craft which makes me believe it could be salvageable." Buckley paused for dramatic effect, allowing Colonel Byrne to continue the narrative.

"I'm surprised no one considered this sooner," he said. "If we're able to utilize the landing craft, we could complete smaller hops around the planet far easier. The two-day journey Commander Pyke is now on could be completed in under one hour. It would be a game changer in our exploration of Mars and allow for the speedier search for minerals.

"We've not spoken to the Russians about this possibility, and I have no intent to either. The laws of salvage in space or other planets have not been written but it would be impossible for Russia to stop us from taking their craft. So, while the commander and her brother are away searching for the holy grail, I want us to work together to formulate a recovery mission using the *Lexington* and a select group of your crew. Only include people you can absolutely trust. For now, there's no need to share this with Commander Pyke. We'll send you the schematics for the Russian craft once we've obtained them, together with instructions in English on how to pilot it. I trust that you will both handle this matter discretely and report only to me with any thoughts or questions you may have. Send me your initial views, together with a list of the resources you may require by this time tomorrow. Thank you for your time."

"What the fuck was that all about?", Mancuso exclaimed, as the screen went blank.

Dunn looked equally dumbfounded. "It sounds like a desperate move. Recovering Russian technology is not what I expected to be doing."

"The colonel's ordering us to steal a spaceship! What makes him think that's the right thing to do? He wants to turn us into space pirates. I can see why he waited for Georgia to leave before he told us his plan."

"What do we do?" asked Dunn.

"I don't know. While I can see the merits of acquiring the landing craft, I'd feel better if the orders weren't secret. Has the colonel learned nothing from the recent disaster? I feel like we need to bring Doctor Betts in on this one. She often has a clearer perspective on tricky matters, and I trust her judgment."

***

"Hey, sleepy head. Time for lunch."

Georgia started at the sound of Jackson's voice as she briefly tried to remember where she was. "How long have I been asleep?" she asked, stifling a yawn.

Jackson smiled as he passed her a protein bar. "Almost two hours. It was a shame to wake you. You looked so peaceful there."

She, still feeling only half awake, looked down at the computer pad resting on her lap. "The rocking motion of the MEV must have sent me to sleep. I didn't realize I was so exhausted."

"You were always the same when we went for long drives with mum and dad. You were always resting your head on my shoulder in the back of the car."

"And I recall you took pleasure in waking me back then too," she replied, smiling at the memory. "What's our status?"

Jackson glanced at the screen in front of him. "We've traveled one hundred and eight miles so far. We're more or less on schedule and power reserves are nominal You've not missed anything, unless you enjoy the endless sight of brown rocks."

Georgia looked out at the landscape which looked depressingly similar to the view from Alpha Base's control room. The only difference was that they were now well away from the edge of the crater, with the sheer cliff walls far less imposing from this distance. For a moment, she suddenly felt very exposed and vulnerable. "I hadn't realized how reliant I'd become on the rock face to provide shelter and safety. I suddenly feel anxious that I'm miles away from Alpha Base and the only moving object on Hellas Plain. It's a very strange feeling."

"You have been living in the shadows of the crater wall for two years so it shouldn't come as a shock. I'm still learning to get used to the ominous cliff face. I keep expecting a rock to fall on me every time I step out of the airlock."

"This is the furthest anyone has traveled since we first landed. I've been so focused on completing the base that there's been no time to explore our new home," she said. "Although, before you arrived, there was no reason to go exploring."

"I hope it's not a wasted journey."

Georgia shrugged. "It won't be. Even if you're right and we don't find sufficient quantities of magnesium or titanium, I now recognize that I need a break. And what better way to spend it than with you." Noticing the time on the main chronometer, she said, "it's time to report back to Alpha Base."

Flicking a switch in front of her, she said, "Alpha Base, comms check."

There was silence for several seconds before she heard Mancuso's voice. "Good afternoon, Georgia. How are you enjoying your road trip?"

"We've not passed any service plazas yet. But, otherwise, nothing to report. Any news I need to be aware of."

"Ground Control have requested regular updates. To be expected on such an important field trip."

"Okay, thanks Joe. I'll perform another comms check in four hours. Georgia out."

***

In Alpha Base's control room, Mancuso looked at Megan. "Are you sure we're doing the right thing?"

Megan nodded grimly. "There's nothing Georgia can do from where she is. They can't afford to return here when there's so much at stake with their mission. Anyway, she left you in charge while she's away."

"But we both know she wouldn't approve of the colonel's plans. I feel disloyal."

"I understand, Joe. It's more than coincidence that Colonel Byrne is telling you his plans. I don't think you have any choice but to follow his immediate orders. All you have to do is pull an operational plan together. Taking the Russian craft requires a number of complex steps before it's approved. Hopefully, someone with an ounce of sense will decide that the risk far exceeds the reward. If not, then that's the time you involve Georgia. I'm happy to tell her it was my idea not to involve her at this stage."

Mancuso was still doubtful but nodded his agreement. "Okay, we play along with the colonel and his consultant for the time being. But that's as far as it goes."

***

Around three hours later, the landscape began to change. Jackson was the first to spot the subtle changes in the rock formations and the lighter coloration of the sand. He would have liked to stop and take some samples but there was no time for that now. He'd have to make do with observing the changes around them and taking plenty of video footage.

Soon, they crested the first of the undulations, and looked across a shallow valley to the next peak. Georgia slowed the MEV, conscious that this new terrain may hold hidden dangers for them. The view in front of her was like nothing she had experienced so far during her time on Mars. She had been used to looking at the flat and featureless plain from the control room window.

"You're the geologist," she said. "What are your initial thoughts?"

Jackson stared intently out of the window, testing his memory for any similar formations on Earth. "From this close the ground appears as if it's been wrinkled. It could have been caused by the asteroid strike that created this crater millions of years ago. Or there could be some sub-surface geological activity at play. It would be an incredible opportunity to be able to conduct some research but that will have to wait for another day. It's not as if this ground is going anywhere."

"I suggest we reduce speed until we understand the composition. I'm relying on you to advise of any possible risks."

The MEV rolled steadily down the slope with no obvious issues. But as they approached the lowest point between the undulations, Georgia noticed that the depth of the sand increased be several inches. The MEV slowed as its wheels dug into the sand, but it continued edging forward.

"There could be rocks hidden just below the surface," warned Jackson. "I wouldn't suggest going any faster unless you want to damage a wheel." As if to prove his point, the MEV shuddered as its front left wheel bounced over a rock. Reactively, Jackson overrode the nav computer and brought the MEV to an immediate standstill.

"I'm not sure that was wise," said Georgia. "We need to keep moving to prevent us becoming stuck. Edge us forward slowly but fast enough to give us some forward momentum."

"Sorry, I wasn't thinking," he replied, putting the MEV back into forward motion. He could sense the MEV's six wheels spinning as they fought to find any traction in the sand, without actually moving.

"What I was afraid of," Georgia said, looking out of her side window. "We're trapped. The weight of the MEV is causing us to get bogged down. Turn the motors off before we sink too far. We need to figure this out before the sun sets in two hours. I'm suiting up to take a look outside. You contact Mancuso and update him."

***

Fifteen minutes later, Georgia stepped gently on to the soft sand. She took two paces forward and noticed that the footprints she'd left behind were almost one inch deep. Opening her comms channel, she said, "Jackson, the sand is as soft as we feared. I'm going to inspect each of the wheels."

She stepped cautiously down the side of the MEV, leaning forward to get a better view of the situation they found themselves in. Each wheel had thick aluminum treads that were designed to cope with most terrains. They had met their match in this sand trap. The pair at the rear didn't look too deeply buried. It was the middle and front pair of wheels that had dug into the sand five or six inches. Small mounds of sand revealed where the wheels had churned the sand. Glancing back, the trailer being towed behind the MEV hadn't reached the deep sand and its four looked to be resting normally on the ground.

Georgia walked past the front of the MEV, keen to know how far the sand trap continued. After thirty feet, she could feel rock beneath her boots again. "This is how far we need to travel to be safe." But, the MEV currently resembled a beached white whale. It was not going to be easy to release it from its predicament. "Any ideas, hotshot?"

"Other than digging our way out? Not really."

"That's my thought as well. There's a shovel attached to the side of the MEV. Give me ten minutes and I'll see if I can get us out of the mess you got us into, little brother."

"You still like to blame me for everything," Jackson replied.

"That's what big sisters do," she said as the unstrapped a small metal shovel and began digging around the front left wheel. After she had compacted a small mound of sand in front of the wheel, she moved on to the right front wheel to repeat the process. After ten minutes she had gone around all six wheels. Although out of breath and sweaty from the exertion, she was satisfied with her work.

"Okay Jackson, this is what I want you to do. You have to get the MEV rocking so that we can use its momentum to escape. I've dug a hollow behind each of the wheels to allow you to reverse about six inches. Then you need to move slowly but steadily forward without spinning the wheels. If you don't get out the first time, be patient and try again."

Georgia kept her fingers crossed that her plan would work; she didn't want to so any more digging and they'd already wasted too much time trying to escape. She looked closely at the nearest wheel as it slowly moved backwards. As the MEV began to edge forward she held her breath, silently willing the wheels to get a grip and allow the journey to continue. As hoped, the MEV continued forward, Jackson adeptly controlling the torque in each of the wheels to minimize any spin.

"That's it, Jackson," she said excitedly. "Keep going for another hundred feet and I'll catch you up. Good job."

***

Jackson parked the MEV at the top of the next ridge. The sun had recently set, and Georgia was not prepared to take any chances driving in the dark. Within minutes, they were enveloped in an inky blackness. The interior of the MEV was dim, bathed only in the blue and green lights from the control screens to save power.

"It's eerie being alone out here," remarked Jackson. "I don't think I've ever felt this isolated."

Georgia was clearing a space to set up their bunks for the night, although the stack of supplies and provisions inside the cabin was not making her task easy. "I understand. Since my encounter with the Sentinels, however, I don't ever feel alone. Part of me believes that we're constantly being observed. I find that comforting."

"But that encounter was two years ago. There's been no sign of them since. And, from what you told me, the Sentinels are in no hurry to re-establish contact."

Georgia slid a box to one side, satisfied she now had the space she needed. "Time doesn't alter the fact that it happened. If the Sentinels have been observing us for thousands of years, they're not simply going to give up and go away because of one chance meeting. They're out there, close by. Making careful notes of every move we make as a species."

"I don't doubt that," replied Jackson, who was now rummaging through a box, searching for the ration packs that contained their evening meals. "But don't you find that creepy? They're basically voyeurs, hiding out of sight."

"How else can they observe us without interfering in our development? I think of it more than a test we have to pass before we receive a ticket to the Universe. Every night, I look up at the stars and am comforted in the knowledge that we're not alone. We now know there is intelligent life waiting to greet us, once they believe we're ready. It's an incredible feeling." She knew she had a look of wonderment on her face, but the thought of alien races always filled her with joy. The hope of meeting them sometime was what drove her every day.

Jackson looked up at the stars through the reinforced glass roof. "All I see are dots of light from unknown and distant stars. I wish I could see and feel what you do."

"Let me attempt to explain it to you. I've not really had an opportunity to do so." The pair of them spent the next few hours discussing alien contact and the possibilities Georgia had in mind. As with most siblings, the discussion was intense but respectful. That night, Jackson had a restless sleep, dreaming of alien abductions.

Chapter 14

After an early start the following morning, Georgia and Jackson arrived at the search location using the co-ordinates provided by the drone. They had spent a frustrating two hours driving slowly across the remaining undulations but had learned how to drive through heavy layers of sand without becoming bogged down. Georgia's spirits had lifted when the terrain has returned to a flat barren plain halfway through the morning, allowing the MEV to travel at top speed.

To Georgia's untrained eyes, the search location looked no different to the landscape near Alpha Base. She couldn't help but feel frustrated. *Maybe I was too eager to hope we would find the perfect spot so soon*, she thought. *This could be a complete waste of time after all.*

As soon as the MEV came to a standstill, however, Jackson enthusiastically jumped out of his seat. He'd also been staring out at the landscape and what he saw filled him with excitement. "This looks perfect. I knew the drones wouldn't let me down," he said as he animatedly checked out his spacesuit.

"It looks identical to any other part of this crater. What am I missing?" she asked.

"Oh, sister. You need to look properly. Can you not see the different shades of sand? There are streaks of darker material that we've not seen elsewhere. And I can see from here that those darker particles are larger than the regular sand and dust we've experienced. It's almost as if they're clumping together."

"I thought that was just iron oxide."

"You're thinking of the small blueberry-type pebbles. What we have here is totally different. The rocks are another telltale sign. They're a more uniform size. This is a fantastic place to begin our field research. I'm starting to think you were right to be so confident."

Georgia's hopes were lifted by Jackson's mood. "In that case, get out there and start pulling together the evidence we need." She reached for her own suit and began to put it on.

***

In Alpha Base's control room, Mancuso, Dunn and Doctor Betts were sitting expectantly for the next message from Colonel Byrne. This would establish how determined the colonel was for the Derzost mission to happen.

"Do you think he'll recognize that we're stalling?" Dunn asked.

"If he's as switched on as everyone says. But remember, he's over sixty-five million miles away and still new to the program. He won't have had time to grasp the realities of being here on Mars." Mancuso was relatively confident his submission and the list of questions should have been sufficient. The unknown quantity was the colonel himself.

At exactly three minutes after ten A.M. local time, the main computer indicated that a message from Colonel Byrne had been received. The three of them looked nervously at one another before Mancuso told the computer to play the message. As the previous day, Colonel Byrne was facing the camera, sitting alongside Kyle Buckley.

The colonel appeared to be more amenable today. "I'd like to thank you both for taking time out of your hectic schedules to pull together your thoughts on the outline plan we shared with you yesterday. I'm sure you were both surprised by the bold intentions we presented to you. No doubt, it is not something that me predecessor would have ever considered." He paused for a moment, as if to allow Mancuso and Dunn to consider that statement, before continuing. "The input you provided will be vital to planning and implementing a successful salvage mission. I can see *Liberty* being an extremely useful workhorse and am amazed NASA ruled out its own small vehicle during the early mission planning."

Another pause and Mancuso noticed the colonel's expression alter subtly. Byrne's eyes narrowed slightly, and he sat more upright and rigid. "Perhaps I didn't make myself clear enough yesterday. This plan will happen, and we will recover the Russian landing craft. Which is why I'm really disappointed in your inept attempt to block this planning process. I'll let Kyle explain why you failed to fool us."

Buckley coughed nervously into his hand before he spoke. "Some of the information you sent through last night was clearly incorrect. For instance, the fuel flow calculations for loading *Lexington* contained an error in the formula that increased the fueling time by two hours. Surely you must have checked the calculations before you submitted your report. You are both chief pilots and I would expect you to have an eye for this type of information. Further delay was included because of the conservative amount of fuel you've assumed. While a contingency of fifteen percent might just be acceptable, your suggestion is closer to thirty-five percent is simply ridiculous.

"We did generally agree with your proposed list of personnel for the mission. It makes sense to take your chief engineer and Lieutenant Molloy. We don't believe, however, that either Base Commander Pyke or Professor Kozlovsky are necessary to achieve our purpose. In particular, we do not want the professor to be in a position to leak our plans to the Russians. We do not know her well enough to understand if she would betray us. And although we closely monitor all the communications between her and Moscow, who knows if they are using any hidden codes to transfer information or instructions."

Colonel Byrne stepped in to take over from Buckley. "As for the base commander, I've received some disturbing information that is likely to make her unsuitable for any further missions until further notice. It has been brought to my attention that she has unknown health issues and is refusing to allow your medical team to perform routine tests to discover what may be the issue. I find her behavior irrational and potentially dangerous to the rest of you. It's fortuitous that she is away from the base at the moment. Over the next few days, I will be promoting one of you to replace her. I'm currently reviewing both sets of records with an advisory board and will shortly make my decision. However, I expect both of you to be more co-operative. So no more bullshit sandbagging. Resubmit a correct and complete plan of action this afternoon or, God help me, I will demote you both as low as you can go. Consider this your final warning. Byrne out."

Mancuso looked accusingly at Megan. "What information about Georgia have you sent to Byrne? It sounds like he wants to crucify her."

Megan looked pale and shocked. "I've shared nothing with him. You should know me better than that. Georgia's my friend."

"What's Byrne talking about then?"

"There were some anomalies in her recent medicals that I could not explain. Relating to her body's healing abilities. But no one was aware of that information other than Georgia, me and Doctor Coleman." Megan put a hand to her mouth as the truth dawned. "I sought him out for a second opinion in order to break the ice between us. I didn't expect Coleman would share her medical records with anyone else. It's unethical. How could he stoop so low as to betray Georgia?"

Mancuso frowned. "We'll talk to him later. Are there any risks to Georgia or the crew?"

Megan was struggling to control her anger. She couldn't believe Coleman's level of deceit. "I don't believe so. Her body is showing amazing recuperative properties which healed her injuries so much quicker and more effectively than I've ever seen before. But, so far, Georgia has refused permission for further examinations to discover why. She can be her own worst enemy sometimes."

"Don't we know it," mused Mancuso.

"You're ignoring Byrne's outburst," Dunn reminded them. "He's given us little choice but feed into his mission. Are we going to just roll over?"

"Not yet," replied a defiant Mancuso. "I don't enjoy being cornered like this. Perhaps it is time to update Georgia. I think she should be aware of the trouble she's in."

***

Megan strode along the corridor toward the medical center, filled with a rage that overwhelmed any rational thought. The focus of that rage was sitting at his desk drinking a coffee as she stormed into their shared office. Coleman's head snapped round as he heard the door slam violently open, keen to see the cause of the sudden interruption.

Megan didn't give him time to speak. She walked right up to him. "What the hell did you think you were doing, betraying the confidence of the base commander? What right did you have?"

Coleman stood up defiantly so that he was staring Megan in the face. "I did my job. As base physician, I have a responsibility to report any medical concerns I have to Ground Control. Especially when it involves command officers. Your close friendship with Commander Pyke has clouded your judgment. Otherwise you would have reported her yourself."

"The medical issues we picked up do not impair Georgia's ability to effectively continue her role. And there's been no suggestion in her behavior that her mental capacity is affected in any way. You made the wrong move. I suspect out of spite. Is it because of the vendetta you have against me?"

"Do not challenge my decisions, Doctor Betts. I made the call because we cannot be certain why the base commander is affected, whether her condition is contagious or even if anyone else here has similar symptoms. I determined, in my personal opinion, that there was a potential and unquantifiable risk to this base. It had nothing to do with the personal animosity between us. It's demeaning for you to even suggest that could be the reason." By now, Coleman's face had turned a deep shade of crimson. "And, for your information, Colonel Byrne agrees with my assessment and thanked me for disclosing Pyke's medical condition."

"I'm sure he did, you little prick." Megan almost spat the words out. "You may have ingratiated yourself with the colonel, but you've just turned most of the base against you. You're going to have a very lonely tour of duty here and your new best friend will be unable to help you. Perhaps you should have considered the consequences of your actions and consulted with me first before playing politics."

"I'm not here to be liked," smirked Coleman. "And I don't appreciate being threatened. I'll make sure your reaction gets a prominent position in my next report."

"You do that. I think we know where we stand." Having had her say, Megan turned and left the office. She returned to her quarters, punching the wall before sobbing in frustration.

Chapter 15

Georgia and Jackson returned to the MEV after three hours of setting up equipment and collecting soil samples.

"Thanks for your help," Jackson said as he carefully removed his spacesuit in the airlock. It was covered in dust and he used a small vacuum hose to remove the worst of it so as not to contaminate the cabin area. "I was able to complete more tasks than I anticipated. Setting up the drilling rig was essential to recovering some meaningful core samples."

"It doesn't mean I understand why you find geology so interesting. It's just the study of rocks and dust," teased Georgia, wiping away the hair stuck to the layer of perspiration on her face.

"That rock and dust will make or break your vision, sister. You should be showing me more respect. I may even have some preliminary results tomorrow morning."

"I keep forgetting how sensitive you are, little brother."

Georgia removed two bottles of water from the small fridge, tossing one of them to Jackson. The work had been physical, and the smell of the dust reminded her how thirsty she was. She sat down, drank half the bottle and checked the chronometer. "Time for another comms check. I don't want Mancuso fretting about us," she said, establishing a comms link to Alpha Base.

"Alpha Base, this is Pyke reporting in. We have returned to the MEV following a productive excursion."

"Good afternoon, Georgia," replied Dunn. "Does that mean you have positive news already?"

"It's far too early to tell. Jackson is testing the samples we collected, and we've set up the drill. He tells me that the initial signs are encouraging but that we need to repeat the exercise across several locations to get a true picture of what's here. You've seen that he likes to be overly cautious. Maybe I need to take a leaf from his book. Is there anything I need to be aware of back at base?"

Dunn hesitated. "There are a couple of matters we need to bring to your attention," he said nervously. "Joe has just returned to the control room. I'll let him fill you in."

The line went quiet for several moments, allowing Georgia to be intrigued by Dunn's message. "Jackson, did she sound uneasy to you?"

Before Jackson could reply, Mancuso's voice came out of the speakers. "Hi Georgia, we have some problems. Colonel Byrne has thrown several hand grenades in our direction. You've clearly pissed him off."

After her last conversation with the colonel, Georgia wasn't surprised. Maybe she should have been more circumspect until she'd gotten to know him better. "Okay, what's he up to now?"

"Firstly, he wants you replaced by Dunn or me. He's citing your medical issues as grounds to relieve you of command. We discovered that Doctor Coleman shared your records, and that was all the ammunition the colonel required."

"That's crazy. There's nothing wrong with me. Coleman knows that."

"Apparently, Coleman has suggested the unknown cause of your condition may put the base at risk," Mancuso replied. Georgia could hear the frustration in his voice. She had little doubt that he and Megan would have confronted Coleman about his actions.

"Okay, Joe. I'll deal with the colonel and Doctor Coleman when I return. Anything else?"

"Yes. Byrne is ordering us to develop a mission to recover the second Russian lander from Derzost. He thinks it will be a useful asset to explore Mars."

"And I'm guessing he's not requested permission from the Russians to do so."

"You got it. I'm sure he realizes it's a provocative act but, as far as he's concerned, the Russians are in no position to object. He sees an opportunity to exploit their current weaknesses, and he's been pushing us to support his plan. We tried several tactics to delay his plans, but he's seen straight through them."

"Damn! What is that man up to? He must have one massive ego. I can absolutely see the merits of having the landing craft. It would be a massive bonus. But there are better ways of acquiring it than by simply stealing it. I don't agree with taking advantage of the Russians, especially so soon after their base and its crew was wiped out. Surely someone has suggested that he make a request to the Russian Space Federation."

"I'm not sure he's that type of individual. He's running a very tight ship and not allowing anyone to question his decision. He seems intent on a complete shake up and stamping his own identity on the program," Mancuso replied. "Easy to do when your competition in in a weakened state and you've been given unlimited authority by the president."

"Yet again, the bureaucrats on Earth are trying to replicate their status quo on Mars," said a frustrated Georgia. "You've done the right thing so far. But I know there's only so far you can push back against the colonel."

"What do you want us to do? Byrne is expecting us to provide a revised submission by the end of the day. One without factual inaccuracies this time! He's brought in an expert to validate what we do."

Georgia quickly thought through her options, realizing they were very limited. "Okay, give him what he's asked for. Demonstrate that you've seen the error of your ways and maybe restore some level of trust. It should take several days for his team of strategists to fully form the plan. I doubt you'll receive a mission profile within five days. By that time, I will be back at the base to thwart his attempts to end my leadership. And there's no way his plan to recover the landing craft will be implemented by us. Not without express approval from the Russians. That's when we find out if he's prepared for a mutiny to be aired in public."

"That sounds like a very high stakes game of chicken," remarked Mancuso. "Byrne knows you don't want public opinion to go against us either. Without that support, we'll all be heading home on the next Earth return flight."

"I would like to think he'll put national interests ahead of his private issues with me. I hope I'm not proved wrong." Georgia was confident that her instincts were correct. But silently, she was willing to sacrifice her career for the future of Alpha Base. "Thanks for the heads up Joe. As I would expect, you and Dunn have the situation in hand. Please keep me updated if Byrne starts playing any other games. Next comms check in four hours. Pyke out."

Georgia took a deep breath. She wasn't sure how Colonel Byrne had been selected for the role, but he was already proving to be an annoying pain in her side. She would have to carry out some research on him and discover why he was so highly rated and who were his powerful connections. There had to be a way to neutralize his capacity to harm the program.

As if reading her thoughts, Jackson said, "Byrne is going to continue getting in your way. If I thought your vision was already impossible to implement, I think it just became ten times harder."

"Agreed. I need to have a working relationship with Ground Control. It's going to be a battle of wills where one of us has to go. I need to have a trump card. Which is why it's imperative that we find large deposits of your previous metals. If we can get the investors on side, that may be enough to swing the balance of power in our favor."

"In that case, let's see what tomorrow brings, sis."

Chapter 16

After three more days of prospecting, taking samples from different locations in the search zone, the interior of the MEV was caked in dust, despite the best efforts of Georgia and Jackson. The dust had permeated everywhere, even into their sleeping bags. It made sleep uncomfortable and Jackson had developed a painful red rash on his left side. They had sent an image to Doctor Betts who had advised there was nothing to worry about and she could treat the rash when they returned to base.

By now, Georgia was eager to return to Alpha Base and face the challenges she had back there. Spending so much times in the modest confines of the MEV was causing her nerves to fray. She had caught herself snapping at Jackson several times over trivial things. She'd known she was doing it but had been unable to stop herself. She knew she was lucky to be sharing the space with Jackson; if it was anyone else, they would have been unlikely to have tolerated her shortened temper.

Jackson was still asleep on his cot as Georgia watched the sunrise. She hoped it heralded the final day in the wilderness before they could head back south. The signs were good. The drill had worked perfectly to recover core samples from various depths up to fifty feet below the surface, although they had used more drill heads than expected. That would be an issue for the miners when they arrived. For now, though, it was a matter of Jackson reviewing the results from the soil tests he'd been conducting. Assuming he could confirm there were sufficient quantities of the minerals, she would be insisting they return to base to issue their formal report.

She leaned forward and gave him a gentle nudge. "You've slept long enough. It's daylight outside and we have plenty to do."

"Go away," Jackson complained, without opening his eyes. "I was having a wonderful dream about surfing in Hawaii with two young ladies. I'd met them in a bar, and they were about to mud wrestle for my affections. Why did you have to ruin it?"

Georgia laughed. "It sounds like they were no good for you. They'd have broken your heart."

Jackson sat up, rubbing his eyes. "You're probably right," he smiled. After yawning and stretching he said, "okay, let's get this done. The soil analysis should be complete."

Although most of Jackson's analysis equipment was located on the trailer being towed by the MEV, they were connected to the on-board computer, allowing the test results to be displayed inside the MEV. Jackson hit several buttons and the computer screen sprang to life. Row of numbers began scrolling down the screen, far too quickly for Georgia to understand. She remained silent, allowing Jackson to concentrate on the jumble of digits on the screen.

Within ten seconds he paused the scrolling numbers to take a closer look. Georgia watched him expectantly, waiting for a joyous exclamation that he'd discovered something. Instead, Jackson began to scroll the numbers again. He immediately paused the screen again but obviously didn't find what he was looking for as allowed the numbers to continue cycling through. Georgia looked at the expression on his face, unable to decipher whether it was good or bad news. After a minute, the numbers stopped moving, and he leaned back in his chair to look at her with a blank stare, revealing nothing.

"Enough with the poker face," said Georgia. "What do the results tell you?"

Jackson could only hold his neutral expression for several seconds before it turned into a beaming smile. "They tell me we hit the jackpot. We're currently sitting on a huge deposit of titanium ore, about forty feet below us. Above that is a layer of magnesite, from which we will be able to extract magnesium. Both of those are on my shopping list. From what we've seen from the different sites, there is an abundance of these metals that justifies mining operations."

Georgia gave Jackson a loving hug, her eyes moist. "Well done. I think you may have just saved us."

"I've not finished yet," he said, returning her embrace. "There are also significant readings for lithium and gold. Probably remnants from the asteroid that formed this crater. We've stumbled upon an Aladdin's cave of mineral deposits. We couldn't have found a more perfect location. And the icing on the cake is that there appears to be a layer of water ice just below the surface which stretches to the west. I deserve a huge bonus for this find."

"Are you confident in your readings? This seems too good to be true."

"Don't worry, Georgia. The results are unmistakable. I'll need to return to the area to conduct detailed mapping and surveying. The mining corporations will want to know their likely returns. But their potential earnings are going to be astronomical. Their planners are going to switch into overdrive over the coming weeks as they prepare the resource and personnel for the next mission. We've found the mother lode"

"So that means we can pack up and return to base?"

"As soon as we've packed and secured my equipment," said Jackson. "You'll be able to celebrate with a shower tomorrow night."

***

Ninety minutes later, with the equipment stowed, the MEV began its return journey. "I've one minor detour," Jackson said. "I want to head west for several miles to see if there is any surface water ice. It's only just below the surface and seems to rise gently as it gets closer to the crater wall."

"That would be an incredible find," agreed Georgia, still feeling euphoric from the earlier find. "If the miners will be able to source fuel and oxygen locally, then their costs will be dramatically reduced. I guess we can make time to confirm your discovery."

The crater wall was less than forty miles away and stood out above the crater floor. As it was still only mid morning, the sun was shining directly onto the cliff face, giving it a shiny appearance. Several wisps of high altitude cloud seemed to glide slowly above it.

They'd been traveling for only fifteen minutes when Jackson slowed the MEV. "Straight ahead," he said, pointing into the distance. "Can you see the terrain change color? It's more gray than orange. That could be what I'm looking for."

It was impossible for Georgia not to see the sudden color change. It resembled a lake, with the gray landscape continuing for several hundred yards before returning to the standard Martian orange and brown. She noticed, with some surprise, that the area was completely devoid of any rocks. It was as if someone had cleared it of any large objects. "Have you noticed the rocks?" she asked.

"The water content must be fairly high," he replied, trying to make sense of what he was seeing. "Anything too heavy sinks, creating the effect we're looking at now. I'd be interested to take a closer look to see how deep it is."

"So it's a swamp?"

"Not exactly, the water here is in a frozen state. It's lowered the density of the surrounding dust and sand, but the ground is still classed as a solid. The best description I can think of is quicksand."

"How close do you want to get?" asked Georgia, suddenly concerned for his safety.

"Close enough that I can stick a pole through the surface. I want to check the viscosity as well as the depth. This is the first discovery of surface ice and we don't know how long it will remain. For all we know, the water could evaporate before our next visit," he replied, stopping the MEV less than fifty yards from the edge of the water ice. "If it's a permanent feature, can you imagine how it can help a mining community?"

"I'm coming with you," she said.

Chapter 17

Jackson cautiously approached the spot where the soil changed color, prodding the ground in front of him with a six-foot long pole that he'd found attached to the side of the MEV. "The ground is still rocky covered by a thin layer of sand. I'm not going to sink into this."

Georgia, followed about five feet behind Jackson, paying close attention to his every step. His words didn't reassure her. Something in her gut was telling her this was a bad idea, but she couldn't explain why. This was one irrational feeling she was going to ignore, at least for the time being.

"I can see the texture of the sand changing," continued Jackson. "The particles are becoming smaller as I get closer to the water ice. The density of that patch must be exceedingly low. I should be able to easily push this pole through the surface." He edged ever closer to the edge, before stopping less than two feet away. "This should be close enough," he said, pushing the pole into the dark gray soil.

The pole slid through with ease. "Like a knife through butter," he said with some disbelief. He almost stumbled forward and lost his balance as the pole carried on until two thirds of it was in the ground.

"Jackson!" gasped Georgia in horror. "I told you to be careful."

"It's hit something solid," he replied, obliviously to Georgia's panic. "Perhaps it's not as deep as I thought. There must still be a huge volume of water here though. It would make a fantastic swimming pool if it was warmer and had an atmosphere. You should ask the engineers to build a dome over the top of it."

"I doubt that's a priority," replied Georgia. "Have you seen enough now? We have a long journey ahead of us."

"I'm intrigued by the composition. I'm going to take a small sample that I can analysis back at the base." Jackson took a container from his pouch and bent over to scoop a sample of water ice. Without warning, the pole he'd been using to take his weight slipped further into the ground, causing Jackson to tumble forward. Instinctively, he stuck his hand out to cushion the fall, but his arm sank into the ground as far his elbow. His other hand, holding the cannister, met a similar fate, and he swiftly found himself laying on his front with both of his arms sinking slowly beneath him. The more he tried to use his arms to push himself up, the quicker they sank. It was if the ground offered no resistance.

"Are you okay?" shouted Georgia, reaching forward to take his right leg.

"Yes," replied Jackson, calmly despite being surprised by the sudden turn of events. "I think I'm stuck though. You're going to have to pull me out."

Georgia grunted as she grabbed Jackson's knee and began to pull him away from the danger.

As both of his arms became free, Jackson reached out to retrieve the tripod leg which still had several inches above the ground. Once he was able to, he rolled over and sat up and laughed. "That was a less scientific approach! A very interesting experience though."

"That wasn't funny," Georgia scolded him. "What would have happened if I'd not been with you?"

"I wouldn't have been so close," he replied.

Before she could chastise him further, she noticed the arms of his space suit were spotless and dust free, unlike the rest of his suit. There was a clear demarcation just above each of his elbows below which the space suit looked brand new. "That's peculiar," she remarked. "Whatever is in that soil mix must have some amazing antistatic qualities. You're going to have your work cut out researching everything out here. Do you want me to assign Molloy or Professor Kozlovsky to provide some assistance?"

"I think you may have to," said Jackson, giving a puzzled look to his suit's arms. He checked that the sample cannister had collected some of the gray matter before standing up. He was about to follow

Georgia back to the MEV when he spotted another unusual phenomenon. The area of water ice was draining away, as if someone had pulled out a plug. It had sunk at least two inches in the past minute, which was impossible for such a large area. "Georgia, wait. Something peculiar is happening," he called out excitedly, taking a few steps away from the area.

"What now?" she replied, turning around in frustration. She was astounded when she saw the reason for Jackson's excitement. "What the fuck is going on? Have you caused that?"

"It's nothing to do with me. There must be a sink hole. It's the only explanation for so much material to be sinking so quickly."

"What set it off? It seems too much of a coincidence that it's occurring now. Did we do something?"

"Possibly," replied Jackson, fascinated by the sight of the ground continuing to sink. It was now almost twelve inches lower than the surrounding terrain. "The vibrations from the MEV may have freed loose rocks. If there's a sub-surface cavity, the rocks could have acted as a stopper. It may mean this whole area is unstable."

"Don't you think we should leave? It sounds unsafe to remain."

"Five minutes, sis. Let's see what happens. We can't leave now. Can you grab a camera from the trailer?"

Georgia retrieved the camera and slowly made her way back to where Jackson was standing. By now, the depression appeared to be three feet deep. She offered the camera to him and he immediately began taking photos of the strange phenomenon.

"This is truly awesome," he said, panning the camera around. "What's that?" he asked, looking through the viewfinder.

Georgia stared at where he was pointing, about one hundred yards to their right, she saw an object sticking out of the ground in the depression. It appeared to be regular shaped and glinted as if it was metallic. "You tell me. You're the one with the camera."

Jackson was silent as he adjusted the zoom controls, hoping to get a clearer image. "It must have been below the surface and only just revealed itself. It doesn't look natural though. Its sides are too smooth. We should take a closer look."

Without waiting for Georgia to reply, he began walking around the edge of the depression to get a closer look at the mysterious object. Georgia ran after him and caught up as he stopped at the closest point to the object.

Now that they were closer, Georgia could see that the object was a green cylindrical tube about four feet wide, with ridges running along its length. It was laying at a thirty-degree angle with five feet of it visible above the ever sinking base of the depression. No sand or dust clung to the object, giving it a clean and new appearance. It looked exceedingly ordinary, yet Georgia could feel her heart racing as she noticed strange symbols on the end of the cylinder.

"This has to be alien," she said, unable to hide her excitement. "There's no way this object came from Earth. I'm not aware of any metals that share the properties we're seeing now. If it was a failed satellite or probe, there would be scorch marks and signs of impact damage at least. But this cylinder is pristine. There's not a mark on it other than those symbols."

Jackson was busy taking photos. "Agreed. But what is it and how long has it been here?" He lowered the camera to look at Georgia. "And what do we do with it?"

"I want to take a closer look. This could be a clue we need to contact alien civilizations." The cylinder was thirty feet from her. Painfully close, yet so far away. But it was an irresistible force, drawing her to it.

"I wouldn't recommend it while the ground continues to sink. We have no idea how deep it goes, and you may not be able to climb out of this hole."

Georgia was defiant. This was what she'd privately been wishing for since she'd said a tearful goodbye to Falmas and Grant. She couldn't simply walk away without taking a closer look. "We need to know what it is. This could be mankind's most significant discovery. Physical and indisputable evidence of intelligent alien civilizations."

"I understand that. But you don't need to risk your life. You can see that the ground is unstable. We can always return with the right equipment. In the meantime, I'll continue to take high definition photos that can be studied. We can also leave some remote sensors behind."

Georgia stood staring at the cylinder, working through the options in her mind. It was incredibly frustrating to be so close to the object without being able to touch it. It seemed like fate was taunting her. Reluctantly, she accepted that Jackson was right, even if it was going to be difficult to leave the object behind. "Okay," she sighed. "Set up what you need and let's set off before I change my mind."

Chapter 18

Jackson drove the MEV as fast as he dared across the Martian surface, kicking up a huge trail of dust. It was now early afternoon, and they were well behind schedule if they wanted to reach Alpha Base by the end of the next day.

Georgia had not spoken for the past hour, instead looking absently out of the window at the endless landscape speeding by. Her thoughts were back with the alien cylinder. Its discovery raised so many questions. Where had it come from? How long had it been in that location? What was it designed for? She knew she wouldn't be able to find any answers back at Alpha Base. A return mission was going to be her top priority and her mind was already planning what she may need.

The sound of Mancuso's voice interrupted her thoughts. "Comms check, MEV. What's your status?" he asked.

Georgia clicked on her microphone, whilst continuing to stare outside. "Alpha Base, this is Georgia. Following our previous transmission, we carried out additional reconnaissance of the area. We're currently trying to make up time."

"I can confirm we're still three hundred and eighteen miles away," added Jackson. "We have a long drive ahead of us."

"Did you find anything else worthy of exploration?" asked Mancuso.

"Before I answer that," said Georgia, "has there been any reaction from Ground Control regarding the mineral deposits? I would imagine the vast reserves will have our corporations jumping for joy."

"Nothing yet, other than a simple 'thanks for the update'. I expected more positive feedback as well. No positive compliments from Colonel Byrne at all."

"Pricks!" exclaimed Jackson. "What more do they want from me?"

Georgia turned and smiled at him, reassuringly. "You did a great job. I'm sure the right people will sing your praises once the news reaches them." She gave Jackson's arm a friendly pat as he returned her smile. "Joe? We made a much more significant discovery this morning. An object that appears to be of non-human origin."

"Alien? How can you be sure? Are you bringing it back with you?" Mancuso asked cautiously.

"Because of the local terrain, we weren't able to get close enough to be sure, but Jackson took plenty of photos. I'll transmit some of them through for you to take a look at. Let Professor Kozlovsky and Lieutenant Molloy view the images as well. There are some markings on the object that may be a language of some kind. We'll need help to decipher them."

"Do I inform Ground Control? They should also be made aware and we'll need their guidance on what we should do next."

After the arrogant behavior of Colonel Byrne, Georgia was reluctant to share any information with him. However, Mancuso was probably right in this instance. It wouldn't look good if it was discovered she had intentionally withheld information on this earth-shattering discovery. She could only hope that the colonel wouldn't interfere too much but realized that prospect was unlikely. "Yes, Joe. Send the images through to Earth also, but using the quantum communications system to encrypt the message. This news has to remain highly confidential until we know what to do next."

"This really could be a game-changer," replied Mancuso. "I'd love to see the colonel's face when he receives the images. I'm not sure how he can dismiss you when you've delivered him evidence of alien life."

"I'm not worried about him. I'm going nowhere, whatever tricks he tries to play. He'll simply see it as another unwelcome problem I've created. Is he still giving you and Dunn a hard time?"

"If you're asking whether the colonel is still busting our balls, then the answer is a definite yes. He's finalized the plan for the acquisition of the Russian landing craft and has gone so far as to name it '*Liberty*'. The plan is substantially the one I shared with you two days ago. I'm confident it will work. Rashid and I have been reviewing the main flying instructions for *Liberty* we believe we can operate it well enough to return safely to Alpha Base. Byrne wanted us to perform the mission before you returned, until I advised him we required more methane to be manufactured by the propellant factory. This is actually true and so he's had no option but wait at least three days until our fuel reserves have been replenished."

Georgia laughed, "that won't have gone down well with Byrne. It's about time he had a reality check. We can discuss more at our next comms check. I'll be interested on the team's feedback to the images. Georgia out."

She accessed an image of the symbols on the end of the cylinder and stared at them on her computer screen while Jackson transmitted the ten images of the cylinder back to base.

"You're already planning the next mission," he said after another fifteen minutes of silence. "You want to retrieve the cylinder, don't you?"

"Am I really that predictable?"

"I've grown up with you. I know how you think and I recognize your body language. You're sitting there now, planning the equipment you need and frustrated at how long the return trip will take. You're fidgety and impatient. This journey must be driving you crazy."

"Thanks for stating the obvious. What if the cylinder collapses into the sink hole? I'm worried we made a mistake leaving it as it was."

"The cylinder will still be there, trust me. In the meantime, we'll have the greatest minds working around the clock to decipher those symbols. They could form a message that will aid our understanding of the cylinder."

"The other thing that scares me is that I'm beginning to agree with Colonel Byrne's plan to acquire *Liberty*. It can carry far more equipment than we can take in this MEV and dramatically reduce the journey time. What's happened to me that I can even consider the ends justify the means?" Georgia was truly appalled at the thought but was unable to deny that the plan was now very attractive. Was she really prepared to do anything to further her vision? The answer appeared to be a resounding yes. And it didn't sit well with her.

***

Mancuso called a small meeting in the control room to share the images uploaded by Jackson. "Georgia wants you to take a look at what she's found and give your opinion. At this stage, there are no stupid or crazy answers."

Anna Kozlovsky, Charlie Molloy and Commander Dunn leaned in to get a closer look at the cylinder. After studying the images in silence, Molloy was the first to speak.

"I don't know what to say. This has to be the find of the millennium. I cannot believe we're looking at an artifact that was created by an alien culture. It's truly incredible. We have to recover and examine it."

"I agree that it is an amazing discovery," said Anna. "But I don't think we should get too close until we know what it is. As it is buried in the ground, we don't know if it is attached to anything else, or if there are any other objects nearby. I would urge more caution until we know more."

"That's a fair point, Anna, " added Dunn. "Until we have a better idea of the origin of that object, it would be unwise to move it. However, I don't think it's our decision to make. We'll require direction from Earth as the implication of this discovery are immense. I'm sure the governments will want to keep this a secret for as long as possible."

"Joe, can you enlarge the section containing the symbols?" asked Molloy. "Maybe they hold the key. If we can decipher even a small part, we will be able to understand the first alien language. There could be a message for us."

Mancuso zoomed onto the end of the cylinder so that the symbols filled the screen. They were a series of gold shapes and figures, seemingly embossed onto the green metal.

"Interesting," exclaimed Molloy. "Although I'm no expert, they appear similar to Egyptian hieroglyphics except that the shapes are nothing I've seen before. I wonder if there is any connection to ancient Egypt."

"It could help explain the pyramids and other ancient marvels," said Mancuso. "I've often thought that it couldn't have been possible to build some of the structures they had with the tools they supposedly had available. And how were pyramids built thousands of miles apart on different continents?"

"I'm not sure we can offer much assistance in that case," added Dunn. "We require some kind of Rosetta Stone to give us the key to those symbols. The experts we want are back on Earth, hidden away in dusty museums and universities. It may take decades to even begin to understand what may be written on that object."

"Let's wait and see what the reaction is back on Earth," said Mancuso. "I'm sure this news will have ruffled a few feathers. I can imagine people panicking as they decide what is the best course of action."

Chapter 19

News of the discovery of an alien artifact on Mars made its way immediately from NASA to the White House. A conference call was hastily arranged between the recently appointed President Ramsay, his national security advisor, the secretary of state, Colonel Byrne and Libby Selznick, the NASA administrator.

"Okay, Colonel Byrne," began the president, staring up at the large screen in the Situation Room located in the basement of the White House. "What are you showing us?"

Byrne coughed nervously as he stared into the camera in his Houston office. "Thank you, Mr President. Approximately ninety minutes ago, we received an encrypted transmission from our base on Mars. Earlier today, while on a field trip surveying for mineral deposits, two of our crew discovered an object submerged in the ground approximately three hundred and fifty miles north of Alpha Base. The object is at least nine feet long, approximately four feet in diameter and appears to be neither naturally occurring nor man-made. The crew were able to take photos of the object but were unable to get closer than thirty feet away because of unstable ground conditions."

The large television screen in the Situation Room changed to reveal six images of the cylinder, each taken from different angles and showing distinct features. The president and the two other men in the room collectively sucked in their breaths at their first look of the object.

"You say that the object is not natural or man-made. Are you telling me it's alien in nature?" asked the president.

"That appears to be the likely conclusion," replied Byrne. "But we are unable to confirm its nature at this time."

"Are you positive this can't be a hoax?" asked Secretary of State Colin Truman, a former director of the Central Intelligence Agency.

"We can't be sure of anything at the time," replied Libby Selznick. "Of course, we need to perform further studies but, due to the location and nature of the object, I find it impossible to think his can be anything but genuine. Which is why we brought it to your urgent attention."

"Who else is aware of this object?" asked President Ramsay, his astute political mind already running through the permutations for his presidency.

"Sir, we've locked down the information in Houston," said Byrne. "Joe Mancuso, the acting base commander sent the images directly to me. Administrator Selznick is the only other person I've spoken to about this. I've instructed Alpha Base to be on communications lock down until further notice. Security protocols are in place to ensure no communications will be released to the public without your personal approval."

"Won't that raise suspicions?" asked the secretary of state.

"We can explain that there are maintenance issues with the communications equipment. We have used that excuse on previous occasions with very little push back except from the conspiracy theorists. And I think the public is becoming weary of continuing alien theories when there isn't any evidence."

"Until now!" said the president, taking a closer look at the images. "Are those letters and symbols on the end of the object?"

"Yes sir, we believe so," said Byrne. "We've not had an opportunity to analyze them. We thought informing you was a priority."

"None of the symbols look familiar. Could it be a message?" asked the president.

"I wouldn't like to speculate at this time," said Selznick. "We would need to involve experienced cryptologists to determine if there are any recurring patterns or themes. We don't have that expertize within NASA."

President Ramsay looked across to his national security advisor. "General McCord. I assume you have access to personnel who could take a look."

"Absolutely sir," replied the general. "I can get onto it as soon as you give the word."

The president nodded grimly. "That takes me to my next question. What do we do with this information? Are we able to keep this discovery secret and should we be sharing with our international colleagues?"

"My advice is that we keep the information to ourselves for the time being. We've been able to control previous information," the general said. "All information and data arriving from Mars is filtered through Ground Control at Houston which has proved very adept at retaining national security. Neither Commander Pyke's previous alien encounters nor the full extent of the Chinese attack have been revealed. I am confident that Administrator Selznick can assure us that she will continue to maintain those levels of security."

"Yes, you are correct," replied Selznick. "I see no reason that any leaks will emanate from NASA."

"As regards sharing the news of this discovery," continued the general, "I see no benefit to America of having other nations know of the presence of a possible alien object. I would rather our experts be allowed to research this artifact and learn what we can from it. It is highly likely we could gather some important technological advances. Do we want to be sharing that with our allies or enemies? And, it will be significantly more difficult for the artifact to remain a secret from the public."

President Ramsay sat back in his chair, continuing to look at the images on the screen. This was a problem he could do without at that moment. His popularity rating since replacing President Wyndham was only thirty-two percent. His advisors had told him he was perceived as weak on foreign policy, particularly with the Chinese.

Domestically, he had yet to make his mark on employment, climate change and food shortages. He felt as if he'd been handed an impossible legacy and there appeared to be no quick or easy fixes.

"Can we bury this object for the time being? Quite literally. Forget we found it and pretend it never happened?" he asked.

"It's possible," admitted General McCord. "But then we could be missing out on gaining a huge advantage."

"You keep telling me that, general," interrupted President Ramsay, slamming the table in frustration. "We don't know for sure that it is alien or that it's of any value. If it was left discarded in the middle of a desert, then it could simply be garbage. Or maybe the Chinese dropped it there to divert our resources."

The room was silent at the president's sudden outburst. Administrator Selznick was the first to speak. "Excuse me, sir. You may be correct, but we have no way of being sure unless we're allowed to examine this object. Allow us some time to at least determine the object's origin. We know for certain that alien civilizations exist and are watching us. If the cylinder is alien then, at the very least, we can learn something about what we're up against. This could be our first real opportunity to study them."

Until now, Secretary of State Truman had been listening to the conversation is silence. He was well known for making considered responses only after having grasped the full facts. His advice was always highly regarded. "Do we know if this object poses any danger to our astronauts on Mars? Is it possible to carry out a risk assessment?"

"That's an excellent point," said Colonel Byrne. "We've had no time to carry out any assessment at this stage. I doubt we have sufficient data to advise our crew's safety. This object has been dormant for the past two years at least, possibly longer as it's never been previously detected on any missions dating back to the nineteen sixties. But that doesn't mean we can safely study it. I support the president's suggestion that we do nothing with the knowledge. At least for the time being."

"Before you decide, Mister President," said Selznick, "You need to be aware that the cylinder was discovered very close to rich mineral deposits. We believe those deposits are more than sufficient to attract the investment required for the next stage of mining and large scale colonization. We wouldn't want one of the mining corporations to stumble across the artifact."

"Shit!" exclaimed the president. "You could have told me sooner. That changes everything. Surely there are other locations suitable for mining?"

"We don't know yet. We've only just begun prospecting the planet. The corporations are pushing for additional information so that they can start planning for the next mission. We'd already told them that the area was a promising location prior to the cylinder being uncovered. Bear in mind the corporations have less than six months to confirm the cargo requirements for Expedition Four."

"In that case, make them wait," President Ramsay replied angrily. "This discovery is of national importance and I won't be rushed into making any decisions until we have more information. Thank you for the update, Administrator Selznick. My decision, based on what you've presented today, is that your crew stays clear of the alien artifact while we consider using robotic devices. I don't want any more fatalities. And we keep a lid on this. Is that clear?"

There were quiet murmurs of agreement before the president abruptly closed the conference call.

Ramsay turned to his secretary of state. "Colin, please can you continue to liaise with NASA? Let Administrator Selznick know we're keeping a close interest on her progress. I don't want them to overstep their remit. There's too much at stake here." Turning to his right, he then added, "General, get your best people to encrypt what's on that cylinder as a matter of priority. We have to know if it really is an alien artifact and, if so, whether we have anything to worry about. Can you also get your social analysts working on the likely scenarios if we were to go public with news that intelligent alien life exists? Thank you both. Now back to real work."

***

In Houston, Selznick was in her office attempting to give a roasting to an unapologetic Colonel Byrne. She was a thin woman, in her early fifties with tight permed brown hair that was beginning to turn silver. She'd joined NASA straight from leaving MIT. Her dreams of being an astronaut had been knocked back because of a hereditary medical condition. But that setback had not dented her determination, which has ultimately led her to being appointed in her senior role eighteen months ago. In a male dominated organization, she had dealt with many people like Colonel Byrne and it pissed her off that such men were still appointed because of their gender or contacts rather than on merit.

"Colonel", she began calmly. "I appreciate you're still new to how we work here at NASA, but I don't enjoy being undermined by my staff, particularly in front of POTUS and his senior officials. If you disagree with any of my decisions, I would prefer we discuss them in private."

Byrne was sitting across from her, his hands relaxed on his lap. If there was one thing he enjoyed most, it was upsetting the apple cart. "With respect, Libby, you were heading down the wrong path and it was impossible to speak candidly with you when the president was looking for decisive support. Surely you've been in your role long enough to recognize the signs when the president is unclear of his next move. Especially a new incumbent who's seeking the popular vote."

"President Ramsay needed guidance to make the right decision in this instance. He doesn't need a crony who will agree with him for his own nefarious ends. I knew it was a mistake when you were appointed."

"Yet here we are. Remove me from my post if that makes you feel better. But remember why I was chosen and then think how you would explain my removal after only two weeks."

"That works both ways Byrne. You'd find it hard to get such another well-paid job with the recommendation I'd give."

"If you want someone who always agree with you, I'm not that person. I may not be right all the time, but I get things done and, despite what you may think, I am prepared to listen. However, on this occasion I do genuinely agree with the president's position that it is best not to be too hasty making a decision until we know what that object is."

"At least General Stockton was a scientist at heart," replied an increasingly frustrated Selznick. She was struggling to remain cool in the face of Byrne's assured calmness, although she was well aware of the game he was playing. "I need someone with an inquisitive mind. You should be seeking out mysteries to be solved rather than hiding them away through fear."

"You're wrong. I have a responsibility for the protection and safety of the crew up there. I'm not prepared to allow them recklessly to study what could be a Pandora's Box. I do want to discover what that object is, especially if it has alien origins. But I won't risk lives to do so. In fact, I'm surprised that you care less for their wellbeing. Shame on you, Libby."

Administrator Selznick had reached her limits. "I think you've said more than enough, colonel," she said angrily as she stood up. "Get out of my office and give the instructions to Alpha Base."

She noticed Byrne smile as he rose slowly from his chair. He oozed contempt for her. If he thought he would be free to get one over on her, then he had seriously underestimated her.

Closing the door to her office, she reached into her pocket and pulled out her cell phone. "Call Evelynn," she instructed and waited the person on the other end of the line to pick up.

"Libby! What a pleasant surprise. I was going to call you to check what you're planning for Christmas this year. What can I do for my big sister?"

"I'm sorry, Evelynn. I've been meaning to call you for the past few weeks. It's been hectic here with several senior changes. But I'm due a long weekend so I was thinking of visiting you and Rob tomorrow night. If that's OK?"

"Absolutely. Rob's away in Europe at the moment and it will be fantastic to have you stay over. You wouldn't fly up to Chicago at this time of year just for the weekend," she said, suspiciously. "What's wrong?"

"There's no getting past your reporter's nose for a story," Libby laughed. "It goes against my better judgment, but I have something to tell you that will blow you away."

Chapter 20

Georgia and Jackson's arrival back at Alpha Base late the following afternoon was met with muted celebration. The latest orders from Earth had not gone down well with any of the senior crew.

Feeling fatigued and dirty after having spent seven days in the confines of the MEV, Georgia was desperate to take a shower to wash off the grime and dust that had accumulated all over her body. She had spent most of the last twelve hours fidgeting in her seat and scratching continuously at random itches. It certainly wasn't an easy life being base commander.

She was looking forward to getting a good night's sleep back in her own quarters, but she knew that an urgent debrief with her team was more important. And so, at six P.M. she gathered Charlie Molloy, Ashley Dunn, Joe Mancuso, Rashid Qadir, Dr Megan Betts and Jackson into the control room.

"Welcome back, Georgia," said Mancuso, with his usual beaming smile. "And congratulations to you both on your discoveries. I think it's safe to say that your expedition was more than successful." He clapped Jackson on his shoulder, nearly knocking the young geologist off his feet.

Georgia stood up to address the room. "Thanks, Joe. And thanks to all of you for holding the fort while I was away. I don't believe there were any emergencies and, if there were, you've hidden them well." She paused for a moment as she considered what to say next. She wanted so much to be positive, but Colonel Byrne's instructions had left her deflated. "I'm not quite sure where to begin. After Jackson's miraculous discoveries in the field I thought we were settled as a colony. He's proved that the resources are available to sustain a permanent settlement here on Mars. That has always been our primary aim, and to achieve it so soon has exceeded even my most optimistic expectations.

"And then we discover what appears to be an alien artifact. And again, that was an enormous discovery. In many ways, it could have a far bigger impact than the mineral deposits. As you can imagine, I was looking forward to returning in order to properly examine the cylinder and determine its origin and purpose. Naively, I thought that was what NASA would want us to do. Yet, Ground Control want to tie our hands and hinder research. I cannot tell you how disappointed I am for all of us."

"I kind of understand NASA's view," said Dunn. "We have no idea what that object could be. You can't blame them for being cautious following the number of fatalities this program has suffered over two years."

"Those deaths were at the hands of fellow humans," Mancuso said. "None of them were as a result of natural phenomena, research or aliens. I'm with the base commander. There's no reason to hold us back from inspecting what's out there. If that object is dangerous, shouldn't we discover what that danger is in case we find any more cylinders."

Molloy stuck his hand up. "I'm more than happy to risk my life to examine that cylinder. I don't care what our orders are. I want to know what that object is made of and what it does. Surely we have a duty to mankind to answer the questions about life beyond Earth. An alien artifact is on our doorstep and we're banned from learning anything about it. It simply doesn't make sense."

Everyone in the room smiled at Molloy's outburst. They had become used to his direct, no-nonsense approach.

"This matter's not over," said Georgia. "I'll be sending my thoughts to Byrne directly after this meeting, clearly stating that we wholeheartedly disagree with his insane instructions. I'm not going to willfully disobey him just yet. I'll give him one last chance."

"I'm not sure he'll listen," said Mancuso. "He's claiming this is a presidential directive. And, I'm sure you're still not his favorite person, especially since Selznick overruled his decision to have you replaced. I think he's still pretty pissed about that."

"Another example of his poor judgment," Georgia replied. "He may feel squeezed by the women in his life, but he needs to work with us. We don't always bite; only when we need to." She noticed Megan and Dunn both nod their approval. "Charlie and Joe? Have you prepared the list of equipment I requested in case I'm able to obtain approval for another mission?"

"Anna and I have raided the science labs and spare equipment racks," replied Molloy proudly. "A full inventory has been packed into crates and ready to be loaded onto the MEV at your command."

"I've prepared two crates with enough supplies for ten days," added Mancuso. "I still need to top up the MEV's water tanks but otherwise your good to go."

"I've downloaded the diagnostics data from the MEV," said Rashid Qadir. "There's abrasive wear on two of the wheels but not enough to prevent a return trip to the swamp. I will swap out the batteries before any more extended runs though."

"Thanks Rashid," said Georgia. "And I like 'the swamp'. It's a good description of what we encountered. We should start using it."

"Wouldn't it be easier to utilize the *Lexington* for a sub-orbital hop?" asked Mancuso. "I know the ship isn't a taxi service and it would require a ton of propellant, but it could be at the swamp within thirty minutes. You could be there and back before the Colonel knew about it."

Jackson immediately shook his head. "I wouldn't advise it, Joe. If there is a sink hole below the alien cylinder, the whole area could be unstable with an unknown number of sub-surface voids. *Lexington's* weight could cause the ground beneath it to collapse and we'd lose the ship."

"Then what about *Liberty*, the Russian landing craft?" suggested Dunn. "We have received all the specifications, and its loaded mass is only twenty-five percent of *Lexington*. Surely that should reduce any risk of subsidence."

Georgia held up her hand. "Let me cut you off, Ashley," she said. "It's a fantastic idea but I'm still not comfortable about stealing that craft. Why can't someone simply ask the Russians if we can borrow it? I would love to have access to that vehicle, but it needs to be done correctly. I'll add it to my report for Byrne." She gave Dunn a reassuring smile. "Before we break up for the evening, I'd like to thank you all again for preparing the next excursion. I sincerely hope we don't have too long to wait. Is there anything else anyone would like to add?"

When it was apparent that there were no further issues, the group began to disperse, leaving only Georgia and Mancuso in the control room.

"You're going to return to the cylinder whatever Byrne says, aren't you," he whispered.

Georgia shrugged, with no hint of remorse. "More than likely. We have to find out as much as we can. It was tough enough tearing myself away from it yesterday, knowing that it could hold the key to understanding more about intelligent extra-terrestrial life. I'm not prepared to pretend that the object doesn't exist simply because that would be a convenient outcome for the president. What's the worst that the colonel can do if I disobey his direct orders?"

Mancuso smiled. "I'd have to lock you up and confine you to quarters until the next Earth transport. But you know I'm not going to do that either. Especially when I agree with you."

"Thanks Joe. I know you've always got my back. I hope I can persuade Ground Control without the need for a mini mutiny."

"I know you can be persuasive when you need to be," replied Mancuso. "Perhaps you should reach out to Libby Selznick. She has your back at the moment."

"It can't do any harm," admitted Georgia, although she couldn't recall having met the NASA Administrator other than a quick introduction at a NASA technology event. "Thanks Joe, I'll let you know how I get on." Feeling exhausted, Georgia made her excuses and returned to her quarters in order to submit her reports and recommendations to Colonel Byrne. It was almost nine P.M. before she'd finished as she struggled to find the right words to influence the colonel's decision. She knew she could never be a diplomat. Georgia had enough energy to send one final communication to Administrator Selznick requesting her assistance to override the orders, unsure what the response would be.

***

"Tell me, what did Commander Pyke have to say?" Anna Kozlovsky slid her trousers off and climbed into bed next to Molloy.

He'd been intently watching her as she undressed in the light of the desk lamp in his quarters, noticing every curve and freckle. He knew that she was aware of his interest, but she didn't seem to care. The crew quarters weren't designed for couples and it wasn't easy to undress in the tight confines of Molloy's room, but somehow, she managed it without losing her balance.

He tried to put his arm around her, but she pushed him off, instead resting her head on her elbow and staring back with her keen blue eyes as she waited for an answer. "You're too easily distracted," she whispered.

Molloy grinned like a schoolboy. "Can you blame me? I'm cavorting with the enemy. A very beautiful enemy. How do I know you're not just in my bed to seduce me for my secrets?"

Anna lifted the sheet and smiled at the reaction of his body to her presence. "That is why I am here," she replied enticingly. "I do not need to know your secrets. Now, what did she say about the alien object? Are we going on a mission to retrieve it?"

"Pyke had nothing more to tell than she'd already shared. She doesn't know any more than us. I can tell she wants to go back. She's clearly frustrated with NASA's reluctance to carry out any research on the alien artifact." Molloy was finding it increasingly difficult to concentrate as Anna gently rubbed her breasts against his chest.

"She is a strong-willed lady. She will find a way to study the artifact. But do you think she will choose either of us to go? We are the only scientists on the base without urgent research projects after all."

"So that's why you're sleeping with me. You want to get closer to the commander! It makes sense that we go. However, technically you're not part of the crew. There may be international considerations to overcome."

"Is that why you are keeping our relationship secret?"

"Partly," he conceded. "But I also like having you all to myself. Now, enough talking, Professor." He leaned over and kissed her passionately, as Anna returned the kiss with equal enthusiasm and passion.

Chapter 21

Georgia had a restless night filled with a recurring vivid dream. It was one she'd been having with more regularity over recent weeks. Although the dream wasn't disturbing in itself, the recurring nature was beginning to concern her. This time, however, the dream had included what appeared to be a replica of the cylinder standing upright near a river surrounded by tall pine trees. A tall figure was next to the cylinder, their features blurred. They seemed to beckon her closer before suddenly disappearing. The musty smell of damp leaves and the blue sky reminded her of Earth. But the distant shiny buildings that reached up into the clouds were definitely not man made. She'd felt lost and confused, unsure where to go. She'd been desperately searching for the blurred figure when the alarm woke her up, pulling her from her search.

She made a mental note to discuss the dreams with Megan, before opening her computer to check for any responses from Colonel Byrne or Libby Selznick. She was disappointed not to see anything from the NASA administrator, and opened the colonel's message with a sense of foreboding.

Fifteen minutes later, she stomped into the canteen for her first coffee of the day. She'd hoped to find someone to share her feelings with. Instead, she saw the two biologists who had arrived on *Lexington*. They nodded to Georgia as she poured coffee into her mug, obliging her to make small talk with them. She felt guilty at not being able to remember their names but was able to bluff her way through by questioning their progress in the aquaponics dome.

She was saved after several moments by Megan's arrival. Georgia made her excuses to the biologists and walked up to her best friend. Megan gave her a quick glance. "The colonel said no didn't he."

"Can everyone read my like a book?" Georgia replied, irritably. "He wasn't even prepared to consider my request to study the cylinder. Instead, he took the opportunity to patronize me, offering to clarify his orders as I didn't appear to understand them. I now have far more sympathy for your situation with Dr Coleman."

Megan sat down at one of the tables with her drink, with Georgia sitting across from her. "There's been a changing of the guard. Byrne is trying to cement his place and stamp his own style following Stockton's departure. He has some large shoes to fill."

"I hope you're not defending him. He's a career bureaucrat who has risen through the ranks on the back of other more successful people. He's disruptive rather than productive. His sole purpose seems to be to antagonize anyone around him. At the moment, I'm in his sights and it's bad for the program. I'm wondering if it would be better for everyone if I stood down." Georgia knew the thought was a knee-jerk reaction to her experiences with Byrne. She didn't want to hinder the Mars program because of personal differences, although maybe it was time for a change. Joe Mancuso would be a perfect replacement; he had the experience, was popular with the crew and would probably have more patience with Byrne.

But Megan would have nothing of it. "That's ridiculous! You can't let Byrne beat you."

"It's okay. I don't have an ego to stroke."

"It has nothing to do with egos. You're the best person to lead this mission. Stepping down would weaken us and strengthen Byrne's position. He can't be allowed to define and shape our future. Someone needs to stand up to him and challenge his decisions. That has to be you. But, if you're not up to the task, then I'd understand after what you're been through. And it would allow me to commence my medical studies on you," Megan added with a wink.

"You're getting nowhere near me," Georgia replied. "But I always appreciate our conversations. You always find a way to put me back on track."

"Have more faith. You keep telling me your goal is to set humankind on a path to the stars. You have an opportunity staring you in the face? Are you really going to let a pompous army colonel hold you up?"

***

"I'm heading back to the swamp to study the alien artifact," Georgia declared at the daily briefing with her senior team, one hour later. "This goes totally against explicit orders from Ground Control, so I'm likely to be going in front of a court-martial for what I'm about to do. Which is why I am looking for volunteers only to join me. I cannot promise the outcome of this journey, so I urge everyone to carefully consider their actions as the wrong decision could be extremely career limiting."

Georgia paused to look around the room and was re-assured by the expressions on almost everyone's faces. Although she had been quietly confident of universal support following her earlier conversation with Megan, she had not taken it for granted.

As always, Mancuso was not short of an opinion. "Georgia, you know that I'll support you all the way. I'm not sure I can add much value to the research trip, but I'll monitor your progress from here and field any objections from our friends back on Earth."

"Thanks Joe, I can't ask any more of you," she acknowledged.

Ashley Dunn was the next to speak. She fidgeted in her chair and looked decidedly uncomfortable as she said. "I'm sorry Georgia. I have a career and family to think about. While I agree in principle with what you are about to do, I'm not willing to take an active part in breach of explicit orders. But I won't try to prevent your actions either."

Georgia nodded. "Thank you, Ashley. I completely understand and have no issues with your position." Dunn visibly relaxed in her chair. "The same goes for everyone else in this room. Some of you have spent most of your lives in the military so I know that you are trained to follow orders without exception or question. And please don't take that as a criticism of you or the system."

"I'll take the chance," volunteered Molloy. "As you've said, it's an opportunity not to be missed. I may be in the army but I'm also a scientist. Though my primary mission has ended, I still have a passion for knowledge. I would also suggest you speak to Professor Kozlovsky. I'm sure you would like to closely examine the artifact as well."

Georgia was taken by surprise. He had given the impression of a strict military person, making him the last person she expected to disobey Byrne's orders. Maybe she had under-estimated him. His scientific background would be extremely useful. "Thank you, lieutenant. I'm happy to accept your offer. You are aware that there will be consequences though."

"Yes, I'm prepared to accept whatever is thrown at me. But no one will be able to take away the fact that I was one of the first people to study an alien object up close. And, hopefully, we'll be able to make some astounding discoveries."

"As regards the professor, I'm sure her scientific background would also prove invaluable. But as a Russian national who is here as our guest, I'm not sure that taking her is the best idea. It brings in a whole new political dynamic."

"But that's another reason why I think Anna will be ideal," Molloy replied slightly too enthusiastically. "She's not part of this crew and therefore, technically, the colonel's orders do not apply to her. And to be honest, we'll all be in enough trouble anyway. What difference does it make if we add some more misdemeanors to our list of transgressions?"

Georgia knew that he made a good point. But she couldn't help but think that he had other motives for wanting the professor to join them on the trip. She'd noticed how he'd referred to the professor by her first name. Were there any personal reasons behind his request?

"You keep telling us that you want Mars to be free of politics and nationalism," Megan reminded her. "This would be the perfect opportunity for America and Russia to collaborate on a mission that affects the whole of humankind."

Georgia could see the satisfaction on Megan's face. They may be best friends, but the doctor was always ready to put Georgia back in her place whenever she felt she needed to. And this time was no different. In fact, it was exceedingly unfair for Megan to throw her own words back at her.

"Okay, I will speak with the professor directly after this meeting. If she says yes, then I think that will be sufficient for the trip. We'll depart at one P.M." Georgia noticed a smile flash briefly across Molloy's face. She hoped that her suspicions of a romantic involvement were wrong; she didn't want to feel uncomfortable sharing the MEV with a couple of lovebirds. "Joe, you may want to consider building a stockade for three people," she joked. "Please make my cell as comfortable as possible."

"I can't promise a room with a view," he replied. "But I'll keep the colonel off your back for as long as I can."

Chapter 22

It was mid-afternoon the following day by the time the MEV rolled up to the swamp, coming to a halt about twenty yards from the edge.

Georgia's excitement had been growing for the past ninety minutes, ever since they'd begun to follow the tracks left from her previous trip only three days earlier. The area looked exactly as it had, with the massive depression visible from several miles away.

"So here we are," she said unnecessarily, looking at the faces of Molloy and Anna as they stared out of the MEV to take their first close glance at the swamp. They had both been quiet for the past hour, checking their selection of handheld sensors for maybe the fourth or fifth time since leaving Alpha Base.

"Where's the cylinder?" asked Molloy. "Do you think it's sunk into the ground?"

"I hope not, otherwise we've needlessly destroyed our careers," replied Georgia. She fought down the irrational fear that the artifact would no longer be here. "You won't be able to see it until we get closer to the edge. It's time to suit up. I know it's only been three days, but I want to find out if there have been any changes since I was last here."

Within twenty minutes they stepped down from the MEV's airlock onto the surface, with Georgia taking the lead. As she drew closer to the swamp, the sight of the metallic cylinder glinting in the sunlight made her breath an involuntary sigh of relief. Stopping several feet from the edge, she carefully surveyed the area, looking for any obvious changes.

"I don't think there's been any further subsidence," she said. "We can check the photos but I'm sure the visible section of the cylinder is the same. I hope that means the floor of the swamp has now settled."

"It is magnificent," remarked Anna, who was standing close to Molloy. "The images you took did not do it justice. I cannot believe

I'm standing near something that was manufactured by another intelligent species. How long has it been here?"

"It is a sobering experience to witness physical evidence of extraterrestrial life," admitted Molloy. "Being here more than justifies my decision to disobey Earth's orders. I wouldn't miss this for anything."

"We just need to get our hands on the cylinder," replied Georgia, her hands on her hips as she considered her next action. "If there's not too much more of it submerged in the ground, we may be able to remove it from the swamp entirely using the MEV's winch."

"That's probably the only solution," agreed Molloy. "Assuming we can reach the object with a cable. I'm willing to give it a try."

"No, Charlie," said Anna. "I should go. I am lighter than you. If the ground is still unstable, then I'm less likely to sink. And you'll be able to pull me out if I get into difficulties."

"I'll make it easy for both of you; I'm going," Georgia said firmly. "Thank you both for being so enthusiastic about recovering the cylinder, but I am base commander and it was my decision to return here. It's my responsibility to take the risk of securing a cable. There's no further debate required. Let's get this done."

***

In Alpha Base's control room, Mancuso and Jackson were debating the extent of the mineral deposits that had been discovered. It had been agreed by the senior officers that everyone, including Commander Dunn, should stay away from the control room in order to protect them from the repercussions of Georgia's actions. The action was unlikely to absolve them in the event of a punishment being meted out, but it was likely to mitigate the situation. After all, there would still need to be a crew to operate the base.

Jackson was standing in his sister's spot, near the large window that provided the perfect view across Hellas Plain. He counted seven dust devils, kicking up spirally wisps of orange dust as they made random paths across the floor of the enormous crater. It was easy to become mesmerized by them.

"I'm surprised the corporations are not on my back for the results of my initial surveys. They were giving me a hard time less than a week ago, Joe."

"We're on lock down," replied Mancuso, grimly. "NASA is controlling all information. They'll have constructed a plausible story to explain your reluctance to share information."

"That's what I'm afraid of. It feels like a siege mentality."

"Byrne won't want to share your information until a long term decision has been made about the alien cylinder. He'll be reluctant to have them planning to mine near to the swamp. Which makes the decision not to study the cylinder all the more confusing." Mancuso took a large bite of his warm salmon and cream cheese bagel. "How's progress going in your new search area? Have the drones provided any positive feedback?" he asked, with his mouth full of food.

"It's too early. I've had to create a new search zone almost one hundred and fifty miles east of the swamp. I can't tell you how frustrated I am, knowing that I've already discovered a perfect spot." As if to enforce his point, Jackson kicked the wall next to him.

The pair of them went silent again, lost in their own thoughts. The silence was broken by the soft chime of the master computer, indicating receipt of a message from Ground Control. This was the third video message so far today and Mancuso didn't need to be a fortune-teller to know what this one was about. In no hurry to listen to Colonel Byrne, he slowly ate the rest of his bagel, savoring every last morsel. After brushing some crumbs onto his plate, he finally hit the play button.

The image of an irate Byrne appeared on the large display screen. "Can someone tell me what the fuck is going on up there? Commander Pyke, I expect you to provide me with an immediate report explaining the current status of the base and confirming that all of my orders are being complied with, to the letter. That does not mean using Mancuso to stand in for you again. I really don't care if you dislike me and my methods, but I will not tolerate insubordination. And if you continue to defy me so willfully, be assured that I will have you replaced by Commander Dunn. I expect your personal report within one hour."

The screen went blank. "Do you think we've pissed him off enough yet?" asked Jackson, raising an eyebrow.

"I think we may have lit the blue touch paper," agreed Mancuso.

Chapter 23

Georgia was impatiently waiting for Molloy to return with a safety tether when Mancuso contacted her to share the contents of Byrne's message. She was surprised it had taken the colonel this long to start threatening her. The delay had allowed her to accomplish the first part of her plan and, now that she was here, she figured there was nothing that Byrne could do to prevent her from completing what she'd set out to do.

"Thanks, Joe, for holding him off as long as you have. You must have been very convincing. You can now reply to him with the truth. Tell him where I am and that I'm studying the alien relic. Let's see what effect that has on him."

"Are you sure that's wise?" replied Mancuso.

"I stopped making wise decisions when I chose to return here. There's no longer any need for pretense. I've had my small victory. Let him throw the book at me. But keep me informed how you get on." At that moment, Georgia realized that Colonel Byrne was irrelevant. He represented a different regime. One that she'd been struggling against for several months with no success. If she couldn't beat that regime then it was time to create her own rules.

Molloy returned with a length of cable coiled over one shoulder and a safety tether over the other. Anna followed close behind him, carrying a large black case that contained a suite of cameras and sensors. Watching their body language as they walked toward her only confirmed Georgia's suspicions that they actually were a couple. Although it had been subtly obvious during the trip from Alpha Base, the pair had managed to retain their professionalism. Although Georgia had not felt awkward in their presence, there was now absolutely no doubt in in her mind.

"So, when did this happen? You two getting together," she asked.

Molloy and Anna stopped in their tracks and looked sheepishly at each other, waiting for the other person to speak.

"There's no point denying it," Georgia added. " I can see how you are around each other. It's quite okay."

Molloy relaxed and grinned. "I thought we were doing really well at keeping it a secret. I didn't want anyone to find out about us."

Anna had a mortified expression on her face. "I am very sorry, commander. We began seeing each other only a few days ago. Charlie has been very helpful at making we feel welcomed at your base."

"It's quite alright, Anna," Georgia assured her. "I'm really happy that some positives came out of the devastation inflicted by General Zhang and his people. No doubt you've been through a harrowing time and you're still coming to terms with the changes in your life here. You're dealing with it very well and you have my greatest respect. And I'm sure you're both professional enough to not let your relationship interfere with your work."

"Of course not," they replied in unison, Anna looking more relieved that her secret was being so well received.

"In that case, let's focus on retrieving that cylinder," said Georgia as she grabbed one end of the tether from Molloy and clipped it securely onto the waistband of her spacesuit. "Charlie, can you lower me down? Then we can see if I can sink or walk."

The drop to the base of the swamp was only six feet and, in any other circumstances, Georgia could have simply jumped down. As Molloy gently lowered Georgia over the edge of the swamp Anna set up the cameras and sensors on small tripods, each facing the cylinder, to record what was about to occur.

Georgia felt her boot touch something solid beneath her. Tentatively, she put one foot down and then the other, waiting for any adverse effects. Looking at her boots, she was relieved to see that she was not sinking. "Keep the tether tight," she called out to Molloy as she took her first step toward the cylinder.

The object was now tantalizingly close, revealing more details on its surface than had been picked up in Jackson's photos. What had looked like a solid green color was actually a swirl of greens, dark blues and black that formed an asymmetrical pattern. There were no obvious seams or joins and Georgia feared it could be one solid block of metal, in which case it may be too heavy to move, even with the assistance of the MEV.

Cautious not to trip on the uneven surface beneath her feet, Georgia finally stopped within touching distance of the cylinder. Her skin tingled, and the air felt as if it was electrically charged. *It has to be emanating from the cylinder*, she thought. *Maybe it's still active!*

That possibility made her stand perfectly still as she visually inspected the cylinder for any clues. Nothing about it appeared to be any different.

Anna's voice cut into her concentration. "Commander, I'm detecting unusual readings in the ultra-high infrared spectrum. They began as you closed in on the cylinder. I would recommend you retreat immediately as your presence appears to be having an effect."

Georgia retreated two paces, noticing that the tingling sensation diminished slightly the further she moved from the cylinder. "Any changes on the sensor readings, Anna?"

"A minor reduction in the intensity of the energy levels. I would say you're definitely causing some kind of reaction. I'm guessing there's some type of proximity sensor."

"It feels like an electrostatic charge. I don't think it's harmful, and it doesn't seem to be affecting my suit's systems," replied Georgia. She was intrigued that the cylinder could somehow sense her presence.

"You don't know that," said Molloy. "It could have some kind of defense mechanism to prevent exactly what we're attempting to do. I agree with Anna. Return to here until we can determine the source of those readings. We don't need to rush this."

Georgia weighed up the options. Molloy's urge for caution made sense but there was something about being this close to the cylinder that was drawing her in. She'd come too far to be deterred. The object looked harmless enough from here. It looked as if it had simply been abandoned.

"I'm going to move in closer just one more time. Let me know immediately if there are any energy spikes." She moved back to where she had been standing. The tingling sensation increased again but there were no other warning signs.

"The readings have returned to their previous levels," said Anna. "There's definitely a correlation between your proximity to the cylinder and the infrared signature being picked up by the sensors."

"Agreed, "replied Georgia, calmly. "I'm going to reach out and touch the cylinder for a few seconds. I wonder what the reaction will be." She slowly lifted her right hand and stretched out until her gloved fingers lightly brushed the cylinder's casing for no more than a second. To her immediate relief, there was no obvious side effect.

"Energy levels went off the scale when you made contact," reported Anna, the nerves in her voice apparent. "I really think you've pushed your luck enough for one day. I was hoping to take a more scientific approach."

"We're not going to learn anything simply by staring at the cylinder," objected Georgia. She could feel the adrenalin surging through her as her heartbeat increased. "We have to be able to remove it from the swamp. I'm sure there's nothing to worry about."

Before anyone could respond, she reached out again, this time placing her hand firmly onto the cylinder and keeping it there. This time, there was a swift reaction. She could feel the cylinder begin to pulsate in a slow steady rhythm, almost as if it was breathing. She fought the instinct to remove her hand, keen to see if there would be any further developments. "It feels almost alive," she said. "Whatever it is, there's something active inside. Either a machine or a generator."

"How are you feeling?" asked Molloy. "There's a faint glow developing around you and the cylinder. Georgia, I think you really should step away."

"Charlie's right, Georgia," added Anna, nervously. "Energy levels have raised exponentially. The radiation is definitely emanating from the cylinder. And the symbols on its end are glowing and transforming into different shapes!"

Anna's warning caused Georgia to turn and look at the symbols. They had become fluid and moved around each other in swirling patterns, briefly stopping to form new symbols before returning to a rippling liquid state. She was fascinated by the way the metal seemed to have an intelligence directing it across the cylinder's surface. She had no obvious explanation for how the metal was moving as if of its own volition. She removed her hand, wondering if it would have any consequences but the gold metal continued its strange dance.

"Any ideas what could be causing this?" she asked.

Behind her, Molloy and Anna shook their heads. They were equally enthralled by what was happening. "It looks alive," said Molloy. "I can only guess it's some form of an alloy containing nano tech that allows it to change from a solid to a liquid. In its liquid state there's strong cohesion with the cylinder that prevents it from dispersing and running down the side. I strongly recommend you don't touch it, commander. You'd become contaminated. There's no telling what properties it may have. I could be corrosive or attach itself to you."

Georgia stepped back from the cylinder to get a better view of the flowing symbols. They now appeared to be forming more regular and recognizable geometrical shapes. "I hope you're recording all of this, Anna. Do either of you have any recommendations?"

"I don't believe I've seen any duplicate symbols," replied Molloy. "But they're changing so rapidly that it's hard to be sure. We'll have to carefully playback the video. It's almost as if they're cycling through every possible combination of shape. There's no telling if this is normal but I suggest we simply observe for the time being. At least until it stops. We may learn to decipher some recurring patterns."

Georgia thought she spotted the letter 'V' form briefly, but she determined it could equally have been a random shape. Maybe her mind was playing tricks with her.

Then, as suddenly as the symbols had started to move, they resolved themselves into two words. Georgia gasped as she read the word 'HELLO' in crisp gold capital letters. She was unable to read the second word which was in Cyrillic script. "I was really not expecting that. Anna, do you understand the second word?"

"Yes, it also is the word 'HELLO', but in Russian. It would seem that the cylinder has been learning our languages."

"But how?" exclaimed Molloy. "And how did it know to write two different languages that we would understand? I have a bad feeling about this. We need to move away from it. There's far more to the cylinder than we could possibly understand. What else is it learning about us?"

Georgia could see his point. The alien object clearly had some unseen ability to learn. It must have been observing them all this time. She'd been fooled into believing that they were the ones doing the studying. It did feel unsettling. Yet, there was still no evidence pointing to any signs of hostile intent. Maybe this was a Sentinel device, in which case she had no cause for concern.

Without thinking it through, she moved forward to run her fingers across the raised lettering. This time, however, she was suddenly shrouded in complete darkness with the sensation of falling rapidly. She felt a wave of nausea almost overwhelm her. This was a darkness like she'd never experienced before. Far blacker than being in space, with a sense of being smothered.

And just as quickly, she was back standing next to the cylinder. However, there was now a tall thin figure facing her, its features hidden in the shadows of a hood. She immediately recognized the figure as the one from her dreams. But how was that possible? Stepping back quickly, she kept her eyes on the figure, but it didn't follow her. "Molloy," she said, her voice quivering. "I could do with some help down here."

There was no reply. "Molloy? Anna?" Georgia turned her head to see that they were both standing exactly as they had been and were staring in the direction of the cylinder. She repeated their names more urgently, but they didn't react.

"Your colleagues cannot see or hear us, Georgia Pyke."

Georgia jumped at the sound of the strange voice. It was a warm male voice, with an assured quality about it. She turned her gaze back to the hooded figure. "Who are you?"

The figure pulled the hood back, revealing a humanoid head with dark brown skin and large blue eye which seemed incongruous with the complexion. There was no helmet and Georgia immediately wondered how the figure could breathe. "My name is Uslaw Haern and I'm originally from the planet Arethusa. You appear to have activated the communication link on my beacon."

"Why are you here on Mars? And what have you done to my colleagues?"

"I don't know what Mars is. Your two colleagues are perfectly fine. I am nothing more than a projection in your subconscious mind. For them, no time will pass. There is no need to be concerned, you are perfectly safe. You have found a probe that was sent from my home world in search of intelligent life in the Universe. You are communicating with me through a cerebral link, created when you made physical contact to the probe. The real Uslaw Haern will have been dead for many years. I am a memory engram of him, downloaded into the probe."

The information that this was only a representation of an alien life relaxed Georgia, but she was still wary. "Can you tell me how long you have been here?"

Uslaw Haern froze for a moment. "Using your own relative measurements of time, the probe landed on this planet twelve thousand and seventy-two years and eighteen days. The journey here took a further two hundred and ninety-seven years and six months. I have remained dormant throughout that time, waiting to be activated by the local species."

"That seems a haphazard way of making first contact. You are lucky we discovered your probe."

"Millions of probes were dispatched. My race decided this was a more efficient means of discovery rather than sending manned vessels."

"What is your mission? There must be a purpose behind your race's decision to make contact and to send out so many probes into the Universe."

"We are a peaceful species. When we encountered other species, we made it a purpose to discover other life in the Universe and to create partnerships between worlds. We believe it is an opportunity for learning for all species involved. More knowledge is positive for everyone. And it is upsetting to know that some intelligent races may suffer or die out through lack of technology that others take for granted."

Uslaw's words chimed with something inside Georgia. This was what she had been seeking since her experience with the Sentinels. And here was an intelligent alien species that was prepared and willing to share knowledge. She sensed a shortcut to achieving her ambitions. Any doubts she may have had were disappearing by the second.

"How many species have the Arethusans encountered? What happens when you discover a new race?"

"When the probe left Arethusa, we had found thirty-eight other species that were capable of space travel and a further four hundred and twenty-nine that you would consider as post-industrial. Our protocols for forming alliances really depends on how advanced that particular civilization is."

"Is there another way of communication, to allow other people to see and hear you?" she asked. "If you can travel between planetary systems, I assume your designers created a better interface."

"You are correct. I was conceived to provide an introduction to my people only. There are instructions within the probe that will help you construct an interface. The ability to build the interface is a prerequisite to determine how technologically advanced your species is. The process acts as a failsafe in case of less intelligent creatures attempting to make contact."

"Once built, will the interface allow us to communicate directly with beings on your home world?"

"Correct, that is the intent. And then arrangements can be made for more formal processes to take place. Is that something you desire?"

"It is," Georgia replied with a smile. "But I'm not sure I have the authority to make that decision. We have a system of government that acts on behalf of different countries on my planet. I will need to confer with them. How do I disconnect from you?"

"Simply remove your hand. To re-engage you must make contact with the probe as you did before."

Georgia made a mental command to move her arm. She immediately felt dizzy and found herself falling to the ground, with Uslaw nowhere to be seen.

"Georgia, are you okay?" She could hear the urgency in Molloy's voice. Before she could reply she felt his arm on her shoulder as he attempted to help her back to her feet.

"Thanks, Charlie. I'm fine. There's absolutely nothing to worry about." She stood up slowly and saw the concern in his eyes. "I think we should return to the MEV. I have something to share with both of you."

Chapter 24

"Do you feel you can trust this Uslaw Haern? You can't be sure what he is or how he was able to communicate with you. How do you know the communications method isn't harmful?" As always, Molloy wasn't holding back. Georgia had only just sat back in her chair inside the MEV and was taking a drink of water when he pounced.

"Uslaw isn't real," she replied. "He's merely a projection of a being who lived over twelve thousand years ago. How can he do me any harm?"

"You should listen to Charlie," Anna responded. "It was a crazy thing that you did. There was no way of knowing what would happen when you touched the alien probe. This is not how I expected the examination to take place. I don't know why you brought either of us if you're going to ignore our recommendations. We need to have more rigor and controls in place. Especially when we're dealing with the unknown. You have no idea of the consequences of your actions."

"I know I took a risk just now. But please don't preach at me when many of the most profound inventions have been as a result of scientists bending the rules or making discoveries by complete accident. I achieved a result. We now know far more than we did two hours ago." Georgia was feeling annoyed at the accusations leveled at her, partly because she knew that Anna was right. Touching the probe had been a reckless act. She hadn't intended it and, in some ways, that made the situation worse. Had she momentarily lost control of her judgment? Or had the probe somehow manipulated her to reach out?

"We know nothing! That's my point," Anna continued. "You're relying on what you've been told by Uslaw. There's no independent verification to confirm that what he's telling you is the complete truth. You say he's nothing more than an elaborate computer program because that's what he told you. His words were written for him before he was blasted out into space. I'm not saying that he's telling you lies. But be cautious. Learn to have some skepticism about whatever you hear."

Georgia nodded. "You're right. I acted in haste and I apologize to both of you. I will ensure you're more closely involved in the remaining study of the probe."

"Did you learn anything about Uslaw's home world or his people? Did he indicate what technology they would be seeking to share or what they want in return?"

"Sorry Charlie, it was nothing more than a brief introduction. I was unable to think of the questions to ask. The strange part is that I've been having recurring dreams and Uslaw has been prominent in them. Tell me, did the probe obtain the image from my memory, as it must have done to learn our language, or have my dreams been premonitions all along? I can't decide which alternative scares me most."

"Very interesting," said Anna, scribbling some notes into the pad resting on her knee. "I will devise some questions for you to ask Uslaw that may help us determine more about him and decide how much of a threat he really is."

***

Georgia was a little surprised when it was Commander Dunn that responded to her next standard comms check. "Where's Joe?" she asked, expecting the worst.

Dunn sounded embarrassed as she replied, "Byrne has stripped him of his duties. He's confined to quarters pending a further decision about your future. He's ordered the same for Doctor Betts. You've also been stripped of your command and I am now acting base commander. I'm sorry it has to be like this but it was always going to happen."

Georgia knew that she shouldn't have been shocked at Byrne's ruthlessness, but the speed of his response was unexpected. She had hoped to at least return to Alpha Base before any actions were taken. "There's no need to apologize, Ashley. I knew exactly what I was doing by breaking the colonel's orders. He's reacted in the only way he could to demonstrate his authority. Although I don't understand why he's punishing Megan. I'm relieved to know that you've not been caught in the crossfire."

"Byrne's first instruction is for me to order your immediate return to base. I'm giving you that order, but I expect you will ignore it. I'd be disappointed if you didn't." Georgia could see Dunn's subtle smile on the monitor.

"Yes, I think we'll be here for several more days yet. We need to determine how and if we can remove the cylinder from the swamp. However, we have confirmed that it is an alien probe. I made contact with what I can best describe as an intelligent projection that explained the probe's origin."

"That's sensational," exclaimed Dunn. "Did you see what the alien life looks like? How did it communicate?"

Georgia spent the next five minutes recounting what had happened to her.

"I'll have to send a report to Ground Control," said Dunn once Georgia had answered all of her questions. "It may help to mitigate your actions in the eyes of some people."

"I understand and thank you for your support Ashley. I know you're doing all that you can. I intend re-establishing contact with Uslaw tomorrow morning. I should be in a position to give you more information after that."

"Good luck to all of you. And be careful."

***

Colonel Byrne watched Dunn's report with an increasing level of anger. It was Saturday night, and he was at home alone in his office, his wife having decided to stay an extra week with her eighty-nine-year-old mother in Baton Rouge. He didn't mind that she wasn't there; they had been drifting apart over the past few years as his devotion to his work had become more important than his marriage. The relationship was now more of convenience for the sake of their three children.

But he was frustrated at not being able to vent his rage at someone. Pyke had gone too far this time. She was acting recklessly with no thought for the safety of her crew. He'd suspected she was up to something but her blatant disregard of his orders, orders that had come from the president himself, was reprehensible. There was no place for it under his command. And the misplaced loyalty placed in Pyke by her senior officers, notably Joe Mancuso and Megan Betts, equally had to be squashed. He'd no alternative but to act swiftly and decisively.

He suspected that Commander Dunn may also have divided loyalties, but he had to give her an opportunity to prove herself. In any event, he had no other immediate options as base commander. He felt as if he'd lost control of Alpha Base and it was urgent that he recovered the situation as soon as possible.

Even though it was almost nine P.M. he decided to contact Libby Selznick and give her a piece of his mind. She was another person who had ignored his judgment and actively supported Pyke's style of leadership. Now it was time for Selznick to learn that those chickens were coming home to roost.

"Hey Google, call Libby Selznick," he said, and took a slug of bourbon while he waited for the call to connect. He frowned as the call went straight to voicemail. "Libby, it's Byrne. Call me back. Pyke is creating more problems for everyone and you need to get on top of it."

Byrne didn't expect that she would call him back that night. The NASA administrator was weak and lacked the clarity of vision that he possessed. She was a simple paper pushed and couldn't see what was obvious to him. If she was going to continue sticking her head in the sand, then it was up to him to do what must be done. Perhaps it was time to test Dunn's loyalty.

***

Libby Selznick checked the caller id on her phone and chose to ignore Byrne. She wasn't in the mood to face him at this time of night. She'd already decided to delay responding to Georgia Pyke's request for intervention until she returned to her office on Monday morning. In reality, she would have liked to knock their heads together and tell them to sort out their working relationship. She'd had a pleasant meal with her sister and had already shared a fine bottle of Argentinian malbec. She didn't want Byrne or Pyke to spoil the evening.

"You could have taken that call. It may have been important," her sister said as she loaded plates into her dishwasher. The kitchen was small but functional, and Libby sat on the far side of the counter, gently stroking the stem of her wine glass.

"It's that pain in the ass colonel I was telling you about, Eve. He knows I'm on leave so he can wait until tomorrow."

Evelynn closed the dishwasher and walked into the living area with her own glass of wine. "Come and sit on the couch, sis. It's more comfortable than that stool. You can tell me the dirty secret you teased me with. You've been here a whole day and not shared it with me."

Libby had been in two minds to say anything and had been grateful that her sister had seemingly forgotten their phone conversation. She should have known that Evelynn was simply waiting for the right time, when she was relaxed and had drunk a few glasses of wine.

"Is this how you get all of your best news stories? By plying your sources with alcohol."

"Of course," laughed Evelynn. "It's the first page in the 'Reporter's 101' rulebook. Lull your victim into a false sense of security, build their trust and they'll reveal secrets they didn't even know they had. There's no point trying to resist it."

"I can see why they made you editor-in-chief at the Chicago Tribune."

"Thanks. I think the Pulitzer had a lot to do with it as well," Evelynn replied, pointing to the framed certificate hanging proudly on the wall.

Libby took a deep breath. "How would you like to win a second Pulitzer Prize? I have something to tell you that will guarantee you serious plaudits and I cannot think of anyone else I'd trust to tell this story properly. Of course, you'll need to find a way to tell it that doesn't implicate me."

"That could be difficult, seeing how we're related. Bu I'm sure I can find a way to ensure you don't have a target on your back. And you do have an exemplary record at NASA. No one would easily believe you're the type to divulge secrets. Can I record this?" she asked, fishing an old Sony handheld recorder from behind a cushion.

"I'd rather you write it down," said an increasingly reluctant Libby. "I trust you to be discrete but there has to be no evidence of my involvement whatsoever."

Evelynn had often found herself in such situations with whistle blowers and had learned to be as flexible as possible in order to get her sources to speak freely. "No problem. It's totally normal to be nervous. And if you change your mind at any time, just let me know. For now, this is between the two of us." She replaced the recorder in its hiding place and picked up a notepad and pen that were laying on the coffee table. "Okay, where do you want to begin?"

A visibly more relaxed Libby Selznick took a sip of her wine and sat back in the comfort of the plush couch. With an air of newfound confidence, she looked Evelynn in the eyes and said in a low assured voice, "We found an alien relic on Mars."

Chapter 25

"Don't you think it would be better if I made contact with Uslaw Haern?" suggested Anna the next morning as she slipped gracefully into her spacesuit. "There are merits to more than one of us having communication with the alien probe as a means of independent verification. We would be able to compare our experiences to ensure that our minds are not misinterpreting the information being passed from the probe. We still have no idea how the interface even works. It could be entirely different for me."

It was obvious to Georgia that Anna had given the matter a lot of thought overnight since they'd made the plans for today's further investigations of the probe. She could see the benefits of sharing the load and she had no intent of being precious about keeping communication to herself. If it helped to understand the alien probe, then she was open to any suggestions. She was wondering if Molloy would also have an opinion. She wasn't disappointed.

"I agree with Anna. I know we discussed that there should be some consistency around the communications but if what you saw is an image projected into your mind from the probe, does it matter? I would like to know if the probe recognizes it is being contacted by a different person. How intelligent is that probe?"

"I don't disagree with either of you," replied Georgia, checking the power levels in her suit were sufficient for the day ahead. "As I would expect, you both make very valid points. You will both get an opportunity to contact Uslaw, but I think it should be me that re-establishes contact this morning. I want to know if he or it recognizes me. At the moment we can only guess that the probe has the ability to learn but we remain in the dark until we know its purpose."

The conversation ended briefly while they secured each other's spacesuits and completed pressure checks to ensure there were no leaks. They silently entered the airlock, and it wasn't until they had walked halfway to the swamp that Georgia brought up the subject again.

"I'll speak with Uslaw now and ask him the questions we agreed on last night. Once I break contact, one of you can repeat the process with the same questions. We can then compare the responses. I'll let you decide which of you wants to be the one to communicate with Uslaw." Georgia couldn't help but smile. It would be a good test of Molloy and Anna's relationship. She didn't want to come between the couple and was more than happy to remain neutral. She knew she'd made the right decision when she noticed the pair of them glance at each other suspiciously, without saying a word.

She climbed down into the swamp with some assistance from Molloy. The sun was still low and the ground between her and the probe was still bathed in shadow. It made her feel cold, and she involuntarily shivered. "Anna, how are the sensor readings?"

"Similar to yesterday. I'll let you know when there are any significant changes."

Georgia took four tentative paces before Anna said, "I'm seeing the same increase in energy signature as yesterday. You're still twenty feet away from the probe. It must be extremely sensitive."

"Thanks Anna. I can see the two translations of hello are still on the side of the probe. I'm taking that as a positive sign." She took the remaining steps until she was standing in the same spot as the previous day. She could just make out the footprints she's left in the soft, dark dust. "Are there any reasons why I shouldn't touch the probe?"

"No more than we had yesterday," Anna replied dryly. All sensor readings are as before.

"I'm holding tight to your tether. At the slightest hint of trouble, I'll have you out of there," added Molloy.

But before Georgia could reach out and touch the probe, she had the same sensation of nausea she'd felt the day before. And Uslaw

Haern was once again standing in front of her, his expression friendly and calming.

"Hello again Georgia Pyke. As you can see, I have enhanced the capability of the interface. It is only possible because your brain is sufficiently advanced. You no longer have to be in physical contact with this probe. I thought it would be more practical for you."

Georgia wasn't comfortable with the idea that Uslaw could enter her mind at will. It was too invasive. "I sense your discomfort," he continued. "I apologize if I have offended you. I was only trying to be more helpful."

"I'm not used to other intellects inside my mind," she replied. "It is not how I usually communicate. I would like to be in control of when I speak to you. You took me by surprise, that's all. I would prefer if I was able to grant you permission."

Uslaw Hearn simply stood and stared at her. She wasn't sure if he was thinking of a response or learning from her behavior. It was unsettling.

"We have some questions. Are you able to answer them?"

"One of my designated responsibilities is to share information and to understand new cultures. I will do my best," Uslaw replied, once again smiling.

Georgia began with one of Anna's specially written questions. "So far, you have answered all of my questions without asking any of your own. Are you not interested in discovering about our species?"

Uslaw's smile reminded Georgia of her grandmother whenever she'd asked questions as a young girl. It was patient, with a hint of amusement. "I was designed to build your trust. We have plenty of time to find out more about you and your planet, but our philosophers believed it important that you knew more about us to begin with. After all, we are likely to be the first alien race that you have made contact with. You're bound to be inquisitive."

The response was unexpected, and Georgia felt it wasn't entirely genuine. Was there more to the building of trust than Uslaw was letting on?

Without pursuing the matter, she continued with one of Molloy's questions. She felt it would be a good demonstration of the probe's intelligence "Do you know what planet you are on and where you are in the galaxy?"

"I do not know the designation of your planet. From an analysis of the star constellations against my original coordinates, I believe I am in a planetary system circling a yellow dwarf star near the galaxy rim, approximately forty million light years from the Galactic Center."

"That's close enough. The planet you're on is called Mars, but this is not my home world. I am from another planet in this system called Earth and the star that we circle is the Sun. How far are we from your home planet, Arethusa?"

"At this moment, we are eight thousand three hundred and eleven lights years from Arethusa."

"That's not possible," exclaimed Georgia. "You stated it took you less than three hundred years to complete your journey. You must have traveled at several times the speed of light. That's impossible." She couldn't do the math in her head.

"I do not understand the limitation you place on the speed of light. We have vessels that are capable of traversing the galaxy within five hundred of your years. This appears to be a technology that you are lacking an awareness of. I shall make a record of it."

"Yes, you do that." Georgia was astounded by the knowledge. What else could she add to the shopping list? But for now, she had to focus on getting more information. "Do you know what species I am? Have you encountered similar species in your travels?"

"There are no details of your species in my data files. You are the first species I have come into contact with, but I can access data from other probes. Since my departure from Arethusa, eight hundred and nineteen new species have been recorded and archived. Of those, six hundred and ninety two are class one intelligence, capable of spaceflight. Ninety-eight percent of those species are carbon based and eighty-three percent are bipeds such as yourselves. Your form, or variations of it, are quite common."

Georgia hoped she would remember all the information. She couldn't believe that there was so much life out in the Universe. Humans certainly weren't alone after all. She wondered how much of the galaxy had been explored by the Arethusans. "Are your species part of the Confederacy?" It was not a question she'd discussed with either Anna or Molloy, but it suddenly seemed very relevant.

Uslaw paused for several seconds and a strange expression flickered across his face. "I do not recognize that name. Are you able to provide more details?"

Georgia was about to explain but her instinct held her back. She didn't want to reveal too much at this time. "I'm sorry, that was my little joke. We have a space opera running on television. One of the alien tribes is called the Confederacy. You wouldn't understand unless you'd seen it."

"What does the Confederacy do?" persisted Uslaw.

"It's just a fictional tribe. It hangs about on asteroids and annoys passing spaceships. There's a different story every week," Georgia lied, more convinced that it was best not to reveal what she knew.

'We will have to study your culture in more detail. Something appears to be lost in translation," replied Uslaw. Georgia thought she detected a note of irritation in his voice. How was that possible in a projection?

"It's my fault. We got side-tracked. Can I ask another question?" Without waiting for a response, she asked. "You mentioned there were instructions within your probe that would enable us to construct an interface with your makers on Arethusa. Can you tell me how to access that information? Do we need any special materials to construct it?"

"Obtaining the instructions is part of the challenge. Georgia Pyke. You will need to provide me with information about your species. I can then determine whether you are significant enough to allow the next stage of the process to be enabled. You must understand that this procedure has been carefully engineered to ensure we engage with the correct level of intelligent species."

"What happens if we fail?" This option hadn't occurred to her until now.

"That would be unfortunate in the short term. However, you are able to continue your attempts indefinitely. Eventually you will succeed."

Uslaw's statement caught Georgia off guard. She had supposed it would be a relatively easy process. All the carefully prepared questions now disappeared from her mind as the prospects of failure dismayed her. "Let me consult with my colleagues. How do I break this communications channel?"

"It is easy. Walk away from the probe and you will move out of range of the interface. Return when you are ready to continue our dialog."

Georgia took a step back. This time she was prepared for the temporary dizzy sensation and was able to remain standing. She felt confused and, at the same time, relieved that Uslaw was no longer in her head. She turned and carefully made her way back toward Molloy who was leaning down, ready to help her out of the swamp.

"Did you change your mind?" he asked, a look of concern on his face.

She shook her head. "Uslaw made contact. He's improved the delivery system so that he can now simply appear when I'm close enough to the probe."

"Were you able to have all the questions answered? Has he revealed anything about his purpose?" Anna was eager to find out if Georgia had been successful.

"Yes and no," replied Georgia, wistfully. "Have you decided which of you is going to make contact?"

"Charlie has decided that it should be him. He thinks Uslaw should see that there is more than one gender of human." Anna was clearly not happy with the decision. "I don't agree that gender should be the deciding factor, but I will concede to him on this occasion."

Georgia could see Molloy squirm. Anna was going to make him pay for his attitude. "Get to it then, Charlie. I want to make sure I'm not hallucinating."

Charlie jumped down into the swamp, striding confidently toward the probe. Georgia watch him hesitate as he approached where she'd been standing only minutes before. He took one final step before appearing to stumble backwards and fall to the ground.

Anna gasped, "Charlie are you okay?"

"Just a bit dizzy," he replied as he quickly stood up, brushing dust from his spacesuit. "You're right, Georgia. The disconnection is disorienting." Molloy turned and walked back toward Georgia and Anna, a look of awe on his face.

"You spoke with Uslaw?" asked Georgia. She couldn't believe how quick the interface occurred. When she was speaking with the alien projection, time seemed to pass normally.

Molloy was effortlessly climbing out of the swamp. "Yes, he looked exactly as you described. Other than the dizziness, the connection is virtually seamless. The probe must somehow link directly into our frontal lobe, fooling the synapses into believing they're having an actual conversation."

"The probe must understand brain waves," Anna said. "That must have been what it was doing yesterday. Calibrating itself to align with our brains so that it can talk in our languages. That is an amazing ability to have if you want to be able to communicate effectively with unknown alien civilizations."

"Provided it is done passively," warned Georgia. "It makes me feel very nervous to know that I can't control when the probe accesses my subconscious. If that device can access our brains, does it have the ability to manipulate our thoughts?"

"We could never know for sure," agreed Anna. "I understand your concern. Perhaps we should return to the MEV so that we can review each of your responses. It's possible that you had different experiences, which would be interesting in itself."

Georgia agreed. "I'm starting to think I made a mistake bringing us here. We'll follow up with Uslaw once we have a new set of questions. But then I'm taking us back to Alpha Base. This probe is potentially far more dangerous than I realized, and we need a better plan."

"Now that I've experienced Uslaw Haern, I agree that it probably a wise option," said Molloy, stepping back aboard the MEV. "Although I doubt any of us will be allowed to take part in future investigations."

"Leave that to me," replied Georgia, although she honestly didn't know how she'd convince Byrne.

***

Libby Selznick waited until she'd had breakfast before returning Byrne's call. She was in no hurry to speak with him and, in any case, the two Tylenol she'd taken had yet to defeat the headache she'd woken up with. She couldn't be sure if the headache was a consequence of too much wine or lack of sleep. It had been almost two A.M. before Evelynn had run out of questions for her.

The colonel picked up on the second ring. "Eugene, you tried to call me."

"That was fourteen hours ago, Libby. Did you not understand when I said it was an urgent matter?"

Libby smiled to herself. She found it much easier to deal with Byrne when she wasn't face to face and it was her turn to have some fun with him. "If it was that urgent, you'd have tried harder. I was out for a meal last night and have only just listened to your message," she lied. "What do you have to tell me?"

"It's Pyke. She's arrogantly disobeyed the president's orders and taken a small group to research the alien cylinder. I had no choice but to promote Dunn as Base Commander. I did warn you that Pyke was unpredictable. But isn't this exactly what you wanted?"

Libby was disappointed by the news. She had chosen to back Georgia Pyke, partly to spite the colonel but mainly because she genuinely believed Georgia was the best person to lead the Mars mission. And although she had not agreed with the president's decision, she had not expected Georgia to so flagrantly disregard them. But were Georgia's actions really any different to divulging the details of the alien discovery to her reporter sister? Either way, it wouldn't reflect well that she may have made the wrong decision to retain Georgia in her post. "I assume you've ordered Pyke and her team to return to base."

"Of course I have. She's reported to Commander Dunn that she has made contact with the cylinder and confirmed that it is indeed of alien origin."

Libby's headache was forgotten about. "Contact? How?"

"If you accessed your messages, you'd have seen the report from Commander Dunn. The probe was somehow able to establish a neural connection with Pyke. Despite her irresponsible actions, Pyke intends further contact with the probe today. To complicate matters further, one of her team is Professor Kozlovsky, the Russian scientist we saved from Derzost. Pyke's actions will have international implications and we won't be able to keep this story secret for much longer."

For once, Libby had to agree with Byrne. What was Pyke thinking? Protocols had been put in place for first contact and she was choosing to ignore them. It was imperative that NASA recover control of the situation. "Who else is aware of the matter?"

"I informed the White House late last night. When you didn't respond, I had no choice. The president is chairing a special session of the National Security Committee in an hour. You may want to get yourself an invitation."

"Shit!" exclaimed Libby. The situation couldn't be any worse for her. She was going to have to use all the skills she'd learned during her long career to get out of this hole. She couldn't blame the colonel for this mess. "You did the right thing, Eugene. Is there anything else I need to know?"

"I don't think so. I think you already know that you fucked up big this time." Byrne hung up abruptly, his words ringing in her ears.

She immediately called the White House who quickly confirmed that she was expected to dial into the president's meeting. After taking a note of the dial-in details she opened her messages and watched Commander Dunn's report with a growing sense of anxiety and incredulity.

Chapter 26

The sleek Sentinel vessel hovered in Earth orbit above the South China Sea. Two hundred miles below, and oblivious to the craft's presence, the American Seventh Fleet was playing a game of cat and mouse with the might of the Chinese navy. The slim silver wakes of the ships were clearly visible against the dark blue of the ocean, revealing the complex series of maneuver and counter-maneuver being ordered by the respective admirals as they tested each other's resolve, without engaging in formal combat.

"In all the years that I have been observing your planet, I still fail to understand your species' desire for conquest against one another," said Falmas as he stared at the viewing screen. "Why the excessive obsession with violence and destruction when you could be focused on far better constructive concepts that would ease the hunger and disease that affects large parts of your home world?"

"I can't argue with the futility of war," replied Jim Grant. "From our perspective here, it's almost a sick joke. One small planet amongst so many in the cosmos and humans spend all their time killing one another. I'm unable to explain it in a way that I understand, let alone make you see the rationale. It is a complete waste of resources. We've been stationed here for two weeks now and I'm becoming weary of what I'm seeing. If only someone could open their eyes to the possibilities that await humankind."

"I believe the future of your world hangs in the balance. I have enjoyed observing some of your great nations rise and fall because there was always progress in your evolution. It has been only in the last one hundred years that I have grown concerned that your world's leaders may have taken the wrong path. One that will lead to complete annihilation."

"You have every right to be worried," I can see the situation has deteriorated in the past two years. America and China will come to blows. I can see that it is inevitable. And if either country is insane enough to use nuclear weapons, then I do not want to be here to watch it happen."

Falmas nodded in understanding. "I would not wish to see my world destroyed either. You're here to provide an insight into the human condition. Can you offer any evaluation of the events developing below?"

Grant had been giving the matter a lot of thought since they'd arrived. He'd watched dozens of hours of news transmissions from around the world and Falmas had intercepted encrypted messages between the presidents of America, China and Russia. He now probably had a clearer understanding than anyone on Earth of what each nation's plans were. With so much information at his disposal, he wished he could return to his home planet and explain to the World's leaders that what they were doing was so wrong. His ideal scenario would have been to kidnap the leaders from the larger countries and bring them together in orbit, but he knew Falmas would never permit it.

"For some time, the Chinese have been attempting to expand their sphere of control. With large investments in several African states and Australia, they're surreptitiously built strategic allies. At the same time, they've built islands in the South China Sea in order to build military installations in beach of various international treaties. For many years, they were supported by Russia but American and Japan have taken a very hard line. With the recent change of American president, China's government have decided to test the new administration."

Falmas was listening intently but was struggling to grasp the rationale "That seems to be a very reckless ploy. What can possible be gained?"

"It's a power struggle. China's ruling party is feeling vulnerable after the fiasco on Mars. They've seen an opportunity to recover some national pride by challenging the new American president. They want to know what type of leader he is and whether he has any weaknesses. I'm ashamed to say we used to do the same thing on a far smaller scale whenever a new kid started school."

"And in the meantime, both countries let people die through malnutrition and treatable diseases?"

"When you say it like that, it does sound totally ridiculous. But standing by and doing nothing doesn't seem any better either."

"We've had this debate far too many times Grant. You won't drag me into it again. We have no remit to interfere." Falmas was about to make an additional comment when a warning symbol appeared at the edge of the screen. He reached out and touched the symbol with his left hand. His body stiffened in surprise as he interpreted the data.

Grant noticed the troubled look on his face. "What's wrong?"

"The ship has intercepted a transmission. It's not a language that I recognize. If our translators can't decipher the transmission, it can only mean the message is not from any species in the Confederacy. I don't understand why we would be picking it up in your solar system.

"Do you know the source of the transmission? Is it close by? Is anyone in danger?" Grant's immediate concern was for Earth. If there was another alien ship nearby, what was it doing?

"Just one moment while the ship processes the information." Falmas closed his eyes to concentrate on the data. "It appears to be coming from Mars, or close to Mars. Perhaps from orbit or one of the moons. It's subspace so definitely not of human origin." he exclaimed in shock. "We must investigate now."

Chapter 27

That night, Molloy's sleep was disturbed by Uslaw Haern. He wasn't sure if he was awake or dreaming or even where he was.

His surroundings were like nothing he'd seen before. A deep orange sun, five times larger than the Sun, was the first thing to catch his attention. He could feel its intense heat burning into his skin. He looked down, surprised to see he was in his shorts and tee shirt, the clothes he's been wearing when he fell asleep in his cot aboard the MEV.

He was standing on a wooden deck, about twenty feet square, surrounded by metal railings. Beyond the railings was what appeared to be a thick forest filled with unusually shaped trees and vegetation. The leaves had an odd red hue that reminded him of autumn. And there was a complete and utter silence. No animal or bird sounds, and no sound of any wind through the trees. He was alone.

"Hello," he called out, anxious as to how he's arrived here. His voice was muffled by the trees and he heard no reply.

Molloy turned slowly around, looking for any clues as to his whereabouts. Walking over to the edge of the platform, he looked down sixty feet to the ground below. He spotted a thin path circling the platform but there was no way down. The sides of the platform were sheer drops, with no sign of steps or other means of escape. He was trapped.

"Is this the one?"

Molloy spun round at the sound of the voice. Uslaw Haern was now standing in the center of the platform next to another figure dressed in similar clothes. The newcomer was shorter and more compact than Uslaw, and his features were sharper. Molloy's first impression was this new figure looked like a fighter.

"Yes, he is called Charlie Molloy. He is a scientist but was also a soldier in one of Earth's armies," said Uslaw.

"You have done well," said the stranger

"Where am I?" shouted Molloy, partly in panic. "How are you talking to me?"

Uslaw smiled graciously. "There's no need to be alarmed. My superior, Tremo Shaern, has taken an active interest in my discovery and desires to speak with you. These surroundings are a replica of Arethusa, but we are only in your mind."

"How can you still be in my head? We severed the connection and I'm halfway back to my base."

Uslaw continued to smile, but it was unsettling. "The connection was not broken. I have been waiting in the shadows, waiting for Tremo Shaern to join us."

Molloy looked vainly around for a means of escape. "Get out of my head. This is an invasion of my privacy. You've no right to be here."

His request was ignored. Instead, Tremo said in a menacing voice, "I understand that Uslaw Haern has answered all of the questions posed by yourself and your colleague. He has been open and freely shared information with yourselves. I wish to ask you some questions and for you to reply in the open and complete way that Uslaw has. That seems reasonable and appropriate."

"It would be if you'd asked me in the correct manner instead of forcibly kidnapping me."

"You are confused. We have not taken you anywhere. Your physical form remains within your vehicle. Once you have answered my questions you will be free to return to your resting state."

"Relax," added Uslaw. "We will not take long."

"My first question I need an answer to is how are your people aligned to the Confederacy?"

Molloy was immediately confused. "I don't understand the question. What is the Confederacy?"

The two Arethusans looked at one another before Uslaw said, "Please do not make this difficult. Georgia Pyke asked me if we were part of the Confederacy. Humans are aware of its existence. We would like to know the relationship."

"I've never heard of the Confederacy. You must be mistaken."

"Do not play games with us. It will not go well for you when we arrive at your planet," continued Uslaw. The smile was now gone. There was no longer a need to keep up the pretense. The two Arethusans approached Molloy, cornering him by the rails. "We do have ways of discovering the truth."

"I don't doubt it. But if my physical being is where you said it is, then this can't do me any harm." Molloy grabbed the rail, hopped over it in one easy bound and fell feet first to the ground below.

***

"We need to get back to Alpha Base as soon as possible. Uslaw Haern is not what he appears."

Georgia sat up at the Molloy's warning. "What's happened?" she said into the darkness.

Molloy turned the lights on in the cab, still shaken and disturbed by his experience. "Uslaw fooled us. He's still in my head. He could be in yours. I was just speaking with him and one of his associates on their home world. They were going to interrogate me. It wasn't pleasant Georgia. I think he's a bigger threat than we thought."

Georgia could sense Molloy's anxiety was real. It wasn't like the big man to behave in this manner. Anna was also staring at him with a concerned expression etched across her face. But his tale seemed far-fetched. "Are you sure it wasn't a dream? Or maybe an echo from your earlier contact. We can't be sure there aren't any side effects from the interface process."

"It was real," insisted Molloy without hesitation. "I was on an alien world. Uslaw told me he'd been hiding in my subconscious waiting to contact me again. The other guy was really unpleasant. He was the one asking the questions. He kept referring to something called the Confederacy. Uslaw said that you mentioned the name to him. They both got angry when I denied any knowledge. Do you know what they were talking about?"

Georgia felt a chill run through her. *What have I done?* "You've just proved it wasn't a dream, Charlie. The Confederacy do exist. Which means we're in serious trouble." She climbed from her cot and fired up the navigation computer. "We should return to Alpha at the earliest opportunity, even though I'm not sure we'll be safe there."

Not in Georgia's worst nightmares had she ever considered she would fear what an alien species could do to mankind. Now, thanks to her thoughtless actions, she wondered what Uslaw and the Arethusans were really up to. As the MEV began its slow crawl through the night, she turned to Molloy and said, "Now, tell me exactly what happened."

Chapter 28

The MEV arrived at its docking port at Alpha Base shortly after eleven A.M. Anna had not been able to stay awake and managed to sleep for most of the journey. Georgia and Molloy had spent the time discussing what Uslaw Haern's revelation meant for them. They had determined that they had insufficient information to do anything other than make educated guesses but, whatever was happening was likely to be disastrous for all of them. Georgia had come to the reluctant conclusion that the only option was to destroy the probe, if that was possible.

As Georgia opened the airlock into the base, she was met by a sombre looking Commander Dunn. "We weren't expecting you until this afternoon. You know I have orders to have the three of you confined to quarters."

"So that will be five of us," replied Georgia, choosing not to hide the disdain in her voice. "We have far more important matters than depriving this base of key crew members when they're needed most. We need to talk."

Dunn acknowledged Georgia's comment. "All three of you come with me. The least you can do is give me a debrief. Byrne appointed me as base commander after all. They followed Dunn in silence up two flights to the control room where both Mancuso and Megan were waiting to greet them with tearful hugs.

"I only said I'd been given orders to have you all confined to quarters," Dunn said with a rueful smile. "I didn't say that I had actually implemented Byrne's instructions. You're all far too valuable to have locked up in our cabins."

"Thanks Ashley," said a grateful Georgia. "I'm sorry if I doubted you. It's me that's fucked up this time. What's the latest from Earth?"

Dunn perched herself on the edge of one of the consoles. "As you'd expect. The White House is incensed that you made contact with the probe against their express wishes. President Ramsay wants your head on a plate, if that's possible. For the time being, he wants us to immediately desist any further study or contact with the alien device and for all your reports to be provided, including sensor readings and any other measurements. He's tasked NASA Administrator Selznick with ensuring that we completely comply with their requests within the next four hours. There's a perceived loss of control on the part of NASA."

Georgia wasn't surprised. Knowing what she now knew, she was regretting being so reckless. Her conflict with Colonel Byrne had become too personal but she shouldn't have reacted in the way she had. Because of her actions everyone on Alpha base was now at risk. "I'll share everything that we have," she conceded. "It may be too late though. I may have let the genie out of the bottle."

***

At about the same time, Falmas' ship arrived in Martian orbit and immediately began to search for the actual source of the mystery transmissions. It proved problematic as the signals were intermittent and had a seemingly random dispersal pattern.

"Have your specialists on Nikari sent any information yet?" asked Grant anxiously. "There must be something in your planet's archives that can help us."

Falmas was concentrating on three different screens in front of him. "It does not usually take this long," he admitted. "The records from our studies are extensive and well organized. It could be that we have encountered a new technology or intelligent species. Whatever is down there is doing its best to remain hidden."

"Georgia and the base could be in danger. Can't we do more or at least warn them?"

"Warn them of what? You're jumping to conclusions, Grant. We need to remain methodical if we want to work this out. In fact, we are receiving information from Nikari now." They both looked at the incoming message as it appeared on the screen. The words 'Extreme Caution' caught Grant's attention.

"Who are the Arethusans?" he asked, sensing the dismay on Falmas' face.

"They are an ancient barbaric race who attempted to conquer this region of the galaxy many thousands of years ago. They were repelled by an allied force that later became the Confederacy. I have read the records from that time and it was an extremely bloody war that lasted for hundreds of your years. The Arethusans had no respect for life and wiped out numerous planetary systems without a thought. In their attempts to grow their army and find new resources to build deadlier weapons, the Arethusans launched thousands of probes and sent them across the galaxy. The majority of those probes were intercepted and destroyed, while some were found by unsuspecting civilizations who were subsequently conquered and forced into servitude, supporting the Arethusans war efforts. This is the first one I've encountered."

"Were the Arethusans destroyed?" asked Grant

"They were pushed back to their own sector of space and a peace treaty was signed. There has been no trouble since that time. Occasionally a rogue probe is found on an asteroid or planet. They contain highly sophisticated stealth technology so are very difficult to locate, and even harder to destroy."

"But you've been able to detect the transmissions. The probe's not hiding now."

"That's because the probe is acting as a beacon," replied Falmas. "It's letting the Arethusan's home world know where it is. Which means the whole of humanity is in danger."

"Why? You said the Arethusans are an ancient race and that there's been no contact for thousands of years. They may have perished or forgotten about their probes."

Falmas shook his head. "There have been rumors circulating that a new force has been building an army far from our borders. If that is true, the Arethusans may be using their remaining probes to gather vital intelligence about the Confederacy as well as build alliances. Our orders are to destroy that probe immediately before the Arethusans detect its location."

"Isn't it too late for that? And what weapons do we have?" asked a concerned Grant. Although he had great respect for the Sentinels, he was now thinking it very short sighted that none of their research vessels carried any weapons, even for self-defense.

"The destruction of the probe will only become an issue when we find it. But I would be grateful if you could give the matter some thought. It may be useful checking the records of our previous encounters with probes to discover what methods we have used. As for timing, based on when we first detected the transmission, our researchers indicate we have another twenty hours before a permanent link is established between the probe and Arethusa."

"So, we have no time to waste. What else do I need to know?" asked Grant. He'd learned that the Sentinels were reluctant to provide him with more information than they thought was necessary. He suspected it was either a trust issue or they viewed him as an inferior species. Challenging Falmas was often the only way of digging out the truth, even if the Sentinel was easily frustrated by the questions.

Falmas hesitated as he read the informatics on screen for further details, a look of confusion developing as he processed the information. "You didn't ask how the probe was activated after so many thousands of years. Our records show the only method we are aware of is when the probe comes into contact with organic life. That means that your former crew have discovered it."

"The probe has to be somewhere on Hellas Planitia," Grant replied excitedly. That's narrowed the search area. If we are able to contact the base, they can give us the exact location. Surely this situation merits a bending of your strict rules."

"It's not that straightforward. There's an artificial intelligence within the probe that is used as a universal translator to communicate with the species it comes into contact with. The program seems harmless enough but in reality it works through its victim's subconscious, extracting tactical information that is relayed back to Arethusa via the beacon. It gives the Arethusans a distinct advantage when they arrive at the new world."

"What type of information?"

"I would imagine it will be related to population, defensive capabilities, key personnel, cultural and physical weaknesses. Anything that can be used to subjugate the indigenous population."

"My god! That could leave Earth wide open to an attack. They wouldn't know what was happening until it was too late!" It was incredible. During his time on Nikari, Grant had been given the impression that all planets in the Confederacy lived in harmony. Not once had he considered there may be other civilizations that threatened that peace. He realized now that he had been very naive. Another example of the Sentinels being selective on what they shared.

"Surely there's a weakness in that scenario," he said, having given it some thought. "What if the person or being that discovers the probe has limited information on those particular subjects? I imagine few people would know much about any of that information."

"You have to credit the Arethusans for their ingenuity," replied Falmas. 'The program is insidious. It acts like a virus, transferring from one victim to another. It lurks undetected in their subconscious, delving through memories until it gathers all the information it needs."

A shiver ran through Grant at the thought of what could be happening to the crew. "Is it dangerous? Can they die?"

"We don't know. There is insufficient information to confirm how each subject reacts. I would imagine it depends on the mental strength of the individual species."

Grant was trying to get to grips with the potential disaster now faced by the human race. The analytical part of his brain took over from the emotions that were threatening to overwhelm him. "If we destroy the beacon, I assume that will cease any transmissions back to Arethusa and will kill the program running in any humans that may be infected."

"That would appear to be a fair assumption. The transmissions would certainly end and, without the beacon's power it's highly unlikely the virus would be able to sustain itself."

"Take us in to a lower orbit above the Hellas crater. Surely, we can locate it from there," urged Grant.

***

The control room was quiet as Georgia and Molloy finished relaying their experiences. Only the buzzing sound of the ventilation system cut into the thoughts of the people as they each considered the implications of what they now knew.

Megan was the first to break the silence. "I'll run some tests on all three of you. Maybe we can detect physiological changes if there are any. Molloy, have you experienced any more contact with either of the aliens you said you encountered in your sleep?"

"No, doc. But it's unsettling to know that they may be in my head. I don't know if they have access to my memories or are able to read my thoughts. They may even be listening to our conversation."

"Okay, thanks Molloy. Professor Kozlovsky, am I right to believe you didn't get close enough to the probe to be able to communicate with it?"

Anna nodded. "That is correct, doctor. I had no exposure so should be the perfect control subject."

"I'm sorry to interrupt you Megan," said Mancuso. "Molloy is right. We don't know what capabilities the aliens have. Shouldn't we be putting him and Georgia into quarantine? I think it's prudent to keep them away from any decision making until we have a better understanding."

Georgia nodded. "I agree with Joe. We're not safe to be around. Their attack against Molloy has shown their true colors. Action has to be taken against that probe, but the less I know, the better for all of us. We'll go with Megan to the medical center while you," she pointed at Dunn, "update Ground Control. Ashley, you now know as much as we do about the probe. You know you can rely on Joe to assist you although you're wise to keep him out of sight for the time being."

"Thanks Georgia. We'll sort this out and get your heads cleared." Georgia noted the lack of conviction in Dunn's voice. She couldn't blame her. They were faced with an unexpected situation with an alien technology that far exceeded anything they could comprehend. Not for the first time in the last twelve hours, she felt a huge pang of guilt at having acted with her gut rather than her head. She hoped the consequences would prove not to be as disastrous as she feared. But she was now powerless to put things right.

She followed Megan out of the control room with an increasing sense of despondency at the realization she no longer had a say in the destiny of Alpha Base and that she may have already set its fate, and maybe the fate of humanity.

Chapter 29

Grant located the beacon one hour later. Falmas has been flying in circles above Hellas Planitia with an ever decreasing altitude in order to triangulate the strongest signals from the device. The search had enabled Grant to appreciate the enormous size of the crater.

"The beacon must be using the crater walls to amplify the signal," remarked Falmas. "It's turned this area into a large transmitter. That's why we have been unable to locate its exact position."

They were still ten miles above the floor of the crater but the image on the main view screen on the flight deck showed the unmistakable clean lines of a metallic cylinder half buried in the ground. As the craft continued its slow descent, Grant said. "The records from Nikari were unhelpful so I've been giving this some thought. If we lack the technology to destroy the beacon, or even disable it, can we move it? It's not a large object. Surely, we can load it into our hold and transport it somewhere safe. That would solve all our problems."

"I wouldn't advise that course of action," Falmas replied. "The beacons are known to have defense systems built into guard against what you are suggesting. I wouldn't want it on this ship while it's operational. We don't know what it would do to this craft or to us. It's simply too big a risk. We must destroy it or, at the very least, disable it where it lays. I will take us as close as I can. The outer casing is primarily an alloy composed of iridium and osmium protected by a magnetic containment field. It has the ability to self repair and is one of the most difficult objects we have encountered with a very high melting point."

That's made my job so much harder, Grant thought with a sigh. Looking back at the main screen he could now discern the unmistakable tracks left by the MEV as well as several trails running to the beacon. Confirmation, if he needed it, that the colonists had discovered the beacon. He briefly wondered where the MEV was now. He would like to be able to prevent it returning to Alpha Base.

He was startled by the sound of an alarm together with the sudden and violent vibrating of the ship. "We're too close to the beacon, "exclaimed Falmas as he punched in some commands to the ship. "It must have detected us and activated its protection system. The ships atmospheric dampeners have gone offline'.

There was no time for Grant to wonder how they had been detected when the cloaking device was supposedly shielding them. The ship was still seven hundred yards above the surface but dropping rapidly. Grant was only an observer as he watched Falmas valiantly fighting to recover control of the ship. Warning sirens were telling them what they already knew. Falmas managed to pull the ship's nose up to take them away from the beacon. But it was too late; the damage had already been done. The ship's momentum ploughed into the ground with a shriek of tortured metal, kicking up a vast plume of reddish brown dust.

Inside, Falmas and Grant were tossed about until the ship came to an abrupt stop. Grant slowly rolled over from the spot he found himself in the corner of the flight deck. He quickly checked himself over and, satisfied that his artificial body had survived the crash intact, slowly rose to his feet to assess the damage. At first glance the ship appeared to be in good shape, considering the force of the impact. Lighting was normal and the single control station in the center of the flight deck had remained in place. He was relieved that the sirens had ceased as soon as they'd crashed; it made it easier for him to think.

He spotted Falmas laying face down in the doorway. The Sentinel hadn't been so lucky. One of his legs had become detached; micro cables hung limply from his torso where the leg should have been, and a thick grey liquid was beginning to pool on the floor. Grant rushed across. "Falmas, can you hear me?" There was no reaction and

Grant began to fear the worse. What was he going to do if Falmas was dead?"

Chapter 30

Georgia noticed Megan's shoulder's slump as she entered the medical center. The reason was immediately obvious. Doctor Coleman was standing behind his desk holding two clear vials. It didn't take a genius to read the look of disdain on his face as he glared at Megan.

"You're supposed to be confined to quarters. I'm going to have to inform Commander Dunn." There was an air of superiority in his tone that Georgia didn't like. She guessed that he had always taken pleasure in winding people up and had probably never been liked as a result.

"She knows!" Megan replied. "I'm quarantining these three patients, so I suggest you make yourself scarce. You can conduct your research in one of the science labs."

Georgia knew that Megan could be formidable when she needed to be. It was enjoyable to watch as a spectator rather than being on the wrong end of her sharp tongue.

Coleman continued to glare at Megan before giving similar stares to Georgia, Molloy and Anna. Seeing that he was outnumbered, he swiftly placed the vials in a tray along with some other equipment and his personal computer before angrily sidling out of the room.

"That was awkward," Anna said, as the tension lifted in the medical center.

Megan laughed. "It's a game we play. He pretends to hate me. I stoke his hatred. We're like an old married couple. I don't think he'll ever accept my presence on the base." She closed the doors leading to the corridor before saying. "I'm afraid to admit that I have no idea what to do with any of you. There was nothing on the syllabus at medical school on how to combat alien possession. I'm sure exorcism isn't a cure."

"We're all learning here, Megan," said Georgia. "I've already learned not to act in haste. But I think it may be too late."

"I don't feel any strange sensations," said Molloy. "Although I am dreading falling asleep again. And now that we're back at base, last night's lack of sleep is catching up with me."

Georgia caught herself yawning. Molloy's comments had reminded her of how tired she was also feeling. The weariness only increased as she watched Megan fold down three bunks from the far wall.

"Okay, I want the three of you laying down so that I can monitor your brain activity. I have Georgia and Charlie's previous records for comparison. We may discover something unusual that we can work with and maybe isolate what's happening inside your brains."

Georgia climbed onto the middle bunk and laid down on the thin black mattress. She watched as Megan applied two pairs of electrodes onto Anna's forehead before she did the same to Molloy. "How long do we need to wear these?" she asked as Megan applied the electrodes to her forehead with a sticky gel.

"I'll start with thirty minutes," replied Megan. "And if any of you have any visions or other sensation, let me know immediately. For now, just close your eyes and relax. I'll be monitoring you from my desk."

To Georgia's amazement, she found it very easy to relax and clear her mind. Her initial anxiety regarding the Arethusans and the future of humanity were quickly forgotten. It was as if an outside force was encouraging her to forget all her immediate problems. She could hear herself breathing and the distant soft whine of the medical computers, but her mind was otherwise a total blank. She hadn't realized she had fallen asleep until a thunderous crash made her suddenly sit up and open her eyes.

Looking quickly to her left and right, she saw that both Molloy and Anna were sitting up and looking as equally startled. But across the room, Megan was slumped face down on the floor. Georgia called out "Megan!" and jumped down from her bunk. She gently rolled Megan over, relieved to see that her friend's eyes were open, although her face was drained of color. "Are you okay?"

Megan looked blankly at her for several seconds until her eyes focused on Georgia's face. "They were in my head! Or I was on their planet. I'm not sure. It's all so confusing. But they asked me lots of questions. I tried not to answer, but they were persistent. They wanted to know everything about human physiology and in the end, I had to tell them. It felt like I was there for hours. I'm sorry Georgia, they wore me down."

Georgia felt sick to her stomach. "No need to apologize. I'm sure you had no choice. Are you going to be okay?"

Megan sat up slowly, looking pale. "It felt so real. I was reviewing your brain patterns and then the next minute I was standing on a wooden platform like the one described by Charlie. Uslaw and Tremo were present. They weren't friendly at all. They accused me of delaying the inevitable when I refused to answer their questions. It was like an interrogation."

"How can that be?" asked Molloy. "You've not been in contact with the probe?"

"I have no idea," replied Georgia. "But if the Arethusans are able to get inside Megan's head then no one is safe."

"They said that they're coming for us," added Megan. "I had their feeling their planning for an invasion. Getting into our heads is just the start."

Georgia was shattered by the revelation. She was the person that lead the human race to its destruction. She had to warn Earth.

***

Grant was relieved to see Falmas open his eyes. He'd managed to drag the Sentinel to the repair bay before activating the ship's automatic recovery system to begin its repairs. He'd watched, fascinated, as Falmas' body was covered in nano-robots, giving him a shiny wet look. They had worked fast. It had taken them less than twenty minutes to reattach his severed limb and heal the deep scratches on his face.

"How's the ship?" Falmas asked.

"If I knew how it worked, I'd be able to tell you. There doesn't appear to be any hull breaches and the alarms have ceased. That has to be a good sign."

"In that case I need to return to the flight deck." Falmas tried to stand. His newly reattached leg, however, buckled under him and he fell to the floor. "Don't just stand there. Help me up."

Grant pulled him to his feet again and acted as a support for most of his weight. They slowly made their way along the corridor to the flight deck where Falmas waved his hands in seemingly random gestures. After thirty seconds he paused and shook his head. "The ship's core has been rendered offline by the beacon. We're stranded here."

"Can we fix it?" asked Grant desperately.

"Not while the beacon remains operative. Its defense systems are confusing the ship's neuron capacitors."

"So, we're going to be here when the Arethusans arrive with their battle fleet. Surely now is the time to let Alpha Base know what danger they're in. There's no other Confederacy ship within range that can save us. We have to help ourselves. You must be able to see that."

"Unfortunately, I have to agree with you this time. But I'm in no state to offer any assistance and we don't have time for my damage to be repaired. You're going to have to find a way to make contact with your human friends. We'll face the consequences later."

Chapter 31

Georgia was consumed by a range of emotions as she waited in the control room for a response from Ground Control to her latest update. In the past fifteen minutes there had been five more reports from personnel across the base that they had been targeted by the Arethusans. All of their experiences were strikingly similar to the one faced by Megan, with threats being made in order to obtain information. So far, no one had been physically injured but the ease and randomness with which the attacks happened was unsettling for everyone. And as each new attack was reported, Georgia was reminded that this situation was all her fault.

She looked across at Dunn and Mancuso who were lost in their own thoughts. None of them had openly said that she was to blame, but she was sure they were thinking it. Even Mancuso, who was always loyal, must be having doubts. She knew she'd let them down.

Jackson strode into the control room, walked straight up to her and gave her one of his special bear hugs. "How are you holding up, sis?" he asked as he pulled away. He frowned as he saw her sorrowful expression

Fighting back the desire to scream in anger, she managed to smile weakly. "Okay considering this is my mess. I wish there was an easy solution to this crisis."

"It's not your fault. We had no clue what the probe was or what it was capable of when we discovered it."

"All the more reason for studying it carefully. Instead, I was trying to prove a point with Byrne. Unfortunately, I proved he was right, and I should have followed his orders."

"That's all well and good. But if you're going to own your mistakes, then you need to take action to put it right. Not sit there feeling sorry for yourself."

"I wish I knew what to do this time. Uslaw and his friend are able to access anyone's mind at will. We're hundreds of miles from the probe and yet Uslaw's targeted several personnel who are at the rear of the base. Two hundred and fifty feet of solid rock is not enough to prevent the attacks."

"You may not want to hear this," said Mancuso, rousing himself from his thoughts. "We have to destroy the probe. I know you thought this was an opportunity to study alien technology, but you can see what it's doing to us. We're all wondering who's going to be next to be interrogated. We have some very frightened people here."

Georgia conceded that Mancuso was right. Destruction of the probe was the only remaining solution. Even then, she wasn't sure if it would be too late. Uslaw had intimated that his fellow Arethusans were on their way and she had no doubts that they weren't going to be friendly. The question was how could they destroy the probe.

"How do you propose we do that Joe?" she asked. "We only have a small stock of explosives that won't even put a scratch on that object, assuming we can get close enough to place the explosives in the first place."

"I was thinking of something more dramatic. Crash landing one of the supply ships directly onto the probe. If we fill the ship with fuel, then we can create a massive fireball. The heat from the explosion, together with the force of the impact may be sufficient."

Commander Dunn nodded in agreement. Excitedly she said, "We could program the ship's navi-computer to target the probe. The software isn't designed for that type of flight profile, so we'd have to override many of the safety protocols. I'm not sure we can guarantee the ship would crash directly onto the probe, but it would be close enough for our purposes."

"I'm sorry but you're wrong." Molloy was back to his usual direct self as he entered the room with Anna by his side. "We've been interpreting the data obtained from the sensors. The probe is made of an ultra-strong alloy. The main components are iridium and osmium and would easily be able to withstand the heat from a rocket explosion. We estimate that the tensile strength of the material is ten time greater than the titanium and steel used for black box flight recorders, making it virtually indestructible from violent trauma. If we try your plan, then we'd simply be wasting one of our supply ships."

"You've got to be kidding me!" exclaimed Georgia. It seemed hopeless. The human race was faced with a threat from alien technology thousands of years more advanced than anything it could conceive of. Before she could sink back into her pit of despair, a video message from Ground Control was received. Forgetting she was no longer base commander she asked Joe to hit the play button.

An image of Colonel Byrne standing next to NASA Administrator Selznick appeared on the main screen. Both of them looked stressed. Selznick was the first to speak and she had no time for small talk.

"The White House has been made fully aware of the situation as you've shared it with us. As you can imagine, President Ramsay is gravely concerned by the threat from the alien probe. His primary concern is for the safety of all America citizens, but he will be informing the United Nations of the imminent danger faced by Earth. It's not the right time for recriminations but be assured there will be consequences if we survive this."

Georgia could see that Selznick looked very uncomfortable. She didn't envy having to advise the president that the end of the world was a clear possibility. She expected Colonel Byrne to be less subtle.

"We're currently looking at all options. We have our best scientists studying the images of the probe together with all the data you've provided in the hope of finding a weakness. They will not rest until that happens. The fact the aliens are able to use a form of telepathy to obtain strategic information from any of you is a disturbing escalation of events." The colonel paused and looked uneasy. "There has to be a way of preventing further details being taken. If we cannot find a way of disabling the probe, we may have to resort to the ultimate solution. That is not what anyone wants but it may be the only way to stop the Arethusans from learning our secrets."

"We'll find a way before that happens," interrupted Selznick angrily. "I won't condone genocide for any reason. In the meantime, give us regular updates. I want them at least every hour, and I promise to do the same for you. Good luck."

The control room was stunned into silence. "Did Byrne really just say they're prepared to sacrifice everyone on the base?" asked Dunn, eventually.

"I can see his point," Molloy replied. "We're currently the weakest link. If it means saving the human race from destruction, then sacrificing twenty-eight people is a small price to pay. I think we can all agree with that."

Dunn wasn't convinced. "Has anyone considered that the Arethusans may no longer even exist. If the probe was dispatched thousands of years ago, who's to say they weren't wiped out in the interim?"

"Are you prepared to take that risk?" asked Molloy. "I don't think anyone on Earth will take that gamble."

"I agree," said Anna. "But I don't like it. Would the Chinese do the same with their personnel at their polar base?"

Molloy nodded. "The Chinese would have no qualms at all if it was for the greater good."

"How long do you think we have before the decision is made?" asked Dunn, looking in Georgia's direction.

Georgia wasn't overly optimistic. "Perhaps a matter of hours. As soon as the president is told there's no other viable solution. The longer he leaves the decision, the greater the risk that we'll give the Arethusans all the information they need."

"Realistically, no one is going to find a way to destroy the probe," said Dunn. "You heard what Charlie had to say. We should advise the crew and allow them to make final preparations. They'll want to send messages to loved ones back on Earth."

Georgia found it impossible not to fault Dunn's logic. Part of her was thinking why wait for the instruction at all. In reality, the scientists back in Houston wouldn't be able to find a solution. The sooner she thwarted Uslaw's plan the better it would be for Earth. She considered attempting to save the crew on the *Lexington* but knew it would take too long to load it with supplies. And there was no telling the range of Uslaw's abilities. If it meant saving seven billion people, then the sacrifice would be worth it.

She was about to share her thoughts with the room when Mancuso jumped from his chair. "We're receiving a transmission from a location on Mars. I'm struggling to get a clear signal but I'm positive it's not from the Chinese base."

"It must be Uslaw," Dunn said. "He must have become bored dipping into individuals' brains. Put him on speaker, Joe. Let's hear what he has to say."

The sound that came from the speakers was initially static with a strange warped whistling noise in the background. "Whoever is transmitting is attempting to modulate their signal. I'll attempt to do the same and hopefully we can synchronize the signals." Mancuso pressed a sequence of buttons which instantly removed the static. Georgia was stunned when she heard the familiar voice speak her name."

"Alpha Base, I need to speak urgently with Georgia Pyke. This is Chief Engineer Jim Grant. Please respond."

"It can't be Jim," said an equally shocked Mancuso. "It has to be Uslaw Haern. He's found a record of Jim and is toying with us."

Georgia listened to the message repeat several times. Although it was over two years since she'd last heard Grant's voice, she was convinced it was him. "It sounds exactly like him, Joe. Why would the Arethusans try to mimic his voice?"

Mancuso looked wistfully at her. "I understand you desperately want it to be Joe. I agree it sounds like him, but don't you think it's too much of a coincidence that he gets in contact when we're under attack?"

She had to admit that Mancuso had a point. There was no telling what the Arethusan probe was capable of. "Perhaps it is a trick, but what more do we have to lose? Open a channel and let's see if we can discover the truth."

Mancuso turned to Commander Dunn for approval. As soon as she gave a hesitant nod, he pressed the transmit button.

Trying hard to suppress her emotions, Georgia said, "This is Georgia Pyke. Please confirm your identity."

"Georgia. Thank goodness it's you. It's me, Jim Grant. I'm on Falmas' ship. You're in extreme danger."

"We understand that. How do I know you're not part of that danger? Can you prove you're really Jim Grant?"

There were several seconds of silence before Grant replied. "You have a birth mark in the shape of a strawberry on your lower back. I saw it the last night I was in Alpha Base."

Georgia blushed as everyone in the room turned to look at her with questioning expressions. Only Megan knew about that one night that she had spent with Grant. And, as the base doctor, Megan was the only other person that knew about her birth mark. "You need to be more specific but preferably on a different and less intimate subject."

"Do you remember the last words I said to you as I plunged to the ground from *Aquarius*? I was looking straight at you in the jetcopter and said, 'you must stop him, Georgia'. Falmas has explained how you defeated Redmayne, so I know you succeeded."

Georgia was transported by Grant's words back to the time she was kidnapped by Tom Redmayne. The loss of so many good people that day had been devastating and she had blocked most of the details. She was sure she'd never revealed Grant's final words. It had to be him.

"Okay. I believe you. What do we need to know?"

"Firstly, thank you for saving my life. Now I'm returning the favor. We know you've discovered the Arethusan beacon. We detected its transmissions when you inadvertently activated it. You need to know two things. Firstly, the beacon has a complex artificial intelligence capability that acts as a method of communicating with any indigenous species it encounters. It connects to a person's brain waves. But more than that, it acts like a virus in that it can jump into other people's brains in order to collect information."

"Yes, we are aware of that. I unleashed the contents of the probe and a number of the crew here have had visions."

"So, you know the type of information it's seeking out. Secondly, the beacon has been emitting a signal to the Arethusan home world. It's letting the Arethusans know it has discovered a new planet with intelligent life. The Arethusans will be coming to conquer Earth unless the beacon is destroyed within the next eleven hours."

"That's where we need your help, Grant. We don't have the capability here at Alpha to even put a scratch on that device. Surely Falmas has something aboard his ship that can destroy the beacon."

"You would think so but no. The Sentinel ships are not equipped with weaponry or any other equipment that could be of use. And, in any case, the ship has been disabled by the beacon. We crash landed less than a mile from the beacon and we currently have no power for the engines. We're marooned here."

"Can't the Confederacy help? This situation must be an exception to their non-interventionist policy." Georgia knew she was clutching at straws. But that was all that was left to them.

"Falmas says that the matter is being debated by their most senior policy makers. He doesn't know which way they will decide. But even their fastest ships wouldn't get to Mars in time to destroy the beacon before the Arethusans learn of our whereabouts."

Georgia looked at the faces in the room. They all realized the situation was beyond recovery.

"Chief Grant, this is Commander Ashley Dunn. Do the Sentinels know what the Arethusans will do when they learn about Mars and Earth?"

There was no missing the sadness in Grant's voice. "They only see these planets as resources to support their own ambitions for galactic conquest. They will destroy any defensive capabilities before enslaving any survivors. They will then plunder all of the resources in this solar system, extracting all the precious and heavy metals for their own spaceships and weapons. And when they've obtained everything useful, any healthy humans will be enslaved to work in their foundries or join their armies. Then they will leave any remaining humans to die in total squalor."

Chapter 32

Commander Dunn had heard enough. "Okay, I think it's time we explained the situation to the crew. Joe, gather everyone in the crew common room in ten minutes. Let's get this over with."

Mancuso reluctantly relayed the message across the base's internal comms system as the others watched him in silence. But he wasn't ready to give up. "There must be a way to destroy the beacon. Humanity can't end like this. And we can't give up without a fight. Grant, can you tell us how the beacon can be destroyed?"

This time, it was Falmas that replied. "Our records show that a concentrated beam of energy that can heat the beacon's casing to a temperature exceeding what you call eight thousand degrees Celsius will be sufficient to overload the magnetic containment field. Once that's completed, the internal technology supporting the artificial intelligence quickly becomes unstable and ceases to function."

Dunn was excited at the information. "The arc welders on the construction robots can reach ten thousand degrees. That's more than sufficient."

Mancuso was less enthusiastic. "That temperature is reached for fractions of seconds only. I doubt it's long enough."

Anna jumped up. "The focused kinetic energy from a pulsed particle beam accelerator is capable of creating temperatures in excess of eleven thousand degrees. Assuming you have sufficient energy and a reliable power supply then the beam can run indefinitely."

"Our particle accelerator was significantly damaged by the Chinese attack on the *Yorktown*," replied Molloy. "It will take months, if not years, to repair. How long do we have Jim?"

"Less than twenty hours until a permanent connection is established between the beacon and Arethusa. They'll then have your coordinates and it will only be a matter of time before their fleet arrives."

"Great!" Georgia exclaimed. "So that rules out another option."

"But there is my particle beam device still at the Russian base," said Anna "It's still in crates but if we can get to Derzost, then we can collect what we need and transport it to the beacon."

"*Lexington* is ready to fly," agreed Dunn. "Thanks to Colonel Byrne, it's fueled and the flight profile is programed in to the navi-computer. We can be airborne within ninety minutes. Because of the ground conditions near the swamp, we would have to transfer to the Russian landing craft, but Joe has been training hard on how to operate it."

"I can fly it," said Mancuso. "We have to give it a try, surely."

Georgia felt the slightest glimmer of hope. There were many hurdles to overcome, but they now had a possible way of destroying the beacon. "That goes without question, although we'll need to find an energy source. Jim, is that something you can help us with?"

Grant had been quietly listening to the conversation at Alpha Base. "I believe so. Bring a long length of power cable and anything you think may be useful to create a transformer. I'm confident I can build something that will hold together long enough for what we need."

Georgia clapped her hands together excitedly as she took control of the situation. "Okay everyone, let's get going. We've no time to waste. Dunn and Mancuso, I'm relying on you to power up *Lexington*. Molloy and Anna, you'll be on the flight with me and we probably need Rashid's technical input. Do we need anyone else?"

Jackson raised his hand. "What about me?"

"Thanks, but your place is here. Help Megan deal with the crew. They're going to need plenty of support if we fail."

***

Seventy minutes later, Georgia found herself laying on her back and strapped into one of the seats on *Lexington*'s flight deck. In front of her, Mancuso and Dunn were systematically going through a condensed set of pre-launch checks. This has to work, she said to herself. This was her final chance to redeem herself.

In the last hour, Ground Control had given their approval to this last ditch effort. They'd also confirmed that their group of scientists had not been able formulate any other plan for destroying the beacon. So, if this didn't work, then there would be no alternative but for the crew to die. The personnel had been informed and were now either leaving messages for loved ones or being counseled by Megan. It been decided not to share details of this mission in order to limit the chance of Uslaw discovering the plan.

The automated voice of the computer counted down the final ten seconds to launch. Georgia felt and then heard the roar of the mighty rocket engines explode into life. Slowly at first, *Lexington* began its ascent into the Martian sky. She gripped the arm rests on her seat as the vibrations caused her teeth to chatter.

Soon, the mid-afternoon sky went from a dusky brown to pitch black and *Lexington* performed a number of small maneuvers to put it on a sub-orbital trajectory toward Derzost on the far side of Mars. After seventy-five seconds, Mancuso declared, "Main engine cut-off" as the ship suddenly went quiet. *Lexington* continued its ascent until, after ten minutes, it reached its apogee and began to free-fall back toward the Martian surface.

Only Dunn and Mancuso spoke, quietly relaying information to each other on the state of the ship's systems and its alignment. Georgia listened intently, waiting to spot any potential problems with the flight but, thankfully, everything was running smoothly.

Eight minutes later, *Lexington* made a textbook landing less than two hundred yards from Derzost. Far closer than would normally be allowed but essential if they were to reach the beacon in time. Within a further five minutes, Georgia was descending the side of *Lexington* in the cradle that hung from the boom extended from the cargo bay. With her were Anna and Molloy. From over one hundred feet up, they had a clear view of the decimation that had taken place at Derzost.

Georgia looked in astonished horror at the large hole that had been ripped open in the roof of the main dome. Debris and bodies were strewn in all directions. "I'm sorry for bringing you back here, Anna. I hadn't realized how much damage had been caused."

"You understand why I had to flee," replied Anna, almost in a whisper. "Many good people were killed and for no reason."

Georgia gritted her teeth. She didn't know how she would cope if this was Alpha Base. "We will return when we have completed this mission. The dead will be shown some respect after death, I promise you."

Anna nodded but said nothing more.

The three of them cautiously made their way toward the ruins of the Russian base, carefully stepping over equipment and twisted metal. Georgia spotted the contorted body of a former cosmonaut laying face down on the ground causing her to detour their route round to the left. She hoped Anna hadn't seen it.

Anna raised her arm and pointed. "There is an open airlock ahead. I used it with Redmayne to escape. I doubt there will be any power inside."

"I can understand if you want to remain outside. I'm sure Molloy can identify the required parts."

"Only if you can read Russian. The components are carefully packed in crates. You need me to identify them and we don't have time for any parts to be left behind." Anna strode forward, taking the lead toward the open airlock hatch.

Georgia was reassured by Anna's strength of character. She was stronger than Georgia had given her credit for. It would definitely be required over the next few hours.

As she followed the Russian professor through the airlock, Georgi was not prepared for what greeted her on the inside of the base. Cables hung limply from smashed ceiling panels. The interior walls had collapsed as a result of the explosive decompression. Dust had already begun to creep into the base, with small orange mounds accumulating against the edges of walls and across the floor. The corridor was pitch black, illuminated only by the powerful flashlights that each of them carried. Anna took them along a corridor that led them directly to the base's control room, what would have been the heart of Derzost. The flashlights caused eerie shadows along the far wall which contained racks of now obsolete equipment. Georgia suppressed a gasp as she spotted a body slumped over a console, its face and hands desiccated by the thin Martian atmosphere. Two more bodies were laid on the ground near a fallen equipment rack, their faces unrecognizable following the effects of having been there for over one month.

Anna stopped to look at them. "The one on the left was Commander Koenig. He stood no chance. None of them did." She glanced up at the hole in the roof that was open to the elements, its ragged edges shaped by twisted metal and severed cables.

Georgia followed her gaze, sucking in her breath as she considered how close Alpha Base had been to suffering a similar fate.

"I never considered the implications of what our particle beam weapons were capable of," added Molloy. "I saw my research as creating a defensive capability, to protect Earth. Seeing this devastation at first hand, with the countless lives lost, I realize how naive and stupid I was."

"You weren't the only one to be fooled, Charlie. But maybe we can put the weapon to good use and save the human race."

"This way," motioned Anna, stepping over a computer monitor and heading down another dark corridor. After twenty paces she stepped into a room on the right. "This is my lab. Or, at least it was.

The crates we want are on the bench. I didn't even have time to open them."

"Is that all of them?" Molloy asked. "I would have expected more for your particle accelerator."

Anna was already sliding one of the crates forward. "Fortunately, the larger components are on the landing craft. These boxes contain power converters, the control pad and all of the connectors. It sounds complex but I think with your help, Charlie, it will take under an hour to construct on site."

"We're going to be cutting it fine," remarked Georgia. "Let's hope it works first time."

***

While the components for the particle beam weapon were transported from Derzost, Mancuso and Dunn were aboard the Russian landing craft, now unofficially renamed *Liberty*. So far, they'd been lucky. The batteries were at eighty-five percent capacity which had made it a simple process to power up the ship's systems. And, so far, everything had been in accordance with the manuals provided by Ground Control.

Mancuso was now sitting in the pilot's seat systematically going through the startup sequence. "I was expecting some modifications that could have caused us some major headaches. Flying this craft should be child's play."

"Rather you than me," replied Dunn who was checking the fuel tanks and pressures using another console. "The controls in here are basic and these seats are really uncomfortable. The good news is that the tanks are full. Anna was right when she said these landers were always ready for an emergency launch."

"That's a relief. I was concerned we wouldn't have enough fuel to return to Alpha once the beacon is destroyed."

"How long until you're ready for launch?"

"Fifteen minutes. Then it's just a matter of waiting for Georgia to load the crates."

Having completed her tasks, Dunn tried to communicate with the crew inside Derzost. "Georgia, how are you progressing with retrieving all of the equipment?"

"We've moved it all outside of the base," replied a breathless Georgia. "Manhandling the crates through the base in the dark has not been easy. Are you or Qadir able to assist us transporting the crates to *Liberty*? We have to complete the journey by foot."

"I'm on my way," replied Dunn. But, before she could leave the *Liberty*'s flight deck, she received a communication from Megan Betts at Alpha Base. "What is it, doctor?"

There was uncharacteristic panic in Megan's voice. "Ashley, the attacks on the crew have recently become more frequent. Uslaw is searching out Georgia again. He knows she's not here and is attempting to find out where she's gone. It has to be only a matter of time before either Jackson or myself are compromised and reveal the plan."

"Thanks Megan, keep me informed." Dunn picked up her helmet and ran for the airlock. They were running out of time.

Chapter 33

Libby Selznick had been watching Byrne nervously pacing up and down in her office for almost five minutes. She was finding it difficult to wait for any updates as well and desperately wished she had not given up smoking five months earlier. She could remember the smell of tobacco so clearly and knew a cigarette would help to calm her nerves. She thought it ironic that she'd quit for health reasons and yet was now facing the prospect of a worldwide catastrophe that was likely to end all life.

She was about to buzz her executive assistant and instruct her to purchase a packet of cigarettes from the canteen when her laptop chimed. It was President Ramsay on a secure line.

Libby beckoned Byrne across to her desk so that they could both speak with the president via video conference. Byrne pulled a chair across and sat at the end of the desk, ensuring there were several feet between him and the NASA administrator.

Libby nervously shuffled a few papers that were laying in front of her. "Good afternoon, Mister President. How was your call with your Chinese counterpart?"

President Ramsay looked harassed. His hair was ruffled and there was a thin sheen of sweat on his forehead. Libby wondered, not for the first time, if he was up for the role of president. "Not pretty. The Chinese president had just received reports from his space agency that members of their Mars mission had received visions from what they reported to be aliens. The description sounded identical to the reports you sent me. The president was extremely displeased at what he sees as American arrogance that has endangered the whole of human life. I have to admit I found it difficult to disagree with his point of view."

"Is he prepared to help us, sir?" asked Byrne.

"Colonel, if you mean is he prepared to sacrifice his Mars base then the answer is yes. Once we've confirmed that our own personnel have taken their own lives. There's still inherent distrust and he wants to be sure we're not playing any games in order to secure Mars for ourselves. It's crazy to think that we would ever consider such a ploy. Where are we on destroying the alien beacon?"

Libby coughed nervously. "*Lexington* landed at Derzost a short time ago. The Russian particle beam weapon is being loaded onto *Liberty* and should be relocated to the beacon within an hour where we intend to establish it with the assistance of the Sentinel craft that crash landed close by. We still have just over eight hours before it's too late and the Arethusans discover our exact location."

President Ramsay took the opportunity to take a drink. "What are the chances of success? Are we just delaying the inevitable and should we be sacrificing the crew now so that we can have a fighting chance?"

Libby was prepared for the question. "Do you want to be known as the president who ordered the deaths of twenty-seven patriotic American heroes? You have to give Georgia and the Sentinels a chance."

"I don't want to be known as the president who missed an opportunity to save the world either, Libby. Your crew has put me in an invidious situation," shouted Ramsay, defiantly.

"Does it really matter if there's no one left, mister president?" Libby almost spat out the words.

"Now is the time for a cool head, mister president," said Colonel Byrne softly. "When all of this is over you can apportion blame as much as you'd like. But I'm with the NASA Administrator on this one. Give our guys the opportunity to put things right. They have all the tools they need at their disposal. All they need is time, and a lot of luck. But I honestly think they can succeed."

President Ramsay glowered back at the screen. "Okay," he finally said. "I want it formally recorded that I am acting on your advisement. Your crew has four hours to destroy whatever that alien device is. After that, I'm ordering the self-destruct of Alpha Base. I'll also make sure both of you are held accountable for this fiasco prior to the aliens arriving to destroy us."

Libby and Byrne looked at one another as the president cut short the conversation. "I think that went as well as it could," she said with a grimace. "Thank you for your support on this occasion."

The colonel scowled at her. "I did it to save my own ass, not yours. Our best chance of survival rests with Georgia and her team. But you still made a poor decision in retaining her as base commander. This situation could have been avoided if you'd instilled more discipline in Georgia and her senior officers."

"My understanding is that you pushed Georgia too far with your unrealistic demands. The only mistake I made was to not block your appointment in the first place. I guess we'll both have to live with the consequences of our actions."

Byrne stood up and headed toward the door. "If we survive this, I'll make sure you're removed from your post. It's time for a change at the top."

Libby had already decided she'd had enough and would be resigning. But she wasn't going to give Byrne the pleasure of knowing. "Good luck, Eugene," she called out after him, but he was already halfway down the corridor.

***

Georgia slumped wearily into the co-pilot's seat next to Mancuso. Next to her, Anna and Charlie Molloy were busy strapping themselves into their own seats. "Okay Joe, over to you. Equipment is a stowed and secured. Ashley and Qadir have returned to *Lexington*. The spotlight now falls on you. Can you fly this thing or not?"

Mancuso shrugged. "You've flown with me many times. You've never doubted my abilities before."

"That's because I've never flown with you when you have the instructions on your lap," she replied, pointing at the small computer screen resting on his thigh.

"I'll admit I'm nervous. The fate of the world is resting on my shoulders. But I know I can do this. Pre-launch checks are complete, and the ship is semi-autonomous so should be easier than piloting the *Lexington*. The countdown is set for sixty seconds on my mark." Mancuso hit a button in front of him and the digital clock at the top left-hand corner of the main screen showed the countdown.

Georgia tried to relax in her seat. She knew that Mancuso was fully aware it was her fault they were in this position. It was unfair for him to have the pressure of success placed so squarely on him. But she knew that he would never blame her and would continue to support her all the way to the end. She just hoped the end wasn't going to be in several hours' time.

To Mancuso's surprise and annoyance, the countdown clock stopped with ten seconds remaining. He pressed several buttons without success before referring to the instructions.

"What's wrong?" asked Georgia. "Is there a malfunction?"

By now, Mancuso was looking agitated. "I don't know. All the checks were completed. I went through them one by one. There's no reason for the launch process to pause like this. Let me see if I can access any error codes." He pressed several more button in a sequence which brought up two rows of letters and symbols on the screen. "What the fuck is this?"

Anna glanced at the screen. "It's a warning. It says you've not primed the ignition flares."

Mancuso blushed at his basic error. Muttering an apology, he cleared the warning screen and reset the countdown clock to thirty seconds.

Georgia wasn't sure what to thank as she noticed that he'd cross his fingers. But, this time, the clock ran all the way down and she heard the deafening roar of the rocket engines before the four of them were kicked deep into their seats by the force of the rapid acceleration.

Being closer to the rocket engines, the noise on the flight deck was much louder than it had been on *Lexington*. But Georgia could still hear the disconcerting creaks of the thick metal deck plates as they objected to the stresses being placed on them. She fought a momentary anxiety attack as the sounds briefly reminded her of her previous flight on a Russian craft. Thankfully, those thoughts were forgotten as Commander Dunn's voice came over her radio. "Beautiful launch, *Liberty*. Good luck with your mission. We'll meet you back at base later."

Chapter 34

The sun was beginning to set as *Liberty* landed close to the swamp with a sturdy bump that caused it to bounce six inches before coming to a rest in a thick cloud of dust.

A clearly relieved Mancuso held his hand up. "Sorry everyone. I misjudged the energy loop back from the landing rockets."

Georgia, who had closed her eyes during the final few seconds of the flight, clapped him on the shoulder. "Great job, Joe. I'm sure you'll get the hang of it." Before he could reply, she unclipped her safety harness and made her way toward the airlock, followed closely by Molloy and Anna.

By the time the airlock had depressurized, the bottom end of the exterior ramp was already resting on the ground. Georgia was the first to walk down the ramp, carrying the front end of a crate with Mancuso carrying the rear end. She looked round for any sign of Grant and felt a pang of disappointment that she couldn't see him. She had little time to dwell on it though. The swamp was one hundred yards away and it was going to take time to get all of the equipment set up.

Georgia spotted the Arethusan beacon as soon as they reached the edge of the swamp. It was an ominous reminder of why they were here. She stared at hit with a growing hatred that was personal. There could be only one survivor. Recovering her focus, she said, "Anna, Charlie. You stay here and start assembling the particle accelerator. We'll fetch the other crates for you." She and Mancuso carefully placed their crate on the ground and raced back to the *Liberty*. "This will be a good test of our fitness," she managed to say, already aware she was starting to breathe heavily.

As she reached the ramp, she heard Jim Grant's voice on her comms. "To your left, Georgia." She glanced over her shoulder and skidded to a halt as she saw him quickly approaching from only thirty yards away. She had been dreading this moment ever since she's heard his voice several hours earlier. Not because she didn't want to see him again but because she feared being overwhelmed by emotions. She had thought of him every day for the past two years and still felt guilty at sending him away. How would he react to her now? Did he blame her?

She could see immediately that he looked different to how she remembered him. There was something about the way he walked that instantly made her think that he looked taller. A chill ran through her as she realized that his limbs were longer. She couldn't help but gasp in shock as she saw his face. Despite the fact it looked like the Grant she remembered, there were key differences. It was much thinner and his skin and his eyes had changed color. He had a blue tint to him now, although it wasn't as pronounced as the Sentinels she had encountered. It wasn't what she had expected when she'd agree to let Falmas take Grant.

He stopped in front of her and then was an awkward moment of silence as they stared at each other. She wished she had been able to meet him under better circumstances. Mancuso, who was standing behind Georgia, was the one to break the tension. He leaned around her and extended a hand. "Hey Jim, it's fantastic to have you back where you belong."

Grant shook Mancuso's hand and smiled broadly. "You look great, Joe. You look like you're still working out."

"And you've grown since we met. You must be what? Seven and a half feet now?"

Georgia was dismayed by Mancuso's directness. "Joe! We've not seen Jim for two years and the first thing you comment on is his height! I'm sorry Jim. But it is good to see you again. I thought I'd never get the chance. You look great." Instinctively, she reached out and wrapped her arms around him before stepping back to take another look at him.

Grant was still smiling. "It's fine. Both of you. I was given some enhancements by one of Falmas' colleagues. They took some time to get used to, but I was told that my injuries were too bad to save my limbs. You did the right thing sending me away, Georgia."

They were the words she wanted to hear. The relief was so overwhelming that she wanted to cry. "You don't know how much I doubted that decision. Falmas promised he could save you, but he said you'd never be able to return. It was a tough call to make."

"I can't lie. I had moments in the early days where I hated you. I felt isolated and so alone." He paused, noticing how uncomfortable Georgia suddenly looked. "But I'll save those stories for another day. Let me help you set up your particle beam weapon."

Mancuso was already pulling the next two crates from the airlock. Grant picked one of them up as if it weighed nothing, while Georgia and Mancuso struggled with the second crate.

"How many more boxes are there?" Grant asked, looking back at Georgia.

"Six I think," she replied, almost running to keep up with him. "And we have a coil of a power cable. I hope that it's long enough."

"It should be. I have brought a portable power supply from Falmas' ship. It's actually eight times more powerful than the reactor that powers Alpha Base." Grant suddenly had a strange far away expression cross his face. "Georgia, you can't begin to imagine the technology and the worlds that are out there in the Universe. I've learned so much. There are so many intelligent civilizations out there, some of them are hundreds of thousands of years old so it's no surprise they're far more advanced than us. You have to get out there and experience it like I have."

"That's been my plan ever since I encountered the Sentinels. Now you've told me what I can expect, I'm more determined," she replied, before adding, "Assuming we survive the Arethusans!"

"If we can transform the power without damaging the particle accelerator, then we have a good chance. I'm positive we can create sufficient heat to breach the beacon's shell."

They reached Molloy and Anna who had already unpacked the first two crates and were setting up a tripod stand. They stepped back when they saw the lumbering figure of Grant approaching. "It's okay," said Georgia, amused by their shocked expressions. "This is Jim Grant. He was our chief engineer on Expedition Two."

As Grant put down his crate, Molloy recovered his composure. "I've read a lot about you, Chief Grant. It's an honor to finally meet you. I'm Lieutenant Charlie Molloy."

"I've not been called Chief Grant for a very long time. Just call me Jim." He reached out and shook Molloy's hand. "And you must be Professor Anna Kozlovsky, the sole survivor from Derzost."

Anna stiffened. "You know my name?"

"We've been observing Mars for some time, and not just the American base."

"So, you saw what the Chinese general did to Derzost. You watched and did nothing as my comrades were slaughtered in cold blood. How could you do that?"

"I'm sorry for your loss, professor. But it was not my decision to make. I'm sure that Georgia has explained the Sentinel's policy of non- intervention. They are not gods and cannot take sides or influence a species' development. It may sound harsh, but I have seen the policy in action, and it does work."

"Not for my friends!" Anna muttered something else in Russian and returned to her work with Molloy. Georgia, Molloy and Grant returned to *Liberty* to collect the next crates of equipment.

Within fifteen minutes, the sun had disappeared for the days and they were working under the lights attached to *Liberty*. All of the equipment for the particle accelerator was next to the swamp in various degrees of assembly. Georgia could only look on as Anna and

Molloy busied themselves with connectors, tubes and electronics. They were finding their clumsy space suits were making it difficult to connect all of the components and they were well aware the delays were eating into their time. Mancuso was busy unrolling the spool of cable and running one end to the power supply provided by Grant.

Georgia was suddenly intrigued by a small box that Grant was working on. "Is that the transformer you mentioned?"

Grant nodded. "It's far smaller than the one we worked on for the base even though it works on similar principles. It will help to govern the energy that powers your weapon. I'm hoping there are no compatibility issues."

"Can Falmas help?"

"I know more on this subject than he does." There was no sense of gloating on Grant's part. It was simply a statement of fact. "In any event, Falmas is recovering from some minor injuries he suffered in the crash. Nothing to worry about. And he does want to meet you again."

Georgia was thrilled. If she got the chance, she wanted to thank Falmas for taking such good care of Grant.

***

It was another forty-five minutes before the particle beam accelerator was fully assembled and ready to be powered up. Georgia communicated the news to Megan, who was eagerly awaiting an update back at Alpha Base. "Libby Selznick has been contacting me every fifteen minutes. She says that the president is getting twitchy and is close to ordering the destruction of the base. You need to destroy that beacon soon otherwise it will be too late for us here."

"You need to get everyone to *Lexington*," urged Georgia. "They'll be safe there. At least for a while."

"It's not that easy. More than half the crew are now in a stupefied state thanks to Uslaw. We can't move them and I'm reluctant to leave them behind."

"Okay. In that case, pray that we're successful. I'll let you know as soon as we have destroyed the beacon."

Georgia looked back at the particle accelerator. It looked fragile and vulnerable, but it was their last chance of defeating the Arethusans. *It has to work.* Grant had connected the power supply to the accelerator and was watching patiently as Anna made some last minute alignments to three glass tubes. After some delicate adjustments, Anna gave a confident thumbs up and Grant allowed power to be transferred.

"This is the minimum setting," Grant said. A row of green lights flashed on the control panel for the accelerator.

"Keep the power levels steady," shouted Anna excitedly as she checked the data on the panel. "I don't want to stress the connectors and we need to allow the argon gas to settle."

"How long?" Georgia asked. She knew they couldn't rush this process but she now more conscious than ever of the time constraints. She had to remain calm so as not to spook Anna.

Anna took another look at the control panel. "Two to three minutes should be sufficient. Then we can begin to increase the power levels in small increments."

The next few minutes passed incredibly slowly. Each of them stood quietly and carefully watched for any sign of a problem with the particle accelerator. Once again, Georgia considered how delicate it looked. The fear of failure was beginning to creep into her brain and she fought hard to remain positive.

"Jim, please increase by two percent," Anna finally said. Georgia breathed a sigh of relief that they were getting the accelerator powered up. She could see the faintest of narrow beams aimed at a point on the side of the beacon. A deep shade of green, it possibly represented mankind's final hopes against an invisible but plausible threat.

The accelerator had increased to fifty percent capacity without incident when Molloy collapsed to the ground without warning. Georgia ran across to him and shouted, "Anna, keep increasing the power. I think we're running out of time." Even though he was unresponsive, she was pleased to see that Molloy's life signs were stable. The bad news was that it meant Uslaw had found them.

Mancuso was the next to collapse silently to the ground. Georgia was staring at him as it happened, and he looked just like a marionette whose strings had been cut. It was shocking. She turned to Anna just at the moment the Russian professor fell limply to the ground. Georgia looked at their slumped forms with dismay. "We're too late!" she exclaimed. "Jim, can you increase the power to seventy-five percent? We need to take a risk."

There was no reply, and, to Georgia's horror, she saw Grant laying unconscious next to the power transformer. She began to run to him but before she'd covered two paces, she was briefly aware of becoming light-headed, her legs buckled and then everything around her went black.

Chapter 35

Georgia blinked at the bright light from the large orange sun shining through the glass roof directly overhead. She instantly recognized it from Molloy's description. With a sense of utter despair, she realized she was now within Uslaw's representation of Arethusa. She had to find a way back to the particle accelerator quickly.

She spun around slowly to get her bearings. She was in a large dome, maybe one hundred feet across. The floor was a featureless gray color, like polished concrete or dull steel. A fine latticework of metal held up the domed ceiling and through the glass she could see the building was located on a beach. She could see the sea, waves crashing onto a sandy beach with spray flying into the air. Away from the water, the beach continued on for miles before it reached a range of mountains. And, beyond the mountains were the tall spires of Georgia's dreams, reaching up into the cloudless sky.

There was no time to consider how she could have dreamed this place. She had to break the link and get back to the real world.

Her thoughts were broken by Megan's voice. "Georgia, over here."

She turned around and where the dome had been empty only several seconds earlier, now stood all of the personnel from Alpha Base along with Molloy, Anna, Grant and Mancuso. Walking up to them she asked, "Are you real or just a figment of my imagination?"

"Oh, they're very real, Georgia Pyke." Uslaw Hearn appeared from nowhere between Georgia and the crew. "Did you expect that we wouldn't discover your plan? I have to admit that it was very ingenious, combining your technology with that of the Confederacy. But we were never going to let you succeed. I've brought you all here so that you can do no harm to our plans."

Frustrated by Uslaw's arrogance, Georgia knew she had to get as much information from him if she wanted to escape. This was only a prison of her mind. All she had to do was find a way to resist. "Where have you brought us? This isn't the same location you used for some of my friends."

"You like it? I've recreated one of the many islands on Arethusa. When I was alive, my favorite place to relax was on a beach very much like this. As a young child, I enjoyed hunting along the coastline with my family. That was until they were taken away for military service. I lived alone on the beach until I became of age. That time taught me to be self-sufficient and ruthless. Ideal qualities for a military commander. And now, I need a prison from which you can't escape. Your friends were too resourceful with my forest jail." Uslaw sneered, revealing thin pointy teeth.

"So, you're just going to keep us trapped here until your army arrives to destroy my civilization?"

A second short figure appeared next to Uslaw. "Not exactly," he snarled. "We still wish to retrieve information from you. There are significant gaps in our knowledge that I'm sure you can help us with."

"Why would I want to do that? I'd be condemning my people."

"You must know by now that they're destiny is already sealed. Your assistance could speed up their deaths and make it less... painful." Tremo said in a matter-of-fact way as if this was an absolutely reasonable suggestion.

"That doesn't sound like a very appealing offer. What happens to my crew and me?"

"You remain in this artificial world until you cease to exist. Your physical forms will simply wither and die over time. And when your bodies die, your consciousness will simply disappear. You won't even be aware that it has happened. We are not the heartless barbarians that the Confederacy will have you believe."

Georgia wanted to keep Tremo talking in the hope that he would reveal something useful she could use to help her escape this trap. "It's still an unnecessary slaughter, however you frame it. Humans are no threat to you. We're thousands of light years from your planet and we don't have the technology for interstellar travel. There is no logic to your actions."

Tremo looked as if he was explaining a basic principle to a child. "The logic is simple. You have the potential to be our enemy. You are already aligned with the Confederacy. The presence of your friend is proof of that." He pointed in the direction of Grant who was watching their conversation with interest. "It is far better to end that threat now, with minimal risk and loss of Arethusans. Once we've plundered your resources, we will know that this area of space is clear of any possible dangers in the future. Do you understand now, human?"

Georgia nodded. "You've made it very clear. Your race is nothing more than cowards. You pick fights with defenseless species. I don't think you'd stand a chance in a fair fight."

Both Tremo and Uslaw laughed. "There is no fairness in war," said Uslaw. "You're either a victor or a memory. You are naive to think there is any other way."

"You fear the Confederacy. Will they consign the Arethusans to be no more than a memory?" Georgia's statement seemed to unsettle Uslaw. He gave Tremo a nervous glance but didn't reply to Georgia's question. Both Arethusans disappeared, leaving Georgia alone with the rest of the crew.

Megan walked up to her and whispered. "If your intention was to aggravate our captors, then I think you succeeded. Your time would have been better spent trying to find an escape route."

"You know me better than that," replied Georgia. "We need to understand the Arethusans if we're going to find a weakness in their armor. No prison is escape proof. Charlie was able to escape from an earlier version."

"They've learned and adapted," said Molloy. "While you were talking to the aliens, I was inspecting the perimeter of this dome. It appears to be hermetically sealed and the dome is made from a very thick glass. There are no objects to manufacture tools. It looks like a perfect prison cell to me."

Georgia quickly glanced around and confirmed that what Charlie said was true. "Okay, from a physical standpoint we're trapped. But remember, this place isn't real. The Arethusans have access to each of our subconscious selves. So, we're not really here. Our brains have merely been fooled into thinking we're in a sealed dome on a distant planet."

Megan shook her head in disbelief. "If we know this place is a lie then why does everything feel so real? I can feel the heat from the sun on my skin. I can hear the waves crashing onto the beach. Whatever device the Arethusans are using to deceive us, it must be highly complex."

"And it's working on twenty-nine individual brains in various locations across Mars," said Molloy, suddenly excited as he began to analyze the situation. "Which means the beacon must be drawing on a lot of power to keep us here."

Georgia saw where he was going with his reasoning. "And so far, we've been extremely compliant. I wonder if the beacon would need to use more energy if we began to resist it in some way. Particularly a co-ordinated challenge. Would the beacon be able to continue controlling all of us and maintaining this dome?"

Grant had a mischievous look on his face. "There's only one way to find out. I'm sure they've not finished questioning you yet. Perhaps we need to be more disruptive."

"Is that wise?" ventured Doctor Coleman who had been sitting quietly at the back of the group. "We're dealing with a technology well beyond our comprehension. You have no idea what will happen if you antagonize the hosts. And don't you think you've committed enough reckless acts already?"

Georgia wondered how the doctor had ever passed the psych evaluations for the Mars program. He was a misfit and was never going to integrate with the team. His attitude was beginning to irritate. "Thank you for your positive input, doctor. I'm well aware of the mistakes I've made and I'm more than prepared to own them. If we're going to save the human race, then we're going to continue taking risks. If the plan fails, we try something different. Again and again, until we succeed. I'm sure everyone here will do all they can to save the Earth. Even you must have someone back home that you care about. Do it for them. I'd really appreciate it if you could support us in that effort."

Coleman seemed to shrink as he felt the crew looking at him questioningly. "I never said I wouldn't assist you. But you have to accept I have the right to challenge your decisions. Especially when you're no longer our base commander."

Dunn stepped forward and stood next to Georgia. "She has my full support, doctor. She's led this base out of several impossible situations before. She'll do it again. Get back in line and offer your full assistance. We have to do this together."

Georgia was grateful for the show of confidence. "Thanks, Ashley. Now here's my suggestion."

***

Colonel Byrne's image appeared on Libby's computer screen. Instead of being in his own office, he was in the mission center, sitting with the rest of the Mars support team. "We've lost contact with Alpha Base," he said, skipping the normal pleasantries. "Doctor Betts should have reported in ten minutes ago."

Libby's mind swirled through all of the reasons why this could have happened. None of them were good. "I assume you're tried to establish contact and checked for any malfunctions in the comms relays."

"I wouldn't have contacted you if I hadn't completed all the standard protocols. We've tried to make direct contact with Georgia Pyke, but we can't be sure if she's switched to the correct frequencies."

Libby ignored the colonel's directness. He was under extreme pressure and, she reluctantly had to admit, was the best person for this scenario. "Do you have any recommendations?"

"You have to inform the president. We must now assume the lack of communication means that something has gone badly wrong on Mars. The crew may be already lost for all we know. My recommendation to President Ramsay is that he orders the immediate destruction of Alpha Base."

Libby was not ready to make that call. "We have no proof they've failed, colonel. Don't you think it's too early for such a drastic decision? There could be a valid reason why contact was lost. I don't want the murder of our colonists on my hands."

Byrne leaned in close to the camera. "Libby, you have to accept that we're in a war with the Arethusans. Tough decisions have to be made and there will be collateral damage. It's inevitable. We lose some battles so that we can win the war. Step aside if you're not up to the job. I'll respect you more for accepting your limitations."

She had more backbone than Byrne gave her credit for. She was not going to back down now. "Thank you for reciting warfare for idiots. If the crew needs to be sacrificed, then I am prepared to make that call... at the right time. I'll report the situation to the president and share your recommendation, but with a caveat that we wait for another thirty minutes. In the meantime, keep trying to raise Alpha Base."

Byrne swore under his breath before abruptly hanging up. Libby took that as a small victory, even if it ultimately proved to be hollow. Taking a deep breath, she keyed in President Ramsay's direct number and hoped he would listen to her advice. The next ten minutes were going to define her career and, possibly, the fate of the human race.

Chapter 36

Uslaw and Tremo soon reappeared in the dome. Tremo moved menacingly toward the frightened group of colonists. "Georgia Pyke, we require more information about your planet's relationship with the Confederacy. There are many gaps and inconsistencies in the accounts given by you and your colleagues. The time for games is over." Tremo pulled a knife from somewhere inside his cape. It glinted in the sunlight and looked incredibly fearsome.

"Tremo can be very persuasive," said Uslaw, his evil smile returning. "I would suggest that you co-operate if you want to enjoy your remaining time here."

"So, it's time for good cop, bad cop," replied Georgia defiantly. "This world isn't real. How can you threaten me in this environment? I've said I'm not going to help you anymore. Your fleet can find out for themselves how well we know the Confederacy."

Uslaw looked more confident than ever. "You're foolish to think we can't inflict pain on you here. You've realized by now that this is a realistic representation of our world. Your brains believe what your eyes and senses see and feel. The pain you will experience from Tremo's dagger will feel excruciating. Do not fight us."

Georgia held her ground, looking Uslaw squarely in the eyes. "You'll learn nothing more from any of us other than how resilient we are. You will fail your masters." She took one stride forward and slowly raised her right arm, giving the signal that her crew was waiting for. As one, they began to advance on the two Arethusans.

Uslaw and Tremo were momentarily taken by surprise by the unexpected show of aggression, taking several steps backward to keep some distance between themselves and the crew. Tremo was the first to recover his composure, firmly planting his feet and waving his dagger in front of him. "That's far enough," he warned.

But the crew, led by Georgia and Molloy took three more paces forward. "I said you were cowards," taunted Georgia. "Now release us." She was worried that the two Arethusans would disappear again. But, at the same time, she was greatly encouraged that the aliens were showing some genuine fear. Perhaps her plan would work.

What she wasn't expecting was for Tremo to lunge quickly forward. She was stunned by the speed of his movement. For his small stature, Tremo's movement was incredibly fast. As he returned to his defensive position, Georgia spotted blood dripping from the end of the dagger. She knew it wasn't hers and was wondering who had been injured when Molloy let out a scream and dropped to his knees clutching his face. She could see a stream of blood running through his fingers and down his arms.

"My eye!" he shouted, angrily.

Georgia could see Molloy was covering his left eye as deep red blood continued to ooze down his face. Megan and Coleman immediately rushed across to see what they could do to help.

"I warned you," said Uslaw. "You can now witness the power of our illusion at first hand. Tell me now that we cannot harm you."

Georgia broke her gaze away from the fallen Molloy, but his screams of agony did not diminish. Her resolve was now being truly tested. But she knew she had to stay strong and ensure the crew were not distracted from the plan.

"That changes nothing. I'm not afraid of what you can do to me. You've taken my freedom and probably my home. There's nothing more that you can take." She took another stride closer to the Arethusans and was reassured to hear footsteps behind her. "I call that a stalemate."

Uslaw leaned his head to one side. "Yes, I can now see that you are not easily intimidated. You are a worthy opponent. But we are aware of your species' emotional weakness. Your sentimentality for friends is overrated." Then, as Georgia had feared, Uslaw and Tremo disappeared in front of her.

She spun around to see where they'd gone, Uslaw's words ringing in her ears. She didn't have long to wait. They reappeared next to Megan who was still kneeling beside the writhing Molloy. Uslaw stared at Georgia and revealed his teeth again in an evil grin. Instinctively, she knew what was going to happen next with a sickening certainty.

"No!" she screamed as she watched Tremo bring his blade down in one swift motion. Megan saw the movement and raised her left arm in self defense. It was the wrong move. Tremo's dagger sliced through her arm, just above the wrist, in one swift motion. Georgia stared in shock as Megan's hand arced through the air and landed on the floor of the dome with a sickly flat sound.

The colonists were stunned into silence as they turned in horror at the sight of Megan's severed hand and a fountain of blood pumping from her arm. Megan looked at her arm in frozen shock, seemingly unable to register what had just occurred.

It had happened so quickly. Georgia managed to suppress a feeling of nausea but noticed that several of the crew were throwing up. Seeing her friend so graphically and callously wounded was too much for her. She was filled with an uncontrolled rage like she's never felt before. Logic and reason were forgotten as she sought revenge for the violence carried out against Megan.

With a guttural roar she leapt at Tremo with all her strength. Most of the crew, including Mancuso, followed her example and bore down on the two Arethusans in outrage.

Tremo lifted his blade and pointed it at the oncoming Georgia. He was mistaken if he thought that would deter her from venting the rage inside her. She saw the sharp blade aimed at her chest, but it meant nothing to her. Her one thought was to tear Tremo apart for what he'd done. She ran headlong onto the dagger as if it wasn't there.

Instead of piercing her body, however, the elaborately carved blade buckled and shattered, leaving a stunned Tremo holding the hilt of the blade.

Before he had a chance to react, Georgia grabbed Tremo around his neck and lifted him above her head with ease. His eyes widened in disbelief at her sudden display of anger and strength. "Uslaw, get her away from me," he yelled in panic, as he waved his arms uselessly.

There was no one to help him. Georgia noticed with satisfaction that Grant was struggling on the ground with an equally shaken Uslaw Haern. And the rest of her crew were waiting to step in if needed.

Georgia glared down at Uslaw as he was held down by Grant. "You're beaten. Now free us and inform your masters on Arethusa that this solar system and its human inhabitants are not going to be bullied or conquered."

To her surprise, Uslaw laughed defiantly. "You still don't understand that this is nothing more than a visual illusion. You can't defeat what isn't real."

"Then why did you both show fear?" she replied, returning his steely gaze. "You're not as indestructible as you'd like to have us believe. I'm going to prove it by breaking Tremo's back across my knee."

But before she could carry out her threat, the dome and Tremo shimmered and vanished as everything around her went black.

***

Libby Selznick had just completed her call with President Ramsay when her cell phone pinged. She picked up the phone from her desk and opened her messages. This one was from Evelynn and it simply read, "It's done sis". *Not that the revelation will make a difference now*, Libby thought, ruefully. *There's going to be no one left to read the article!*

She called Byrne, who answered on the first ring. "What's the president's position?" he asked.

Libby sighed, disappointed that it had come to this. "We have twenty minutes. Then you can blow the hatches on the base and pray that we've done the right thing."

"Understood. It can't be the wrong thing if it saves the planet." Then, unexpectedly, his tone softened. "Libby, it's twenty-eight lives versus seven billion. If I have to carry out the order, I will but I will not take no joy in sacrificing good people. I promise to carry on with our attempts to re-establish contact for as long as I can. Don't give up all hope just yet."

Libby forced a grim smile. "Thanks Eugene." She closed down the call, knowing that what he had said were empty words. In her heart she knew that all hope was lost for the colonists. It was almost unbearable to accept the reality of the situation. All she could hope for was a miracle. Sitting alone in her office with the world potentially about to end, she wondered if it was too late to rediscover her faith.

Chapter 37

Georgia lashed out with both her fists and brought her knee up, directing all of the rage and aggression she was feeling into striking Tremo. Somehow, none of her strikes hit their mark. She opened her eyes and saw she was rolling around on the ground near the prone body of Grant. She'd been punching thin air and had been fortunate to not connect with the power transformer. She stopped moving, feeling the adrenalin still surging through her body. It took her several moments to gather her thoughts and realized she had managed to escape the Arethusan's trap.

Scrambling quickly to her feet, she saw that Mancuso, Molloy and Anna remained unconscious on the ground. She ran across to Molloy and was relieved to see there was no blood inside his helmet. Thankfully the injury to his eye had only been a part of the artificial world created by the probe. The sensations had been very realistic but had just been part of her subconscious. Which meant that Megan hadn't lost her hand either.

It was still dark, but she had no clue how much time she had left. Checking the chronometer on her spacesuit, she estimated she'd been inside the artificial world for about thirty minutes. More time wasted that they didn't have. Turning her attention back to the particle beam accelerator, she was reassured that it was still functioning. The control panel continued to show a series of green lights and the weapon was still powered at fifty percent capacity. Georgia could see the green beam of light had increased in intensity but was having no effect whatsoever on the beacon. The Arethusans attempt to prevent her from using the accelerator was an indicator that it would work, if only she could get sufficient power to it.

She was about to return to the transformer when she noticed Grant stirring. He sat up, shaking his head. "Did we make it?" he asked.

"The two of us have," she replied as she helped him to his feet. "Our coordinated attack seems to have worked in overpowering the beacon's system. It wasn't prepared for such naked aggression."

"There was something else too. I saw how the dagger's blade shattered. It was as if you'd suddenly become as hard as a diamond. You have some type of ability that the probe is unable to handle."

"I'm not sure about that. I was just lucky. But does it mean they can't take us again? All they need to do is delay us for a while longer and then the connection with Arethusa will be made. We need to finish this now."

Grant nodded. "You monitor the particle accelerator. I'll ramp up the transformer."

Georgia paid close attention to the accelerator's control panel as Grant increased the power first to seventy-five percent and then one hundred percent. She ignored the warning lights flashing across the panel. They were in Cyrillic anyway. She was focused solely on destroying the beacon at any cost. Surely the particle accelerator would do its job. But her heart sank as she saw no effect on the beacon other than a white hot glow where the now intense beam was attempting to cut through its defenses. There was no telling what temperature the beacon was now at, but it seemed to be withstanding the energy from the accelerator. It was indestructible.

"We need more energy," she shouted in desperation. "Jim, you need to turn it up further.

Grant adjusted the controls on the transformer, increasing the power by a further thirty percent. The accelerator's glass tubes were now glowing white hot and Georgia feared they would explode at any moment. But she began to feel some encouragement as she noticed that the casing of the beacon was beginning to warp and blister under the intense heat being generated by the particle beam. She willed the accelerator to hold out for a few more seconds.

Grant increased the energy one final time. The particle accelerator was now at one hundred and fifty percent capacity. Well past any tolerances that the Russians may have designed into their weapon. Georgia could feel the static energy sizzling in the air all around her. Her skin was tingling, and she noticed the top layer of dust on the ground was vibrating so much that it was bouncing off the surface.

Without warning, the particle accelerator exploded spectacularly, sending a shower of molten glass into the air. Georgia looked at the sad remains of the weapon and sank to her knees with a sense of abject misery. She'd failed. The weapon had been mankind's final hope and it had destructed in the most dramatic way possible. It was now nothing more than a smouldering mangle of metal and wires. The irony was she had been so close to destroying the Arethusan beacon. But that counted for nothing. The human race was now doomed.

As she despaired at her predicament, a movement out of the corner of her eyes quickly caught her attention. Anna was moving her arm. Georgia watched in amazement as Anna sat up, looking confused and dazed. Molloy, did the same, raising one hand quickly to his helmet.

Georgia rose to her feet and walked to the edge of swamp where she could see the Arethusan beacon was now nothing more than molten pile of metal. She watched in awe as metal slowly ran down into the sand before solidifying. Wisps of smoke rose into the air, giving a strange spooky appearance under liberty's spotlights.

"You did it," exclaimed Mancuso who had also recovered and was sitting up. "You destroyed the beacon."

Georgia couldn't believe her eyes. Had she really succeeded? A flurry of sparks from the remnants of the beacon were confirmation that the threat really was over.

But to be absolutely, sure she turned to Grant. "Can you check if the beacon is still functioning?"

After quickly conferring with Falmas via his comms device, Grant said, "we can't detect any signals emanating from the beacon. It was close, but you managed to neutralize it."

Georgia's relief was short-lived as the image of Megan's severed arm flashed through her mind. "Alpha Base, please respond. Megan are you okay?"

After ten seconds of silence that felt like an eternity, Georgia worriedly tried again to make contact. Still nothing. She saw Anna and Molloy looking nervously in her direction.

Moments later, the tension was released as Megan's voice came through their headsets. "Sorry for the delay. I had to deal with Colonel Byrne before he hit the destruct button. I take it you succeeded."

Georgia could only cry tears of joy at hearing her friend's voice. Composing herself, she was able to say. "The beacon is destroyed. Inform Ground Control that the area has been made safe. The human race isn't going to be wiped out today."

Chapter 38

Falmas was resting in his ship's medical room still waiting for his leg to become fully operational. Georgia followed Grant into the room, immediately recognizing it as the same room in which she had encountered the Sentinels. The irony of the role reversal didn't escape her attention.

Falmas lifted his head and gave her a friendly smile. "Congratulation are in order, Georgia Pyke. You've saved the lives of your people."

"Thank you Falmas, but we both know that we wouldn't be in this situation if I hadn't foolishly attempted to discover the properties of that beacon. My blind desperation to seek you out almost caused a catastrophe. I escaped by the skin of my teeth. It could have been such a different result. It almost doesn't bear thinking about."

"That is true," acknowledged Falmas. "But if you hadn't found the beacon, then someone else would have done, eventually. And they may not have been so resourceful as you. The beacon is a relic from a different time in our history. The Arethusans wanted it to be found so that they could sow discord and disharmony. The probes they sent across the galaxy were designed to be irresistible to intelligent life. It is likely that its artificial intelligence was already in your brain before you knew it was there. It was there, influencing your decisions."

Georgia shook her head. "The decision was mine alone. I take full responsibility. Tell me though, is the human race safe?"

Falmas frowned and thought carefully before he answered. "From itself? Definitely not. From the Arethusans? I honestly don't know. Destroying the beacon has given you a good chance. The Arethusans will pick up the beacon's signal and will know of your existence. But, because you prevented signal lock, they won't have your exact location or know a great deal about your species. They may decide to not take the risk of commencing a campaign against the

Earth. My guess is they will send more probes to this region of the galaxy in the hope of pinpointing your home planet."

Georgia wasn't sure if she should feel reassured by the news. Falmas' words seemed to indicate that the Arethusans could still come to conquer Earth. It was therefore imperative that Earth's leaders unite. "Surely the Confederacy must help us now. They wouldn't want an enemy to destroy us and strip the solar system of all its resources."

"I wouldn't count on it," said Grant, who had been listening carefully to the conversation. "I've experienced the Confederacy. They're leaders have been in power for centuries and do not like change. After thousands of years of peace, they've become soft and complacent. Passively observing new species suits them perfectively. And they don't permit new members to the Confederacy unless those members are prepared to uphold those ancient values."

"Views are changing," Falmas admitted. "There are rumors of small conflicts on our furthest borders. It is believed that some of our enemies are testing the Confederacy's taste for war."

"Okay, I get it," said Georgia. "You have your problems to deal with and we're on our own for now. That means I need to escalate the matter with my president as well as other government leaders. Maybe finally they'll see there is a threat to our very existence. And, just maybe, they'll do something about it."

"I think you're what your colleagues would regard as a dreamer. You have noble ambitions, Georgia Pyke but you have a mountain to climb. I which you luck."

Georgia shrugged. "I prefer to see myself as a visionary. But I do accept that I need to control my enthusiasm if I want to keep humanity safe. I now know what damage one bad decision by one person can do."

"You had me worried for a while," admitted Falmas. "Especially when you were all taken by the probe. I wasn't sure if you'd be able to escape. I cannot tell you the feelings I had when I saw that you and Grant had found a way."

"What can I say? We're both very ingenious. But that does remind me that have to thank you for saving Grant. I wasn't sure you'd be able to heal his injuries. He was in such a mess. However, you kept to your word and I can't tell you how good it is to have him back looking so healthy. I can't wait to have his knowledge and skill back at Alpha Base."

Falmas and Grant exchanged knowing glances. "I can't return," said Grant, quietly. "Look at me. I'm seventy-five percent alien technology. My presence would make it impossible to deny the existence of advanced alien civilizations. It would only take one leaked message or accidental photo for the public to discover the truth. And can you imagine how many scientists and engineers would want to get their hands on my components? Don't try to persuade me otherwise, Georgia. It's taken me a long time to realize it, but the Earth is better off without me... for now."

Georgia was crestfallen. She'd found Grant, only for him to be snatched from her grasp. "It's my fault again. Jumping to conclusions. When I saw you earlier, I assumed you would also be resuming your time with us. We need you."

"No, you don't," he replied, holding her hand and looking softly into her eyes. "You have more abilities than you give yourself credit for and you'll be able to carry on without me. I was so lonely following my accident but Falmas has taught me that I have a place in the Universe. I think I've found it. I truly believe you're close to finding your own place. And I won't be far away. We're assigned to study Earth and humanity for the foreseeable future. I'm sure our paths will cross again."

"I think you're wrong but thank you for attempting to ease the pain. I don't know that the knowledge you're both close will help me. Perhaps in time. I'd much rather have you by my side. The information you've learned, and your enhanced body would make so much difference to the base and to achieving my dreams."

Falmas sat up. "Georgia, there's something you should know. We've held this information and I probably shouldn't be sharing with you. We think you're different. When we healed you, our nanobots may have altered some of your DNA. It was unintentional and we're not sure of the side effects. However, it may explain how you were able to overcome the Arethusan trap and escape the beacon's containment field. Have you noticed any changes over the last few weeks and months?"

Georgia didn't know what to say. Falmas could just have resolved the mystery of her extraordinary healing abilities "Are you telling me I may not be human?"

"You're still human, Georgia. There just may be parts of you that are beyond the standard human physiology."

Georgia looked at Grant. "Did you know about this?"

"Only recently," he admitted. "But it's purely hypothetical at the moment. The Sentinels carried out some computer modeling of what they did to you. They discovered several interesting scenarios."

"Should I be worried? Are there any long-lasting effects?"

"We don't know," said Falmas. "We will need to conduct some tests on you to determine what changes, if any, have been made and whether your body has accepted those alterations. This is a whole new field of research for us. Our scientists are very excited about the prospects."

"I can't say I'm very enthusiastic at the prospect of being the subject of medical experiments by alien scientists. Am I able to say no?"

"We won't force you to do anything you don't want to. But the tests won't be invasive or painful. Just some scans and some analysis by our chief researcher. We think this could be an important step in human evolution."

"Because you've made me different? I need to let that sink in before deciding what to do."

"Georgia, you can trust them," Grant said. "I'm living proof of what is possible. And I've not made it easy for them."

"I understand your concerns," added Falmas. " You have time to let the information sink in. For now, you must return to your base and re-join your colleagues."

She knew Falmas was right. But standing there, with Grant and the Sentinel that saved both their lives, she wanted nothing more than remain on the alien vessel.

Reading her thoughts, Grant said, "Georgia, you won't help your cause by staying here. Go back and start converting the crew and then the people of Earth. Have faith."

"I've never been great at goodbyes," she replied, before bursting into tears.

Chapter 39

Libby Selznick handed in her resignation at eight A.M. the following morning. She'd had a sleepless night thinking about how close she had come to losing personnel. She had worked her way up the ranks in NASA because of her zest for knowledge and exploration. During her career she had always felt she was making a positive impact. She couldn't say the same now when she looked at her reflection in the mirror.

But everything had changed over the past week. She knew in her heart that she was no longer cut out for the role. She hated to admit it, but Colonel Byrne was correct. Earth was now facing a war and impossible decisions would have to be made. She knew she would never be able to make the life or deaths calls that Byrne seemed so easy to order.

She called Byrne to her office at thirty minutes later to inform him of his decision. Sitting at her desk, staring at the various photos of space rockets and astronauts on the walls, when felt at peace with her decision. She had no idea what she would do next but was sure that private companies would be lining up for her services once they discovered she was available.

Her thoughts were interrupted by a knock on the door as the colonel walked into her office. Now that the immediate emergency was over he seemed less sure of himself; a shell of the decisive man of action he'd been less than twenty-four hours earlier. "Thanks for coming over, Eugene," she said with a genuine smile. "Take a seat."

"Thank you, Libby. You look as if you had as much sleep as I did. If you were wanting to see my latest report, it will be with you shortly. I've got one of the tech guys running some numbers. However, it appears as if the emergency has passed. The Alpha crew have reported no alien visions overnight. Some of them are still shaken up by the whole experience but that's to be expected and we will be arranging counseling for those individuals."

"Thanks Eugene. Actually, I wanted to let you know I've resigned my post. It's been a tough few days and I think it's time I stepped aside for someone better qualified to take NASA into the future."

The colonel's face remained neutral as she shared her news. "Has this got anything to do with your sister's story this morning? The discovery of the relic is across all media sources this morning. I did wonder how she knew so much detail."

"I don't know what you mean, colonel. I'm sure that Evelynn has a vast network of sources for all of her stories. There are so many ways she could have got hold of the information. And she knows better than to approach me when I've dedicated my life to space exploration."

"Okay, have it your way," replied Byrne. "I'm sure the government will be publishing denial stories and the matter will be forgotten within a few days as another conspiracy theory. It's the one thing the government is very good at. Nothing will have changed as far as the public will be concerned."

Selznick managed to keep a straight face. She was going to make sure that the news remained in the public space. And the photos her sister had published online had not come from her. Evelynn had another high-level source who wanted the truth to be shared. That thought was exhilarating. Byrne and the government were going to have their work cut out for them over the coming months.

***

Mancuso managed a smoother landing of *Liberty* close to Alpha Base causing a cheer from Molloy, Anna and Georgia. They'd spent the night in the craft, next to the swamp. It was a relief to be back at what they called home. Now that she was here, Georgia knew it was where she needed to be. Amongst her closest friends and brother.

The crew had gathered in the common room to welcome them back. A few of the crew looked ragged and agitated from their harrowing experience. Georgia felt a pang of guilt at what she'd put them through. She hoped that they would forgive her as she promised herself to never make the same mistake again. She would definitely think of others before acting recklessly.

Once the immediate celebrations were over, Commander Dunn ushered Georgia into a corner for a private conversation. "I have some mixed news for you. The good news is that Colonel Byrne has seen sense and is reviewing your status. None of you are under arrest for the time being and are you're free to carry on your duties. However, I am to remain base commander pending full inquiries of what occurred."

"Thanks Ashley, I'm happy with that," Georgia replied, "You've shown superb leadership under very trying circumstances and you have my full support. What's the bad news?"

"I've just received word that Libby Selznick has resigned her post. Rumors are that Byrne will be stepping in to cover her role until a replacement is found."

"Yes, that's not good for us or the program. If the colonel gets hold of power, he's not going to relinquish it. And that spells disaster for me."

"I understand it's not what you wanted to hear," said Dunn. "I thought you ought to know."

Jackson must have spotted the two of them because her strolled up behind Georgia. "Hey sis, there's no need to look so glum," he said, wrapping his arms tightly around her shoulders. "I've just heard that the mining corporations have been instructed they can carry out operations. Everything is back on track and I'll be spending more time over the coming months carrying out a detailed survey of the mineral deposits. Maybe you can join me."

For Georgia, Jackson's news more than made up for Byrne's potential promotion. Finally, there was a guarantee that Alpha Base would continue as a human colony. However, she didn't feel as excited as she thought she would. There were too many other important things in her life to consider, not least of which was how to deal with the bombshell news Falmas had shared with her. "That's fantastic news, Jackson. It really is. Thanks for the invitation, but I'm not ready to go back there just yet."

She saw the disappointment in his eyes. She knew she'd have to take the time to explain her reasoning, But, at the moment, she felt she was stretched so thin that she'd snap at any moment. And she wasn't sure if she'd ever be the same again.

***

On Nikari, Director Mortak stared out of his office window at the thick covering of snow and ice as it glistened under the twin moons. He didn't see any beauty in the scene, only coldness and emptiness.

He was deeply disturbed by the latest news coming from the Confederacy. After thousands of years of peace, it appeared as if a war was inevitable. The two Lorkan peace envoys sent to Arethusa had been missing for three days, only to be discovered in the wreckage of their spacecraft, drifting in interstellar space. He wished he'd not read the report. The images of their mutilated bodies were going to haunt him for a very long time.

"So Mortak, you really are convinced we're going to war," his companion said, more as a statement than a question.

"Jillnap, if I showed you what I've seen then you'd have no doubts either. It's purely a matter of time. The Confederacy is revising its battle protocols as we speak and is building a fleet of battle cruisers to enhance what it already has."

"That's never happened in living memory. I'm not sure we're ready for a war."

Mortak nodded. "Which is why we can't wait any longer to test the human. You leave tomorrow and I pray that our suspicions are confirmed."

"Have no worries," Jillnap replied confidently. "If she possesses the abilities, I'll find out."

<<<THE END>>>

IF YOU ENJOYED RELIC

My Mars Frontier series charts the progress of human colonization on Mars. Book 1 of the series, Discovery, is available on Amazon now.

DISCOVERY sees Mission specialist Georgia Pyke arrive on Mars with bold intentions to establish a legacy, unaware one of her colleagues has been holding a grudge for six years. How far is that person prepared to go to exact their revenge?

The mission quickly becomes a matter of life and death for the twelve astronauts as they struggle to establish a foothold on Mars. While Georgia and her crewmates fight the elements as well as their personal demons, something is lurking out of sight. Something that will change them forever.

WHAT READERS ARE SAYING:

"This book is an easy read. It's well paced and sets the scene for the next books in the series. The characters are well formed, believable and very human. There is just enough technical talk to make it all seem real without turning the reader off. This is the first book I've read by this author and am looking forward to finding out what happens next! Highly recommended" – J. Bee

If you're looking for a fast-paced action adventure, get your copy of Discovery today!

[Amazon US][1]
[Amazon UK][2]

---

1. https://www.amazon.com/dp/B07Z6NTP7F
2. https://www.amazon.co.uk/dp/B07Z6NTP7F

GET EXCLUSIVE CONTENT

Building a relationship with my readers is the very best thing about writing. I occasionally send newsletters with details on my current projects, new releases and special offers.

And if you sign up to the mailing list, I'll send you a copy of Deception, my prequel to the Mars Frontier series. You can receive this novella, for free, by signing up at www.paulrixauthor.com[3]

---

3. http://www.paulrixauthor.com

ABOUT THE AUTHOR

Paul Rix is the author of the Mars Frontier human colonization series. His online home is at www.paulrixauthor.com[4]. You can connect with Paul:

on Twitter at www.twitter.com/PaulRix8[5]

on Facebook at www.facebook.com/paulrixauthor[6]

or email at paul@paulrixauthor.com if the mood takes you.

---

4. http://www.paulrixauthor.com
5. http://www.twitter.com/PaulRix8
6. http://www.facebook.com/paulrixauthor

Printed in Great Britain
by Amazon